A Cinderella Christmas

Contents

Mistletoe Maiden

SABRINA JEFFRIES

For my dad, who passed away a year ago:
Thanks for being a reader and a storyteller who passed those abilities and skills on to me.
I miss you, Daddy!

Chapter 1

London
December 1814

Thirty-year-old Noel Davenant, the Viscount Cokesbury, stared into the shop window at the print he'd been searching for all morning. He'd hoped he might find it if he ventured beyond Mayfair, and his persistence had been rewarded.

Every bit as evocative as the others engraved by a Mr. Beasley, this latest Beasley-engraved print showed a girl hard at work at her sampler. Noel meant it to be for his mother as a Christmas gift, to take her mind off the death of his sister Natalie. The girl even looked like Natalie at that age.

Lately, Mother's needlework seemed the only thing that brought her out of her grief. It had been two years, yet Mother mourned his sister as if it had been only two days. So did he.

He leaned forward to see if he could make out a price, then felt a hand slip into and out of the coat pocket that held his wallet. What the devil?

As he patted his now empty pocket, he whirled around just in time to see a poorly dressed lad race off down the crowded road.

With a muttered curse, he ran after the thief. Clearly, the boy was a very bad pickpocket, or Noel wouldn't have felt his hand. That was the only reason he didn't call, "Stop, thief!" He doubted the lad was yet a hardened criminal.

Still, a few boys were warily watching the chase, wise enough to stay well out of it. By the time Noel caught up to the guttersnipe and grabbed him by the arm, he realized the lad was no more than eight or nine, well-groomed and clean, despite his shabby clothes.

Nonetheless . . .

"Give me my property!" Noel growled.

"Dunno what you mean, you blasted gentry cove!" the boy had the audacity to say. "I ain't got naught of yours!"

"Then why were you running?"

"Uh . . . to . . . uh . . . I gots to meet a gentry mort."

"A gentry mort?" He snorted. This *child* wasn't meeting any woman, that was for damned sure. "Then you won't mind if I search you." He began digging in the lad's capacious coat pockets.

"Leave off, you bloody whoreson!" the boy cried, trying to wriggle away.

"James William Archer!" a female voice cried from a slight distance ahead of them. She coughed for a moment, as if the very effort of pronouncing his name hurt her throat. "I don't want to hear you using such language ever again! What in heaven's name is wrong with you?"

Instantly curious, Noel lifted his gaze to the woman, only to be arrested by the sight of the most beautiful, auburn-haired creature he'd ever seen. Granted, her flamboyantly embroidered green pelisse was patched and her flimsy green bonnet too thin for the weather, but otherwise she reminded him of the three red-haired young sisters whom everyone called the Mistletoe Maidens. When those impudent lasses appeared in Covent Garden with their green cloaks and mistletoe wares each year in December, everyone knew Christmas was just around the corner.

Unlike those freckled and ruddy-cheeked maidens, however, this one had creamy skin and angelic features, even with the frown marring her perfect brow. She looked to be in her twenties, although younger than he by a good measure, and a thick scarf of red wool engulfed her neck.

"Well, Jimmy?" She coughed once more, then cleared her throat. "What do you have to say for yourself?"

"Don't be angry, sis. The other lads tease me something awful if I talk the way you want me to."

Another amazement. The boy spoke the purest English now, without an ounce of guttersnipe in his accent. What the devil?

"The other lads?" She glanced about as she gave another cough, but the older boys he'd seen earlier had melted into the alley across the street. "Those miscreants you call friends, you mean? Where are they? I assume they're lurking about here somewhere."

Then she seemed to realize that Noel still held her brother fast, and she fixed her irate glance on him. "And who are you, sir, to be manhandling my brother so?"

He wondered if the pair did this dance often, a sister and brother pickpocket team, but she simply didn't look—or sound—like a woman of that sort. Perhaps that was what made her so effective.

Somehow, he found his voice. "Your brother just stole my wallet, madam. I am merely trying to get it back."

"Oh, Jimmy!" she cried, a fetching blush spreading over her cheeks. "How could you? Return the man's wallet to him at once!"

Noel waited to see if the boy would continue to protest his innocence to his sister's face.

"We need the money!" young James cried. "You know we do!"

"Not badly enough for you to turn thief. Papa must be turning over in his grave."

"Don't say that," James muttered, looking genuinely hurt.

She snapped her fingers. "Give it to me *now*, young man!" she demanded, then punctuated the command with another round of coughing.

Noel tensed, the repeated coughing so familiar that it dragged him back in time to the worst period of his life. Consumption. God, he hoped this radiant woman did not have Natalie's disease.

Unlike his sister, however, she didn't have the look of a consumptive. She appeared slender, to be sure, but her skin lacked the translucent paleness of Natalie's in her final days, and her shape was as womanly as any man with blood in his veins could want.

Good God, he was lusting after some strange woman, and a confederate of a pickpocket besides. Had he lost his mind?

Meanwhile, her persistent cough apparently affected young James, because all the fight went out of him. "All right," he muttered and dug into an inner coat pocket Noel hadn't yet searched. Pulling out the wallet, James handed it to her sullenly.

After using her embroidered handkerchief to dust off the leather, she held it out to Noel. "I know you have no cause to trust us, sir, but I sincerely beg your pardon for my brother's behavior, and I promise this will never happen again."

Somehow, he doubted she could promise anything concerning her brother's behavior, given the merry chase James had led him on.

"Please don't call the constable," she asked, her holly-green eyes darkening with concern. "It will break our mother's heart if James is arrested."

Releasing the boy, Noel took the wallet and shoved it inside his coat. "He's a child," he grumbled. "I wouldn't have called the constable regardless. I just wanted my property back."

"You . . . um . . . should probably check to see that everything's there," she said with a hint of embarrassment, coughing more delicately this time.

"I had only a few notes in it, anyway," he said with a shrug.

"Heavy notes," James mumbled.

He eyed young James balefully. "And a miniature of *my* sister that I did not wish to lose." As the lad hung his head, Noel returned his attention to the lady. "But he didn't have time to remove anything, trust me. No need to fret over it."

She blinked, then gazed at him more closely. "Mr. Davenant? *Noel* Davenant?"

Thrown off guard, he didn't tell her he was Lord Cokesbury now. "Do we know each other, madam?" Because he would certainly remember this incandescent female if they'd ever met.

"You probably don't recall," she said almost defensively, her cheeks pinkening again. "I only recognized you because your sister was also always saying, 'No need to fret over it.' Although this makes matters rather more mortifying. I almost don't want to tell you who I am."

"It's a little late to deny the acquaintance, don't you think?" he said, casting her a cold look.

It didn't keep her from laughing. "If you say so. I'm Natalie's friend, Eve."

The two names, James William Archer and Eve, suddenly snapped together in his head, and he groaned. "Little Eve Archer? Who used to chide me for being 'the worst brother in Christendom?' "

"Well," she said matter-of-factly, "you *were*."

"That's not how I remember it," he said, keeping his expression as impassive as he could when his heart hurt.

"Oh?" Her eyes twinkled at him. "How do *you* remember it?"

He hardly knew. She was confusing him with her beauty and her laughing gaze and the cough she couldn't seem to squelch. But one thing he had to determine. "Did *Natalie* see me as 'the worst brother in Christendom'?"

She smiled softly. "Of course not. She adored you. That's precisely why I called you that awful name back then. Because she wanted you to take her along everywhere and have fun with her, but you had far more important things to do than tolerate your sister and her friend."

That much was certainly true. He'd been so busy trying to mitigate the worst of his wastrel father's excesses that he'd ignored his baby sister entirely. Not making time for Natalie was something he regretted more deeply than he could express.

"But I'm sure you've improved with age," she said, as if sensing his somber mood. "You were only nineteen, after all."

"And you were only thirteen, a tart-tongued, skinny little thing. Now you're . . ." He couldn't prevent his gaze from drifting down her from the top of her pretty head to the soles of her well-worn half boots.

"Older," she said, laughing.

He'd been going to say *breathtaking,* before he'd caught himself. She'd obviously fallen on hard times. Besides, he was on the verge of offering marriage to Lady Margaret Tipton—an attractive, serious-minded female who did *not* make his blood race and his heart tumble over in his chest.

That was preferable. Hearts were fragile. If they weren't, his would have mended by now. But after his father's and Natalie's deaths, his heart seemed to have broken permanently.

"I'm still tart-tongued, however," Eve added with a twinkle in her eyes.

"Aye, that's true," James said.

"Quiet!" he and Eve ordered the lad together. Then they shared a rueful smile.

"How *is* Natalie?" Eve asked, then coughed again. "I would have paid a call on her before now, but . . . well . . . between our arrival in England, and trying to get my stepmother and half brother settled here—"

"Oh, right. I forgot. You and your family were détenus." He was delaying the moment when he had to tell her Natalie was gone, but who could blame him? His sister had been very close to Eve.

"You know about the détenus?" she said, looking surprised. "Many Englishmen have no idea."

"Natalie used to read your letters from Verdun aloud at the dinner table—at least until Napoleon cut off all communications between England and France. And I also happen to be acquainted with another détenu—the Duke of Falconridge." When she looked blank, he added, "You might have known him as Lord Jonathan Leighton. He became duke after his father and brothers died while he was detained in France. He only learned of his new title upon his return."

After eleven years in a detainee camp. It still astonished him that Napoleon had kept civilian Englishmen—and women and children—captive for eleven years once the Peace of Amiens abruptly ended.

"Oh, yes!" she said brightly. "Lord Jonathan was the one who introduced my father to my French stepmother in Verdun."

"Ah." From what he'd heard, it hadn't been unusual for détenus to make new French friends in Verdun. And her father had already been a widower back when Noel had known Eve.

Suddenly, he realized they were drawing a crowd. "Can I accompany you and your brother anywhere?" He found himself loath to end the conversation . . . because of her connection to Natalie, of course. Nothing more.

What a liar he was. When she looked hesitant, he added, "It will give us a chance to catch up."

"In that case, we were just on our way to Lincoln's Inn Fields when I stopped to talk to a friend, and my brother decided to disappear on me."

"I'm right here," James said sullenly.

"And you will stay beside me until we get to the square, you little rascal."

"Stay beside *us*," Noel said, offering her his arm and foolishly praying she'd take it. When she did, he let out the breath he'd been holding.

They began to walk, with James trudging along beside his sister. She coughed into her handkerchief a couple of times, tearing at his equilibrium.

When she got her coughing under control, she said, "You haven't yet told me about Natalie and how she is."

Damn. She had him all out of sorts. And he was never out of sorts.

He dragged in a harsh breath. It felt wrong, cruel somehow, to tell her of Natalie's consumption when she seemed to be fighting a similar affliction. But he had to say *something*. "I suppose I should have mentioned it sooner, but Natalie died two years ago this Epiphany of . . . an illness."

"Oh no! That is awful!" Eve stopped short to stare at him, her shocked expression showing she truly meant it. "How your parents must have suffered!"

Not quite ready to admit his father was dead, too, he said, "It has been hard on our family."

She seemed to notice the stiffness of his words. "Forgive me. I'm sure it was hard on *you* as well as your parents. I know you and Natalie weren't close, but—"

"Eleven years is a long time, Miss Archer. Natalie and I became closer as she got older." *And sicker.* He forced a smile. "We had little choice in the matter since you were no longer around to be her friend, through no fault of your own, of course."

Tears glittered in Eve's eyes. "I missed her so much in Verdun, and now I shall never see her again."

The sorrow in her voice was unmistakable, and it touched him deeply. "We would have written you, but we'd already heard that Napoleon had stopped the flow of mail between our two countries. So there seemed no point."

They walked a few moments in silence. Then she shivered, and he realized she shouldn't be out here so flimsily dressed.

"Take my greatcoat," he said, shrugging it off. "It's deuced cold out here."

She hesitated, then allowed him to put it on her. She had such a fresh, clean scent—some sort of citrus was involved, he would guess. And how thin she seemed. Was it because she didn't eat enough or was that just her natural shape?

Not that he should care. He'd spent the past two years trying not to care about . . . anything. His state of blessed numbness made it easier to go on without his father and his sister.

Still, he felt the opposite of numb as he continued with Eve down Holborn Street. Just seeing her reminded him of his sister before her illness—how the two girls had giggled at his ridiculously pompous pronouncements, how they'd groaned in unison when he'd chided them like a typical older brother. He had to find some way to help her. Natalie would want that, wouldn't she?

"Do you often go to Lincoln's Inn Fields?" he asked, hoping to figure out how she and her family had come to this pass. The carriage traffic cleared, enabling them to cross.

Her features softened. "As often as I can. Even in winter, there's enough greenery to cheer the soul." With a sudden smile, she nodded to her brother. "And this one likes to run about in the gardens. There wasn't much of that in Verdun. Papa was afraid of him straying too far."

Her soft spot toward her rapscallion of a brother was endearing, to say the least. "How did you end up in France, anyway? I can't remember if Natalie ever said."

"Papa was determined to take me there during that brief period when the war halted. He had some notion of improving my education by exposing me to architecture and the arts in Paris. Sadly, we'd only been there a month when it was announced that the war was back on and Napoleon made his decree concerning the English who were still in France."

The decree that sent them all to detainee camps. "Your father must have been disappointed to find himself restricted to a Verdun détenu camp for so many years."

"You don't know the half of it. He nearly got into trouble over a pamphlet he wanted to publish concerning Napoleon's outrageous behavior. Lord Jonathan—I mean, the duke—talked him out of it. And when His Grace saw I had an interest in embroidery, he recommended that Papa engage my stepmother to teach me sewing, too." Her face lit up. "She was wonderful for Papa."

His heart sank. "*Was*?"

She stared off down the street. "I should have mentioned that, I suppose. Papa is also . . . gone. He died on our journey from France."

That struck him hard. He was painfully aware of how deep such grief could run, and to think she had suffered, too—"I am so sorry to hear that. Your father was a good man." As opposed to his own feckless father, who'd nearly wasted the entire family fortune enjoying himself, never meeting a horse race he didn't wish to put money on.

"Thank you," she said, looking distressed. Once more, he'd banished the joy from her face, which he hated doing.

"And now, *I'm* the Baron Archer," James announced, puffing out his chest. Then his face fell. "Or I'm supposed to be, anyway. If I hadn't been born in France."

"What does he mean?" Noel asked Eve as they approached Lincoln's Inn Fields. "James being born in France shouldn't change his claim to the title. It might impact his ability to serve in Parliament, but—"

"Jimmy," Eve said, shooting Noel a quelling glance, "could you run ahead and see if Mr. Washburn is in this morning?" She grabbed James's arm before he could leave. "And no picking pockets, do you hear? Or there will be no gingerbread for you when we get home."

As James nodded solemnly, then ran off, she sighed.

"No gingerbread?" Noel said dryly.

Apparently misunderstanding his point, Eve said, "One of my mother's customers has a cook that makes the most heavenly gingerbread, and sometimes she's generous enough to give us some. It's Jimmy's favorite treat."

"Still, *that's* your idea of a punishment for picking pockets?"

Her cheeks flamed as she released his arm. "I know it's inconceivable to a man of your standing that anyone should feel so desperate," she said, the words pouring out of her, "but the lad is trying to fill rather big shoes—our papa's. He thinks it's his duty to provide for me and my stepmother. And it's not as if he could find a job at his age . . . unless it's dangerous, like sweeping chimneys or working in a bootblacking factory where—"

"I wasn't advocating *that*," he said quickly.

"Weren't you?" She walked briskly ahead.

"Of course not. I merely didn't realize things had become so bad for your family." He mused a moment. "I wish you had come to me. It's not as if you don't know where I live. I might have been able to help." Even as he heard himself say the hasty words, he groaned. The last thing he needed was to get involved with a woman who clutched at his heart with every cough.

"You would hire my pickpocketing half brother as a footboy, I suppose?" she said with a shaky laugh.

"That might not be a bad idea," he quipped, willing to say almost anything to keep her laughing. "A light-fingered footboy could steal a rose for my mother from the neighbor's garden, slip my uncle's flask of fine whisky out of his pocket and into mine, and remove eggs from beneath our hens without alarming them."

She eyed him askance. "Surely you do not actually keep chickens in Mayfair!"

"No. Only at our estate."

"In that case, I can't allow Jimmy to work for you as a light-fingered footboy," she said teasingly. "We would miss him too much if he moved to the country."

"I see. Then I shall just have to settle for trying to help your family some other way." He sobered. "I was thinking more in terms of loaning your stepmother money until such time as the matter of James's title is settled."

Her face reddened with embarrassment. "They've told us it could be years. Forgive me, sir, but we don't need your charity."

Yet he wanted to do *something* to help. Not that he blamed her for her pride. She'd gone from being a wealthy baron's daughter to *this*. Still . . . "Let me at least find out more about the legal aspects of James's situation."

"Oh." She softened. "That would be useful. I know nothing about these things, and my stepmother knows even less, so we have to rely on Mr. Washburn, our attorney. He's supposed to be making sure James gets his due, but he hasn't been able to do much."

"Why not?" Noel asked.

She shrugged. "According to Mr. Washburn, Papa's brother, Uriah Archer, is disputing James's claim to the barony. Uncle Uriah says his elder brother would never have married a French seamstress, and even if he had done so rather than simply making her his mistress, how can the court be sure James was born on the right side of the blanket?" She scowled. "It's maddening how certain he is of my stepmother's poor character when he hasn't even bothered to meet her."

"Surely your stepmother has proof of the marriage *and* of James's birth."

"The marriage and birth records are in France at the church where Papa wed my stepmother and James was baptized. They hurried us out of Verdun as soon as Napoleon abdicated, so there was no time to get official copies."

"Witnesses?"

"So far Mr. Washburn hasn't been able to find them. Everyone left Verdun at different times once we were released, and all of us had to make our own way to the coast. One of the witnesses had died, anyway, but Mr. Washburn has had no luck finding the other in England."

She sighed. "Besides, we didn't expect Papa to perish on the journey home. He would have been able to prove it all eventually, and in the meantime, he could have supported us." She shook her head. "Now someone has to return to France and get the priest to attest to it in a legal document and such. We can't afford it, but that's what Mr. Washburn says must happen."

His eyes narrowed. "Mr. Washburn doesn't sound like a very good attorney."

Her shoulders drooped. "To be fair, Uncle Uriah has had access to Papa's funds for some time. He just refuses to give us any. Papa hadn't changed his will to reflect his new marriage, I'm afraid, or the letter doing so never made it to England. And he wasn't expecting to die so young."

Noel's father hadn't been, either, but that hadn't prevented a carriage from striking him as he'd crossed a street. Meanwhile, Natalie had known to expect her death. They'd all known. Few people survived consumption.

But it had been shocking and devastating, anyway. Even when death was expected, it was a surprise.

Suddenly he realized something. "You're not coughing anymore."

"No. I don't cough in this part of town, or in most parts of town, really. Only in Holborn."

Odd. Her cough hadn't seemed feigned—of all people, he ought to know—but that bad a cough couldn't suddenly be suppressed.

Then the rest of her statements sank in. "Wait, are you *living* in Holborn now?" It was a decent area of shabby gentility, but certainly not a neighborhood for the likes of a baron's daughter and her family.

Her cheeks turned bright red, yet she forced a smile. "We did try to find a place in Mayfair, but they expected us to actually pay for our lodgings," she said flippantly. "Can you imagine?"

How could she joke about such a thing? "And you live free where you are?" he asked, in all seriousness.

She lifted her eyes heavenward. "Of course not. But our lodgings are far less dear than yours, I daresay."

"No doubt, if you're in Holborn."

"I did not say that's where we live," she countered, rather nervously.

"Miss Archer—" he began, but before he could press her further, her brother came running up to them.

"Mr. Washburn isn't in," James said. "He's in court."

She snorted. "I doubt that. One of the clerks told me yesterday he would be in his office today. He's just avoiding me."

"Who recommended Mr. Washburn to you?" Noel asked.

"One of the other détenus," she said.

"A fellow who's sweet on Eve," James said sullenly.

That news delivered an unexpected punch to his gut. He fought to ignore it. "Doesn't surprise me. I'd be shocked if all the détenu males aren't sweet on your sister."

She looked startled by the compliment. "That's laying it on a bit thick, don't you think?"

"Only half of the males, then," he said with a smile. "In any case, I think a disinterested party like me should look into Mr. Washburn's credentials and reputation, don't you?"

She stared at him as if weighing the wisdom of it. "If you can be discreet about it," she finally said, "Maman would greatly appreciate it."

"And you? Would *you* appreciate it?"

She cast him a shy smile. "Of course."

"Good." He offered his arm. "Now, why don't you let me walk you home, so you can get out of this cold?"

Alarm filled her features. "No need. I have Jimmy to accompany me." Quickly, she shrugged off his greatcoat and handed it to him.

Reluctantly he put it back on. She was determined not to let him know exactly where she lived, wasn't she? "At least give me your direction, so I can pass on whatever information I find out about Mr. Washburn."

"As you said, I know where *you* live. I'll pay a call on you and your mother in a few days' time to find out what you've learned." She smiled at him. "Thank you, Mr. Davenant, not only for looking into Mr. Washburn for us, but for not dragging James away to the constable. Again, I must apologize for—"

"You have nothing to apologize for." He caught her hand and lifted it to his lips to kiss. "I look forward to our next encounter."

She seemed surprised by the courtly—and decidedly not English—gesture, but not nearly as surprised as he was. It wasn't like him to do such a thing. Yet he couldn't help noticing she trembled as she took her time about pulling her hand from his.

That gave him immense satisfaction. Which was rather worrying. He didn't want to feel such emotions right now. He wanted to continue to take refuge in feeling nothing.

She turned to her brother. "Come, Jimmy. Let's go home."

As if the hounds of hell were at her back, she hurried away. He was still watching her, wondering how to follow her without her knowledge, when young James stopped her to say something, and then, at her nod, ran back to Noel.

"We live in Hatton Garden, next to the dye factory," James whispered.

So, definitely Holborn. "Did your sister tell you to say that?" he whispered back, rather amused by the air of secrecy.

"No, she don't . . . *doesn't* . . . know I'm telling you. I said I wanted to apologize for stealing your wallet."

"And are you apologizing?" he asked.

James looked him in the eye with a pride much like his sister's. "We've got to eat, don't we?"

The lad is trying to fill rather big shoes—our papa's. He thinks it's his duty to provide for me and my stepmother.

"I suppose you do." Realizing that Eve was watching them closely, Noel held out his hand to shake, and James took it.

But before the lad could draw it back, he pulled him closer and said in an undertone, "All the same, your family's situation will be markedly damaged if you end up in jail for thieving. Thieves are often sent to the hulks, even at your age." He waited until James's eyes widened in alarm before adding, "So, if I hear you've been picking pockets again, I'll make sure your sister and mother keep you locked up if they have to. Let me see what I can do to help your situation before you go trying to steal things again, understand?"

The boy bobbed his head. As soon as Noel released his hand, he darted back to his sister.

She flashed Noel a tremulous smile, and he returned her smile warmly. He had a perverse desire to beg her not to go. That wouldn't be wise, however.

He would help the young woman and her foolish brother, if only because of what she'd once meant to Natalie. And because he wasn't made of stone.

But anything more would hurt his plans for a more settled life—a more settled *wife*—than could possibly be found in a woman who came with untold possibilities for difficulty and pain: a rascal brother with a dubious claim to a title, a foreign stepmother, and that alarming cough. Not to mention a woman who roused such intense feelings in him that she could easily shatter his heart.

What was left of it, anyway, after losing his sister. He mustn't let Eve into his heart, or *her* loss from that cough of hers would finish it off.

Sadly, he had to repeat his reasoning to himself all the way home before he could put Miss Eve Archer's parting smile out of his head.

CHAPTER 2

The morning after encountering Mr. Davenant on the street, Eve had donned her father's old coat and was gathering up her charcoals and dyes, preparing to work outside while the dye factory's vats were spewing steam into their joint alley, when Jimmy grabbed her arm.

"You didn't tell Maman about yesterday, did you?" Jimmy asked her plaintively.

"Not yet. But if you don't behave today . . ."

"I will, I promise!" He made the sign of crossing his heart.

But when he then reached for a third slice of toast, she caught his hand. "You've had enough. The loaf has to last us the week." She coughed into her handkerchief, cursing whatever dye the dyeworks was producing today that aggravated her asthma more than usual. "And Maman hasn't yet had any this morning."

Just then, Maman came up behind them. "Hasn't had any what?" she asked in her thick French accent. Maman had been working on bettering her English ever since she'd met Papa.

"Toast," Eve said. "We have butter for once. You should eat."

"You eat it, my dear. Mrs. Beckford always offers me pastries when I take her gown for the fitting, so I will eat there. And while I'm gone, be sure to watch your brother."

"Of course. Speaking of Jimmy . . ."

Jimmy kicked her under the table, and Eve glared at him.

Maman sighed. "What has the scamp done this time?"

"Nothing." What a blatant lie. "I was just wondering if I could take him with me over to Lincoln's Inn Gardens again, so I can pick some sprigs of holly off their bushes to use as models for my new Christmas design. We . . . er . . . didn't make it there yesterday." Unfortunately, such a long speech meant she had to cough repeatedly afterward.

Maman frowned. "Your asthma is bad today, no? I shall purchase more thorn apple mixture at the apothecary on my way home."

"We can't afford—"

"Mrs. Beckford will pay us well. She liked your embroidery design, and I know will love the finished gown." Maman chucked Eve under the chin as if she were still a child. "You must have your herbs. It helps you breathe, no?"

Tears filled her eyes as she nodded. Because her own mother had died bearing her, her stepmother was the only mother Eve had ever known. Eve loved her dearly.

"I only wish we could live somewhere better than this, but the rent is so cheap—"

"That's all that matters. Perhaps once we finish these latest gowns for Mrs. Beckford, we can look for a better place."

"Perhaps. And yes, of course you may take your brother to pick holly." Maman lifted the huge case she kept gowns in and headed for the door. "Just keep an eye on the little scamp."

Ever since Maman had heard the word "scamp," she used it often to describe Jimmy. Which was certainly appropriate.

Maman opened the door, then hastily closed it again. "There's a man in the alley, Eve," she whispered in French. "He's staring at your latest pattern on the wall."

Eve ran to their only other downstairs room, which acted as their sitting room. The window in it looked out onto the wall of the dyeworks, where she generally sketched all her embroidery designs. And standing between her and the wall was—

"Jimmy, you . . . you *scoundrel*!" she hissed as she hurried back into their kitchen/dining room. "You told him our address?"

Jimmy was polishing off the last piece of toast. "Oh, is the gentleman here?" He jumped up. "P'raps he'll take us to the gardens in his carriage!"

"Is that the man James was telling us about last night?" her stepmother asked Eve.

"Mr. Davenant, yes." Eve sighed. "I didn't want him to see how we live." Although he'd genuinely seemed sympathetic about the parts of their situation she'd revealed. Still, she feared that one more truth laid upon the scale would tip the balance of their worth in his eyes, making him return to being the thoughtless, self-important fellow he'd been in her youth.

Maman shrugged. "If he looks down upon us, it's best to know that now." She opened the door to peek out. "Your young man is very handsome, from as much as I can see of him. And he must be rich. That greatcoat alone—"

"Maman! He's not my young man." Though he was, indeed, attractive. She hadn't thought so at thirteen, but he was leaner than she remembered, and far more solemn. His head of unruly raven curls made her think of King Arthur of old. Not to mention those blue eyes of his, the color of cloudless skies . . . Oh, heavens, a woman could die happy in them.

"I believe you could make him your young man if you wished. He found you here, didn't he?"

"It means nothing," Eve said, remembering how fiercely he'd gripped Jimmy's arm yesterday, terrifying her that he would drag her brother off to the constable.

"Come, dear. Introduce me." Maman's face darkened. "Unless you're embarrassed to be seen with your French *maman*."

"Never." Eve kissed her cheek. Steadying her shoulders, she walked outside, followed by Maman and Jimmy. "Good morning, Mr. Davenant."

"There you are!" He whirled to face her. "I thought for certain I had the wrong place. Until I saw this." He swept his hand to indicate her drawing. "It's a pattern for embroidery, is it not?"

"It is, indeed." She coughed. "How could you tell?"

"Well, the cross-hatching, for one thing. You forget that my mother and sister always had patterns lying about the house. And I remember how keen you were on needlework."

"You do?" she said, incredulous.

He shrugged. "I wasn't entirely an oblivious older brother, you know. I almost never saw you without your head bent over your tambour." He gestured to her design. "But why draw the pattern on the wall?"

"Because paper is—" Maman began.

"—not big enough for me," Eve broke in before her stepmother could say *costly*. "I like my designs writ large." She coughed again. "Then I can gaze at them out the window as I work and tell where every stitch must land."

"Don't the owners of the dyeworks mind?"

"No, they're very kind, since we rent from them. Besides, I always wash it off when I'm done." And the workers gave her the bits of charcoal and dye powder she used to make the designs.

Her stepmother nudged her.

"Mr. Davenant, may I present my stepmother, Lady Violette Archer?"

"I'm honored to meet you, Lady Archer," he said with a courteous nod. "I was very sorry to hear from Miss Archer of your husband's demise."

"Thank you, sir," Maman said.

"In fact," he went on, "my mother was always so fond of your stepdaughter that she has asked me to invite the three of you to dinner tomorrow night."

"That is very kind of her," Maman said, clearly surprised. "We would be delighted to accept."

"Maman," Eve said in a low voice, "we don't have clothes fine enough to dine with the viscountess and her husband." And what if Eve had forgotten how to navigate a proper table setting and how to behave as a gently bred lady in company?

"It will be quite informal, Miss Archer," Mr. Davenant put in. "She has known you for years and would be disappointed if you couldn't join us."

Eve would love to see Lady Cokesbury again. The viscountess had treated Eve like a daughter at a time when Eve had lacked a mother. Indeed, it had been she who taught Eve all those manners in the first place. "Very well. If you're quite sure she and your father won't take offense when we arrive dressed less impressively than they're used to."

"She could never take offense at seeing a friend, no matter how informally that friend is attired." He looked suddenly uncomfortable. "But . . . um . . . there's something I should have told you yesterday. My father won't be joining us for dinner. He passed away about a year before Natalie fell ill."

Her emotions bounced all over the place. First, she was sad for Mr. Davenant, then astonished he hadn't told her right away, and then . . . Oh, good Lord. If his father was dead, Mr. Davenant was the viscount now. She'd been treating him like the mere heir. Could this get any worse?

She blinked at him, then turned to her stepmother. "I'm sorry, Maman, but I didn't introduce the gentleman properly. This is Noel Davenant, the Viscount Cokesbury." She coughed a moment. "Forgive me, Lord Cokesbury, but I didn't know that you . . . that your father—"

"Please," he said hastily, "I'm the one who should ask forgiveness. I was enjoying our conversation so much yesterday that I forgot to mention it."

She sensed there was more to it but didn't wish to discuss it in front of Maman.

"And speaking of that," he went on, "I looked into your Mr. Washburn. From what I could learn, he doesn't have a good reputation. With your and your stepmother's permission," he said, pausing to smile at Maman, "I'd like to have my own attorney research your situation."

"Thank you, my lord," Maman said stiffly, "but we cannot afford that. Besides, if my late husband's brother were to hear of it—"

"My attorney is quite discreet," he assured her. "As for the money, I pay him a yearly retaining fee, which he earns whether or not he does a thing for me." He flashed Maman one of his brilliant smiles. "So, it won't cost me any more than I've already paid. I will tell him only to do what is covered by the retainer, all right?"

"Oh," Maman said with a questioning look at Eve. "I do not understand this word *retainer*. I thought it meant someone who was beholden to a lord."

Eve had never heard of a retaining fee, but that didn't mean much. Doubtless it was something only rich people did, and it had been a long time since her family had been considered rich. "I think the viscount is saying that his *attorney* is beholden to him . . . precisely because His Lordship gives the man a yearly fee."

Lord Cokesbury smiled. "Very good, Miss Archer."

Eve warmed beneath the sunshine of his smile.

"Then that would be kind of you, sir," Maman said. "But now it is I who must ask forgiveness. I am on my way to deliver a gown to a customer and must not linger. Perhaps you could stay a bit so that Eve may work on her design outside? When I am gone, which isn't often, she usually sits inside and locks the door. It is not safe for a woman alone, no? But if you are outside with her, she will be fine."

Oh, Lord, now Maman was trying her hand at matchmaking. "Surely there's no need for Mr. . . . for Lord Cokesbury to stay around, Maman," Eve said hastily. "Jimmy and I will walk with you and then go to Lincoln's Inn Fields to pick holly."

"I require Jimmy to go all the way with me to help carry my case, I'm afraid," her stepmother said blandly. "But you should not walk alone."

"I'll walk with Miss Archer," Lord Cokesbury put in. "Or stay here if that is her preference."

"Thank you, sir," Maman said, beaming at him. "That would be most helpful." She turned to Jimmy. "Come along, my little scamp."

"Do I get pastries, too?" Jimmy asked as he took the other end of the case.

"If Mrs. Beckford wishes to give them to you." Maman turned to Lord Cokesbury. "It was lovely to meet you, my lord."

He bowed. "I can see that Miss Archer is in good hands with you, madam. I will send a carriage for you and your family tomorrow night at six."

With another smile, Maman hurried out to the road with Jimmy.

An uncomfortable silence fell after the two of them were left alone.

Eve ventured a glance at him to find him watching her with an odd concentration. "You don't have to stay with me, my lord. I'm fine."

When she followed that statement with a couple of deep coughs, he frowned. "Clearly, you're not fine. You're coughing again."

"You can't help me with that." She narrowed her gaze on him. "And you seem inordinately interested in my cough."

Alarm lit his face. "Not interested. Worried. That is—"

"I have asthma. The fumes from the dyeworks aggravate it."

"Asthma!" Relief filled his voice. "Of course. Thank God."

She blinked. "I beg your pardon?"

"Not thank God that you have it," he said hastily. "I mean, thank God that you . . . I thought it was . . . *feared* it was . . . well . . ." He looked rather adorably flustered. "Natalie died of consumption."

"Oh! I-I'm so sorry to hear that. Fortunately, I don't have consumption. The doctor assured Maman of that."

"Good, because it's a dreadful way to die."

"So I've heard," she said softly.

He must have detected the pity in her voice, because he drew himself up and swiftly changed the subject. "This design of yours is astonishing." He gestured to her pattern on the wall. "That's Father Christmas, is it not, in the circle of holly?"

"I'm surprised you can tell it's holly," she said ruefully, coughing a little. "I can't seem to get the shape right. I'm doing it from memory, and it's been so long since I saw any that I can't remember how it actually grows. But, yes, that is Father Christmas."

"You ought to surround him with chubby-cheeked little urchins. Your brother would be the perfect model."

"Only if the urchins are picking Father Christmas's pockets," she said dryly. "And I mustn't encourage such behavior during the holiday. Especially in my brother."

"Duly noted," he said, though his eyes twinkled.

She'd never seen his eyes twinkle. It stirred something warm in her blood.

"What colors do you mean to use?" he asked, looking genuinely interested.

"Father Christmas will be in green and brown, but I can't decide whether to use white thread to indicate snow on the ground or just leave the background all white from the fabric."

"I vote for snow," he said. "Nothing demonstrates Christmas like fluffy-looking snow. And holly, of course."

"*If* I can get it right."

"It looks perfect to me already, although you do need some holly berries in red."

She nodded. "I was already intending to add the berries once I was done with the leaves. I've been putting off finishing everything because it's been so cold, but now I have no choice. The embroidery design is for a gown Maman completed sewing days ago. I've nearly finished embroidering the Father Christmas figure, so I must start on the holly soon. Maman is sewing dancing slippers to go with it, and then I'll have to repeat the design on those."

"Can you fit Father Christmas on dancing slippers?"

"I can. As long as he is quite small."

"That would require very small needles and fine needlework, wouldn't it?"

"Yes." She arched an eyebrow. "Do you doubt I can do it?"

"I wouldn't dare." He grinned at her. "I fear you'd stab me with one of your needles if I did."

"And don't you forget it, sir," she warned, trying to look serious and failing. She coughed a few times. "Maman's most important customer, Mrs. Beckford, is attending a Christmas Day affair at a friend's house, so that's what the gown and the slippers are for. Fortunately, the dyeworks next door is spewing lots of steam today and keeping the alley moderately warm, which is why I was hoping to get work done outside."

"Even if it makes you cough."

She nodded.

"Also, it isn't 'moderately warm' out here. It's freezing."

"It's not so bad," she lied. "Not with plenty of warm clothes on."

He lifted an eyebrow but didn't remark on that. Instead, he returned his gaze to her design. "I take it your stepmother supports you three with her sewing? And you do the same with your embroidery?"

"Yes." She shrugged. "I would embroider things regardless since I enjoy the art, but why not earn money for it?"

He seemed to be pondering something. "I'd love to see some finished examples of your needlework."

She couldn't help laughing, especially after all the questions he'd asked regarding her design. "The Viscount Cokesbury has an interest in embroidery. How droll."

"Please don't stand on ceremony with me," he said, his beautiful eyes gleaming as he walked up to her. "Call me Noel, as you and

Natalie did when you were girls. After all, you and I are old friends, aren't we?"

She arched an eyebrow. "Are we? You never wished to see my embroidery when I was thirteen."

"I never wished to kiss you then, either," he said bluntly, "but things change."

A delicious shiver swept over her when he tipped up her chin with one finger and pressed his lips to hers.

Her heart pounded in her chest from the sheer surprise of it. It wasn't like any kiss she'd ever experienced. Lips supple as kid leather caressed hers as he slid a surprisingly powerful arm about her waist to pull her close. Everything about it intoxicated her—the feel of his hard body against her, the taste of coffee on his breath, and the smell of spicy cologne that clung to him and settled into her, a familiar scent after she'd smelled it on his coat yesterday.

Then he slanted his mouth over hers, coaxing it open so he could plunge his tongue inside. Her heart thundered in her chest. Such wild heat spread from where their mouths were joined to where he was holding her that she thought she might burst into flames. He tangled his tongue with hers over and over, rousing an unfamiliar hunger in places that had never felt hunger before, prompting her to throw her arms about his neck.

Groaning low in his throat, he kissed her more fiercely, as if he couldn't get enough. Or perhaps it was she who couldn't get enough . . . of the sensual strokes of his tongue and the feel of his soft curls beneath her fingertips.

He broke the kiss only to scatter a succession of kisses down her chin to her throat, making her gasp at the thrill and yearn for more. His hat fell off, as if tempting her to thread her fingers through his gorgeous hair, so she did. He pressed a warm line of kisses along her neck and up to her ear.

Heavens. What lovely kisses he gave!

Suddenly, a sharp noise sounded in the street nearby, jerking them both back to their surroundings.

She was the first to pull away, to draw her coat about her and avoid his gaze, embarrassed that she'd behaved like a veritable wanton with him. Thank God no one was likely to notice them in the alley, especially since the dyeworks windows were high up, but still . . . this was very public.

He dropped his hands, then bent to pick up his hat and knock it against his thigh before placing it back on his head.

For a moment, the only sounds in the alley were of the steam from the dyeworks and their heavy breaths.

At last he cleared his throat. "Forgive me, Miss Archer. I shouldn't have taken advantage of you."

Such a gentlemanly thing to say after he'd just been kissing her with such abandon. It rather amused her. "If I am to call you Noel," she said with a teasing smile, "the least you can do is call *me* Eve. And you didn't take advantage, I assure you."

He gazed at her steadily. "Didn't I?"

"No." To be honest, she couldn't remember the last time a man had kissed her. Father had been so strict that he'd rarely let any of the détenus near her. And it wasn't as if she could find the right sort of man here in Holborn. They were all mostly married, or shopkeepers who looked down on her family for their meager existence.

But the few times she'd been kissed in Verdun had been nothing like this. She fancied she could still feel Noel's mouth against hers, and she slid her tongue along her lips to see if she could still taste him there.

For a moment, he followed the sweep of her tongue with a hungry gaze, and his eyes seemed to heat. Then, as if willing himself to ignore whatever he felt, he shuddered, and an impenetrable veil dropped over his features. "All the same," he said regretfully, "it must not happen again."

His words both startled her and told her only too well what he thought of her. She ignored the tears stinging her eyes. She would not give him the satisfaction of seeing her cry over it. "I agree—it must not," she said, when what she really wanted to do was ask *why* it mustn't happen again.

Unfortunately, she knew the answer. He was a viscount, and she a poor nobody now, the daughter of a détenu baron whose will apparently hadn't even provided for her and her family. She ought to have realized she was far beneath his notice, only worthy of a dalliance. Clearly, he was too much of a gentleman even for that.

Except when he was kissing her.

"But I do wish to see your needlework," he said, his tone softening, as if he'd realized he'd hurt her feelings. "My mother still has the apron you embroidered for her as a girl for Christmas."

"With the red ribbon and gold bells?" she asked, willing to say almost anything to keep from discussing their kiss. Although truly, she was surprised to hear that his mother had kept her embroidery. "It wasn't as well-done as I'd prefer. I'm much better at needlework now."

And she was babbling. But what else could a woman do when faced with a man who kissed as intoxicatingly as the viscount and then wanted to forget it ever happened?

"My mother thinks that apron is beautiful," he went on, "and treasures it as one of her favorite things. She won't even wear it for fear it will get dirty. In fact . . ." He paused. "I'd like to pay you to make another just like it, so she can have one to use and one to keep."

He might as well have slapped her in the face. Now, he wanted to be her *customer*? That was how little the kiss had meant to him?

Instantly, she cloaked herself in her pride. "I see. So, that's why you wanted to view my present needlework. To see if you might employ me?"

He blinked. "Good God, no! I only meant . . . That is not what I intended at all. I merely thought that you and your mother could use—"

"The funds." She crossed her arms over her chest, struggling to hide her anger. "So, you *pity* me, is that it, my lord?"

"Don't call me that, for God's sake," he muttered.

"Why not? It's who you are." And the sooner she got that through her thick skull, the better off she'd be. "I suppose, since I refused to let you outright give money to my stepmother, you now mean to have me embroider something for your mother so you can pay us for it. But either way, it's charity, and I won't take charity from you."

"It's not charity," he said firmly. "Christmas is coming, and I want to give a gift to my mother that I know she'll appreciate."

"I'll be happy to embroider another apron for your mother,"

she choked out. "I remember her fondly. But it will be my gift to her. You will not pay for it."

"You're going to be stubborn about this, I see."

"I'm afraid I must."

He stared down his nose at her. She stared up his nose at him.

At last, he shook his head. "Fine. At least I can accompany you to Lincoln's Inn Gardens."

"No need. I shall wait until Maman and Jimmy return, and then I'll go."

"Why wait?"

Because you've made it very clear what you think of me, and I need to be away from you before I really am tempted to stab you with one of my needles. "Because I'm sure an important man like you has better things to do than wait on the leisure of a tradeswoman like me."

"You are no more a tradeswoman than I am a merchant," he bit out. "I was not trying to say that."

"True. You weren't *trying* to say it at all. You were succeeding, and quite handily, too."

He muttered a curse under his breath. "Eve, I swear I meant you no insult."

"Just go home, my lord," she said wearily. "You may have nothing better to do with your time, but I certainly do."

His eyes glittered at her. "Very well. Then I shall see you tomorrow evening." When she merely stared at him, he looked a bit more uneasy. "I *will* see you tomorrow, won't I?"

How she'd love to refuse, but she dared not. "My stepmother has already accepted for the family, and I wouldn't for the world gainsay her." Maman would assume that Eve was embarrassed by her.

"You'd come to dinner for her, but not for me?" he pressed her.

"Why would I do it for you?" she managed to choke out.

"Because we're old friends," he said, his gaze dropping inexorably to her lips before he seemed to catch himself and jerk it back up. When she blushed, he drawled, "And it's a little late to deny the acquaintance, don't you think?"

It infuriated her to hear him repeat the line he'd said yesterday, the one that had prompted her to tell him how she knew him. Angry with herself for blushing, she said, "Watch me."

Then she marched right back into the house, shut the door, and locked it. But even as she heard him call out, "Good day, Miss Archer!" and walk away, she was tempted to open the door and beg him to come back.

And that would be the height of folly.

CHAPTER 3

For the hundredth time since yesterday morning in Hatton Garden, Noel chided himself for being a fool.

He shouldn't have kissed her.

Even now, as the carriage headed closer to Eve's lodgings, he wondered how else he could have reacted to her teasing him and looking like an angel, even in her patched gown and too-large coat.

He'd had to kiss her, damn it, even if it was only the one time, because otherwise he would have driven himself mad wondering how she would taste, how she would feel in his arms. Except now he was driving himself mad wondering when he could do it again.

What insanity. Although the kiss had gone rather well at first, he had somehow managed to bumble through what had come after, thinking only that he shouldn't be kissing her when he intended to offer for Lady Margaret one day soon.

Suddenly, she'd looked stricken and called him "my lord" and made him yearn for what he'd known he dared not have. Then he'd panicked and tried to fix matters by offering to hire her to do some embroidery. Any other woman in her situation would have welcomed the work. Right?

Then again, what he knew about young ladies could be put into a thimble with room left over. He and Natalie hadn't been close until she'd fallen ill. Even then, it had taken her three years to die, and with Father already dead, Noel had spent most of that time trying to figure out how to keep the family solvent and Natalie alive, trying every doctor and remedy that might keep her from death's door. He'd neglected his estate so he could be there for his family. Not that he regretted it, but it was only more proof that caring for someone came with a high cost.

After Natalie had finally lost her battle with consumption, it had been a relief to spend his time shoring up the viscountcy finances. It was better than dwelling on how he'd failed to save her. On how he'd lost years of closeness he might have had with her if he hadn't behaved like a typical heedless older brother when he was young.

Over time, his own grief had settled into a blessed numbness that kept him from pain. He sometimes thought he and Mother moved through their daily lives in a dance that never altered its rhythms or patterns.

It was only at the end of the most recent Season that he'd gone looking for a wife. He wasn't getting any younger, after all. He had to sire an heir.

His ideal candidate had been someone who wouldn't tie him into emotional knots, because he didn't have the strength for it anymore. He could barely keep his own mother from her grief. He certainly couldn't shower love and affection on some woman he hardly knew.

So, he'd started courting the first woman who'd seemed sensible and responsible, a tall order among the usual crop of young hopefuls. Lady Margaret would never make him feel or yearn or risk loss. She would run his household and bear him children and never expect more from him than he could give. She would never spend him into penury. She would make the perfect viscountess.

He sighed. But it hadn't been Lady Margaret he'd lain in bed last night craving. God, he'd barely been able to sleep thinking of Eve's soft lips, soft body . . . soft everything. Of her teasing smiles and her amazing talent for drawing.

Of the fact that he'd insulted her and still wasn't entirely sure how.

The carriage shuddered to a halt, and he groaned. Now he'd have to endure an entire dinner with her and her family while she sat staring daggers at him. Which was preferable to her flashing her sweet, melting smiles at him that threatened to overrun his control.

With an oath, he climbed out and headed for the door of the skinny building sandwiched between a larger building and an alley, one wall of which held her sketch. He couldn't see it now that darkness had fallen, but he smiled to remember her beautifully rendered Father Christmas. The twinkle in the fellow's eyes had brought him to life, and that was hard to manage in an embroidery design, even one "writ large" on a wall.

He knocked on the Archers' door and James answered. "Cor, you look dashing!" he cried.

Noel chuckled. "You look rather dashing yourself, young man." It was true. The lad wore woolen breeches and a matching coat, not to mention an embroidered waistcoat with fleurs-de-lis dotting it. All of it appeared well-worn, and the suit was clearly a decade out of fashion, but it was far better than what Noel had expected the boy to be wearing.

James preened a bit. "Mother got the breeches and coat from Mrs. Beckford—they used to be her son's, the lady said. Sissy made the waistcoat a while ago from one of Father's old ones. And I already had the shirt and gloves." He tugged on the collar. "It's tight, though, on account of the cravat. I don't like a cravat."

"No one likes a cravat, trust me. Cravats look great, but—"

"Feel like a noose."

Noel blinked. "You could say that." He only hoped the lad never had to make the comparison in real life. He tried to look past James. "Are the ladies ready?"

James rolled his eyes so dramatically it was a shock they didn't pop out of his head. "They're ladies. They take *forever* to be ready."

The boy had certainly picked up an understanding of some things in his few years. "Then may I come in to wait?"

"If you wish, my lord." He turned to walk toward the table that sat in the middle of the small room.

"Call me Noel," he heard himself saying and marveled at his casual tone. He'd never been one to be havey-cavey about following the rules of societal behavior, so this was a first.

"Mother and Sissy said I have to call you 'my lord.' "

"Ah, but you're the Baron Archer—or you will be one day—so that makes us equals," Noel said and winked at the boy, something else he never did.

"All right, then," James said, and tugged at his cravat.

Noel stood gazing around what was apparently the kitchen. At last, he'd advanced to the inner sanctum. It appeared that the only other room was a parlor. Everything was clean and neat as the queen's drawing room, showing that both Eve and her stepmother did their best with limited resources, where another pair of women might have given up in despair. Still, the fact that there were only two rooms downstairs disturbed him.

He'd gone to the Baron Archer's town house in Mayfair once in his youth, when the whole Davenant family had been invited to dine there. The place had been three times the size of this at least, and well furnished. It sobered him to see how easy it was for a family to be laid low. At least his own father had made sure no one would dispute Noel's right to the title.

And what the devil was wrong with Eve's uncle that he wouldn't provide for his niece, at the very least? She was certainly the legitimate daughter of his brother.

"I take it that the bedrooms are upstairs?" Noel asked.

"We've got two," James said proudly. "It's better than in Verdun. We all slept in the same room once Papa's credit ran out."

From what Noel understood, there'd been a lot of that going on in the detainee camps.

James's face fell. "Being as we're equals and all, I should offer you tea, but we don't got . . . don't *have* any. Sorry. We ran out this morning. Besides, Mother won't let me make tea. She thinks I'll burn myself." He crossed his arms and frowned. "I'm not a baby, but she thinks I am."

"I doubt that. She's just being a mother. Mine is like that, too."

The lad's eyes widened. "Does your mother scold *you*?"

"She does." *Or rather, she used to. Before Father died and left us on the brink of financial ruin, and Natalie died, snuffing out the candle of our joy. Before Mother stopped caring about anything but her grief.* "I like it when she scolds me."

James blinked at him. "Why?"

"Because it shows that she cares." He strolled through to the sitting room or whatever one called a room holding a misshapen couch and a hard wooden chair with a cheap table. Sprigs of holly lay strewn about the chair as if Eve had been drawing them in different positions. And on the table was a heap of embroidery pieces.

"Are these your sister's work?" he asked as he looked over a series of beautifully done scenes and designs and even some ribbon embroidery. She was an artist with a needle, no doubt about it.

"Hunting for examples of my needlework again?" asked a female voice lightly from the doorway.

He turned to see Eve standing there with her mother, both practically swallowed up by their worn woolen cloaks. He couldn't tell from her tone if she was still angry over yesterday's kiss and his words afterward.

So, he decided to pretend nothing was amiss. "Do you mind if I take some of your work to show my mother, Miss Archer? You may not remember, but she's interested in embroidery in all its forms."

"We would be honored, my lord," her mother said. "Wouldn't we, Eve?"

"Of course," she said in a chilly tone, though she *looked* incredibly vulnerable. He had an insane urge to take her in his arms and ask if she'd spent all night thinking of him the way he'd been thinking of her.

But that wouldn't be wise.

So, after tucking a couple of her smaller embroidery pieces inside his greatcoat pocket, he stepped up to offer Lady Archer his arm, leaving young James to accompany his sister out the door. Moments later, they were all climbing into his carriage, where hot bricks wrapped in flannel helped keep it warm.

As soon as they were situated, with Eve and her mother across from him and James, Noel unfolded some fur blankets and threw them over the laps of everyone.

"Will you look at this, *mon ange*?" Lady Archer said to Eve. "These are nice and warm, are they not?"

"Furs generally are, Maman." As his coach set off, Eve gazed out the window, her face in shadow inside her cloak's hood. "Lord Cokesbury, you didn't need to fetch us yourself. You could have just sent the carriage."

"Why would I do that, Miss Archer, and forgo the pleasure of your company?" Since one fur blanket lay across both his lap and hers, he was able to nudge her knee without anyone seeing. When she swung her head around to raise an eyebrow at him, he had to suppress a laugh.

"It *is* very kind of you to come," her stepmother put in hastily. "I feel safer with you here, my lord."

"*I* will protect you, Mother," James asserted. "I've got Papa's pocket pistol right here." He patted his coat pocket, as if that were the most natural thing in the world.

"Good God, lad," Noel said as the ladies expressed alarm. The very thought of him haphazardly carrying a loaded pistol in a closed carriage with his mother and sister chilled Noel's blood. "Give it to me," Noel demanded, and held out his gloved hand.

When James hesitated, his mother said, "Do as the man says, son!"

"All right," James said sullenly and handed it over.

Noel checked to see if it was loaded, then handed it back to the boy.

"What in heaven's name are you doing?" Eve cried. "He can't be running around with a gun!"

"It's not loaded," Noel said.

"It's not?" James asked, gazing at it. "But I put a ball in it."

"Doesn't do anything, lad, if there's no powder." Noel sat back in his seat. "You and I must have a serious discussion about guns later."

"I told you we should have sold the thing," her stepmother said to Eve in a low voice.

"It's the only item of Papa's left that James could have, Maman," Eve said. "We sold everything else. It wouldn't have been right to take that from him, too."

God, her generosity to her family made his heart hurt sometimes. She protected her rascal brother even at risk to herself. He couldn't help admiring her for it, no matter how much he disagreed with her approach. She really was a wonder, wasn't she?

Somehow, he couldn't see Margaret going to such lengths for a sibling. Then he chided himself for such a disloyal thought.

Eve cast Noel an anxious look. "Are you quite sure the gun won't . . . go off somehow?"

"Quite sure," Noel said, trying not to smile. "I hunt regularly on my estate."

"You've got an estate?" James asked and gazed up at him in awe.

"I do. I'd be there now except that Mother has a charitable affair she participates in every year. We come into the city for December so she can be part of that."

James peppered him with questions about his estate that he answered as best he could. Even the ladies asked a few here and there.

The conversation stopped as the carriage halted. "We're here," Noel said.

Stepping out first so he could help the ladies down, he offered his hand to Eve, who took it readily, though she wouldn't meet his gaze. Before releasing her hand, he squeezed it, which finally garnered him a soulful look and a hesitant smile. After James jumped out and Noel helped Eve's mother out, Lady Archer grabbed her son by the shoulder and held him back a bit, leaving Noel and Eve to go ahead together.

They climbed the steps while Lady Archer and James stood back to admire the house. Eve murmured, "Thank you for handling Jimmy. Ever since Papa died, it takes us both to corral him. We haven't known what to do with him."

"How could you? A lad his age doesn't know what to do with himself. He doesn't even really know what he wants. He wants to be a boy and a man at the same time, to get treats like a child but be considered the protector of the family. It takes a while for him to find his place, especially if he has no father."

She nodded. "Did you know what *you* wanted at his age?"

"No." He stared down at her until she gazed up at him, then added, "But I know now."

"Oh?" she said, arching one eyebrow. "What might that be, sir?"

You. God, he had to stop wanting to say provocative things to her, stop thinking of her as his. There was no point. Eve would make him feel things, when he would rather not. He was considering a witty retort that would hide his true emotions, when the door opened and his mother hurried out to greet them.

Mother was even smiling, which she seldom did these days. "Here you are! I am so delighted to see you, Eve," she said as she took Eve's hands in hers. "And haven't you grown into a beautiful woman, my dear? Don't you agree, Noel?"

"I do," he said, wishing it weren't too dark to see if Eve was blushing.

Then his mother turned to the other two Archers with another rare smile. "I'm delighted to meet the pair of you, too, of course."

Noel made the introductions, then added, "But we should probably go inside, Mother, before we all freeze to death."

"Oh, pish," his mother said, "the cold never bothers you and you know it."

"I'm wearing a greatcoat, aren't I?" he told her.

"For once." Mother sniffed as she ushered them into the town house. "Half the time you walk around with the thinnest attire possible, risking your very life."

Now *that* sounded more the way his mother used to be—overprotective and worried about him, thank God. Not walking about in a fog of grief.

He removed Eve's embroidered pieces from his coat before letting the footman take it, then tucked them under his arm as he bent toward James. "You see what I mean, lad? She scolds me often."

"Not often enough, apparently," Mother said. "And when I do, it's because you deserve it."

He chuckled. "No doubt." He turned to their guests. "Welcome to Cokesbury Place."

Meanwhile, James was staring about him. "God bless me, you live in a palace!"

"Don't say that in front of the queen. She would not agree." Noel glanced over at Eve only to find her reddening, clearly embarrassed by her brother's behavior. "Your sister used to come here quite a bit, James. Do you think it has changed much, Miss Archer?"

That must have been the right approach to lessening her mortification, for she cast him a grateful smile. "Hardly at all. For one thing, I remember that staircase well. The finials are so lovely. Although I see that your entrance rug is new. It's quite pretty."

"Father bought it after winning money in a card game," he said tightly. It had been one of the few times he'd won, and Noel had wanted to spend the money on the tenant cottages. But as usual, his father had refused to do such a practical thing.

With a veiled look at him, his mother stepped in, making sure everyone else shed their coats, scarves, and hats and handed them to the footmen. When Eve faced him once more, he caught his breath.

Her red sarsenet gown ornamented with fading ribbons clearly wasn't new, nor was it richly made. But it fit her perfectly, pushing her breasts up just enough to make his mouth water. And it had embroidery all about the bodice, as if to draw attention to the treats inside.

He wanted treats. He dared not have them. Still . . .

"What my son is trying to tell you with his rude stare, Eve," Mother said, clearly amused, "is that you look lovely in that gown."

"You do," he managed to choke out.

"Is the embroidery yours, dear?" Mother asked. "It's quite good."

"Thank you, Lady Cokesbury," Eve said, sparing a soft glance for him. "Yes, I embroidered everything on our clothing. And I owe my skill, such as it is, to you. I must thank you for all you showed me. I learned so much from you during those days when Natalie and I were together, plying our needles and giggling over nothing."

Noel tensed and glanced at his mother, but she barely reacted to the mention of Natalie, which surprised him. He'd been walking on eggshells around her ever since his sister's death, trying not to speak of Natalie or hint at things from that time. Perhaps he should have spoken of her more.

Suddenly, he remembered the other pieces he'd brought and handed them to his mother. "These are Eve's . . . I mean, Miss Archer's, too, Mother."

His mother examined them, then broke into a broad smile. "You were right, son. These are perfect." She gestured to the Archer family. "Come, come, let us all go into the drawing room. I have something important to discuss with Eve before dinner."

Eve shot him a quizzical look, but he merely smiled as he accompanied her into the drawing room.

Once there, his mother offered glasses of sherry to all but James, who had to be content with punch. Then she bade the ladies sit on the settee. She perched next to Eve on one side while Lady Archer sat next to Eve on the other. That left him and James to take the chairs opposite.

Mother patted Eve's knee. "Noel has been raving about your intricate embroidery designs."

"Lord Cokesbury *raves* about things?" Eve said in a teasing tone. "I confess I have trouble imagining that."

"I raved about your Father Christmas design," he protested. "I called him 'astonishing.' "

"You also suggested changes to the art, like chubby-cheeked urchins and holly berries."

"I was joking. For the most part, anyway." His gaze narrowed on her. "You know that I was."

She burst into laughter. "You, sir, take things entirely too seriously."

"He does," Mother said. "At least in recent years."

"That's not true," he grumbled. But it was, and he knew it. Until now, his mother had joined him in that seriousness. Tonight, however, she was bright and cheery, as if Eve's very presence had stirred up her natural instinct to live happily.

It wouldn't last. How could it? The losses still lay heavy on them both.

"Didn't you have something to discuss with Eve, Mother?" he snapped, annoyed for some reason he couldn't explain.

"Of course, son," his mother said soothingly. "I'll do it right now."

Thank God. He only hoped she'd have better luck at convincing the Archers to let her help them than he'd had thus far.

CHAPTER 4

Eve stared at Lady Cokesbury. What was this all about? The most she'd been hoping for was to reminisce with Natalie's mother about Natalie while her family got a nice, filling meal for a change. But it appeared even the meal wasn't happening right away.

"My son tells me that your family has had difficulty establishing your claim to your brother's rightful inheritance," Lady Cokesbury began.

Tensing, she glared at Noel.

"Hear her out," he said with a faint smile. "Please?"

The way he said that last word, as if he truly meant it, was the only thing that kept her from jumping up and leaving. Well, that, and her respect for his mother.

She sighed. "Yes. I assume that your son told you why?"

"He did, although I do not understand why your father didn't leave any sort of inheritance for *you* at least."

"Mr. Washburn says he requested information on it from my uncle but has not received any response."

Noel snorted. "One more reason I don't trust the fellow and why my own attorney is looking into the matter."

"Which we do appreciate, my lord," Maman put in.

"That will have to be handled by the lawyers, I suppose," the viscountess said. "But in the meantime, I'd like to help in another area. And I think when you hear what I have to say, you will agree that my plan is a good one."

"And what is your plan?" Maman cut in, looking a little insulted herself. After all, she prided herself in keeping the wolf from the door as best she could.

"I want Eve to enter her embroidery in a competition of sorts," Lady Cokesbury said.

"I beg your pardon?" Eve asked.

"Before I explain, let me just say that your work is exquisite," the viscountess went on. "Then again, it always was."

"No better than Natalie's," she murmured, then could have kicked herself when she saw pain flash across Lady Cokesbury's face.

But the lady recovered quickly, taking Eve's hand in hers. "Please don't misunderstand what I'm about to say. I loved my daughter with my every breath, but I wasn't blind to her true interests and abilities. Needlework was a mildly entertaining pastime for Natalie, not the passion it seems to be for you and me."

A passion. She'd never thought of it that way, but she supposed it truly was that for her. She was never so happy as when plying her needle.

"You have original ideas for design," the viscountess went on, "and you execute them well. That is the sort of thing Her Majesty is always looking for."

Eve blinked. "Her Majesty! Whatever do you mean?"

Lady Cokesbury patted her hand. "I assume you have heard of Mrs. Pawsey's School for Embroidering Females?"

"Of course," Eve said. "I wanted to apply for a position there as a teacher, but I was told it has moved to Ampthill in Bedfordshire."

"Yes, well, despite being under the queen's patronage, Mrs. Pawsey found that she could expand the school and take in more pupils if she moved it out of London. Anyway, Queen Charlotte has been encouraging young ladies to practice needlework as an art form. So, every year for the past ten, she has held a charitable auction on behalf of the school. Ladies twenty-five years of age and younger submit embroidered items to the auction. Then the queen chooses an item for herself, to be displayed or worn at her royal affair on

Christmas Day. As you may realize, it's considered a great honor for any young woman's piece to be chosen."

Eve's heart began to pound. "I can only imagine."

"The other items are auctioned off," Lady Cokesbury went on, "and the proceeds go to the school. But many young ladies vie for the privilege of having the queen wear or display their item at her party. I think *you* should submit a piece."

While Eve was still sitting there in shock, Noel leaned forward. "If you win, it will give you a chance not only to gain royal patronage for your own work but to plead your brother's case and enlist Her Majesty's help in making sure James is given the title that is his by right."

Eve laughed wildly. "*If* I win. Forgive me, but you are both quite daft to think I could win such a competition against ladies with undoubtedly more skill, experience, and time to practice than I have."

The viscountess squeezed her hand. "I attend this affair every year, my dear. Your needlework easily rivals that of any of the other ladies, trust me. Why, I still have that apron you gave me."

"Besides," Noel said, "even if you didn't win, you'd still get to meet the queen and argue for James. It's worth a try, isn't it?"

Trying not to be heartened by his and his mother's arguments, she glanced over at her stepmother. "Tell them they're both quite in error about my abilities."

"I will not," Maman said with a glint of pride in her eyes. "Your work is exceptional, *ma chérie*. I have always told you that you don't value it enough. Why not give the idea a chance?"

Eve gazed at Jimmy, then Noel. "What about materials? The thread would need to be of the finest kind, not to mention the fabric, and I'd need smaller needles if I am to do the more exquisite sort of embroidery."

Lady Cokesbury nodded to a footman, who brought a huge box and set it before the viscountess. She turned to Eve. "This is all of the many threads and needles and fabrics I bought for Natalie in her final days that she never got the chance to use. I haven't been able to bring myself to get rid of them, but she would be dancing in heaven to know that *you* are making good use of them."

A lump stuck in Eve's throat. It would also give her time to grieve Natalie, since Eve hadn't had much chance to do so. If not for Natalie, Eve might never have had someone to giggle with about boys, never have known the fun of occasionally breaking the rules.

She might never have discovered her love of embroidery.

Tears stung her eyes. "It *would* be a way of honoring her."

"Yes, exactly," Noel said, his gaze soft on her. "And of helping your brother."

"Don't do it for *me,* Eve," Jimmy said stoutly. "Do it so you can meet the bloody queen!"

"Jimmy!" she and Maman cried at once. Then Eve turned to the viscountess with an apology on her lips only to find the woman silently laughing.

Noel, on the other hand, cast Jimmy a quelling glance. "I can see that you, young man, will have to learn better manners before *you* can meet the 'bloody' queen."

Her stepmother sighed. "I wish you luck in attempting to teach him any. Eve and I long ago despaired of it."

"Leave that to me," Noel said. Then he actually winked at Eve.

Her jaw dropped. She'd been unaware that Noel even knew how to wink. It hadn't seemed in his nature.

Of course, what did she truly know of his nature? She barely knew the man. Except for the fact that he kissed exceptionally well.

She fought the blush stealing over her cheeks.

Suddenly, the butler entered to announce that dinner was served. As they rose, Lady Cokesbury squeezed her hand. "At least promise me you'll think about it. And before you make your decision, give me the chance to answer any questions you might have."

"I do have several," Eve admitted.

"And I have answers. This is my main charitable cause every year." As the viscountess led her to the dining room, with the others following behind them, she said in a lower voice, "I have one apology to make to you, however."

"I can't imagine what you would have to apologize for, Lady Cokesbury."

"I should have searched for you and your family as soon as word arose of the détenus coming home. But after Natalie died, I could scarcely bring myself to do more than stare out at the garden and wander the house like a wraith. I just couldn't—"

"Say no more, please," Eve put in. "I know how destitute I felt after Papa died. I daresay it is even harder to lose a child than a parent. You have no reason to apologize, trust me."

The viscountess smiled at her. "As a girl, you were always sweet and generous, my dear, and you're even more so as a grown woman. I cannot say how much your being here has lifted my spirits."

Eve could only blush and say, "I'm glad I could help."

They entered the dining room and took their places, with Noel at the head of the table and his mother at the foot, while Eve and her stepmother sat on one side and Jimmy on the other. As the servants served the soup, talk returned to the auction.

"What questions do you have for me?" the viscountess asked Eve, whom she'd seated next to her.

"The most important one is, when *is* this charity auction?"

"On Christmas Eve."

"That's a week from now!" Eve nearly choked on her first spoonful of soup, which would have been a shame since it was the most heavenly chestnut soup she'd tasted in some years. "I can't complete a piece fit for such a competition in a week."

"Could you do it if you could embroider somewhere away from the dyeworks?" Noel asked. "You could come here and bring James with you. He and I could work to improve his . . . er . . . manners enough for him to meet the queen, and you could embroider in better light, without the dyes provoking your cough."

The thought of spending every day in Noel's company, trying not to yearn for his attentions, struck her with panic. "But Maman needs me to—"

"As long as Her Ladyship will make sure you are properly chaperoned," her stepmother said, with a quick glance at Noel, "I see no issue. Besides, it might be better if you and Jimmy were not home, anyway, so I could finish sewing the rest of Mrs. Beckford's order. *You* are a help to me, of course, but you cannot help when you have embroidery to do, and Jimmy . . ."

"Is a hindrance?" Noel quipped. When Jimmy began to scowl, Noel added, "I'm just guessing."

"I did not say *that*," Maman retorted, eyes twinkling. She ate some soup. "Not exactly, anyway."

Jimmy was wolfing down his own soup, but still managed to halt long enough to grumble, "I help sometimes."

"Of course you do, *mon ange*," Maman said soothingly. "I didn't say otherwise, did I?"

Eve had to bite her lip hard to keep from laughing.

"Then that's settled," the viscountess said. "Eve and James will come here every day. I will help Eve with her submission in whatever ways I am allowed, and Noel will help James learn to be a proper gentleman."

"What do you mean by ways you are allowed?" Eve asked.

"I'm not permitted to so much as show you a stitch, my dear. It is against the rules. The submission must be fully yours. But I can fetch you thread or tea or anything else you require."

The idea of a viscountess fetching her things *really* made Eve want to laugh. "If I'm here, won't people assume you're giving me the wrong sort of help?"

Lady Cokesbury sniffed. "They'd better *not* assume such a thing. I've been part of this endeavor since Her Majesty first started it. Why, Natalie submitted something in the year before she fell sick. She didn't win, of course, but no one questioned her right to submit a piece, even though she was my daughter. The committee does recognize that women, not just gentlemen, have honor, too."

"I'm glad to hear that, because I quite agree," Eve said.

At that moment, the footmen brought in the next course, a lamb ragout, along with fried potatoes, and Maman nearly swooned. "A *ragoût d'agneau*? Lady Cokesbury, you have just made this French woman very happy."

"I asked my French cook what you might most miss from France, and he suggested this."

"Cor," Jimmy said, "there's more than the soup?!!" He tore into his serving of ragout as if he hadn't had a good meal in a month. Which was actually close to the truth.

Her stepmother stopped eating at once. "James, you must slow down! It is rude to shovel food into your mouth like that."

"Pish," the viscountess said, "you should have seen Noel eat at that age. One time I found him in the kitchen late at night with a roast chicken that he'd reduced to a carcass all by himself."

"Good God, Mother," Noel said, "must you tell all my secrets?"

Eve couldn't resist teasing him. "Is that what you meant when you told me, 'a boy of that age doesn't know what to do with himself'?"

"Great," he grumbled, "now you're *both* conspiring to tell my secrets."

"What secrets?" Jimmy asked through a mouth full of lamb.

With a roll of his eyes, Noel glanced at Jimmy, and added, "The first lesson we'll have to give you, lad, is table manners."

All the women laughed. Jimmy merely shrugged and continued to eat.

The lamb course was even more heavenly than the soup. Eve had just finished a delightful mouthful of the fried potatoes when Noel's mother asked, "Do you have any more questions about the competition, Eve?"

Dabbing at her lips with her napkin, Eve said, "Actually, I do. What are the sorts of items I can submit? What about a dress or a wall hanging, for example? I do have a mostly finished embroidered gown I could offer."

"You are thinking to submit Mrs. Beckford's gown?" Maman paused in her eating to ask. "Oh, I don't know, *ma chérie.* What if she attends this affair and takes offense?"

"You mustn't worry, Lady Archer," the viscountess said. "Eve cannot submit a gown or anything that large, anyway. Otherwise, one lady could submit a gown and another lady could submit a reticule, and the reticule would suffer by comparison because, well, a gown takes longer to embroider, depending on the design."

"You could submit the dancing slippers that go with the gown," Noel proposed as the footman whisked away his empty plate.

"Dancing slippers would be fine." His mother picked at her food. "The rules allow for any accessory—gloves, reticules, turbans, stockings, even capelets, and the like."

"But the dancing slippers might take me more than a week," Eve said woefully. "The design is so intricate and small. Besides, if Maman does not wish me to use something meant to go to her client—"

"I do not think she will care as much about slippers," Maman said. "Those are not so noticeable as a gown would be."

"Are there other pieces at your home, Eve?" the viscountess asked. "Perhaps you have something else you have already done. We should pick the best. Why don't you bring everything tomorrow, including your latest design for the slippers, and we can look through it all?"

"Eve prefers to design things in charcoal on the wall of a dye-works, Mother," Noel said in a faintly amused tone. "Something to do with wanting it 'writ large.' So, unless you wish to travel to her home or have me do a life-size rendering somehow—"

Maman snorted. "What nonsense. She doesn't want it 'writ large.' It is merely cheaper to draw on a wall than on paper, my lord."

Noel looked completely taken aback. Apparently, he had taken Eve's explanation at face value.

That both gratified and embarrassed her. "Please, Maman," Eve said in an undertone, feeling her cheeks heat.

"No, *ma chérie*," her stepmother said, "we must be honest if you are to do this. The viscountess and her son must be made to understand that we cannot afford the sorts of things they take for granted. Otherwise, it will all be for naught."

"Lady Archer," the viscountess said warmly, "I would never ask your stepdaughter to do anything beyond *your* means. There have been times in our lives, too, when money wasn't readily available, so I do understand."

When she exchanged a glance with her son, Eve wondered what she was talking about. Would he tell her if she asked?

Lady Cokesbury went on. "But this opportunity could open doors for all of you. I merely want to support the talent of a young lady who deserves every chance to make use of it." She patted Eve's hand. "If you feel I'm overstepping my bounds, please tell me. It's just that Eve reminds me so much of my late daughter, and I greatly miss Natalie. In helping Eve succeed, I feel as if I am keeping my daughter's memory alive. That is worth more than gold to me."

Maman took that in but didn't say a word. Then the next course was brought in, and she was obviously torn between devouring the suet dumplings or fighting with the viscountess over Eve's soul. Or Eve's *something*, anyway.

"Besides, Lady Archer," Noel put in, "we have all the paper Eve could need—big or small. I daresay some is in that giant box of items Mother bought for Natalie. Someone might as well make good use of those, don't you think? Otherwise, they go to waste."

Eve started to retort, but Maman laid a hand on her arm to stop her. "I have to ask, sir, what is *your* particular interest in this? You are not a needleworker, I would assume. So why would you help my stepdaughter meet the queen?"

His gaze locked with Eve's. "Because I couldn't help Natalie reach *her* dreams. Because I spent so many years consumed by my own affairs that I failed to notice how she needed me until it was too late." He turned his gaze to Eve's stepmother. "Helping Natalie's closest friend is something I *can* do—something Mother and I both can do. So, why not let us?"

Maman stared at him, then at Lady Cokesbury, and finally at Eve. "What do you think, my dear? Do you still wish to do this?"

"I don't think we have a choice, Maman. The longer we go without Jimmy's right to the inheritance being resolved, the worse things will get. Any introduction to the queen is bound to help. And I can do the work. I shall just have to labor for long hours."

Her stepmother cast Noel a veiled glance. "But you will come home every night, Eve, will you not?"

"Certainly. And Jimmy, too, of course."

"Very well. In that case, I will allow it."

Eve let out a long breath, hardly aware that she'd been holding one until that moment. Because the truth was, the longer they discussed it, the more excited she became. To have a chance at showing her abilities to the *queen* . . . how wonderful was that? Even if she didn't win, she would know that Lady Cokesbury considered her worthy of participating.

That Noel considered her worthy of participating.

No, she mustn't think of him in those terms. He'd made it clear he didn't think of *her* in those terms yesterday.

But today, well, anything seemed possible. *If* she won the competition.

Lady Cokesbury beamed at them all. "Now that we have come to an agreement, why don't we talk about something else? I should like to hear all about your time in France."

"I suspect that will take more than one meal to relate," Noel murmured, but said nothing more as the three women began to discuss life at Verdun. Instead, he grabbed Jimmy's hand as the boy reached for the dumpling on his plate, then closed Jimmy's fingers around the handle of a fork.

Jimmy looked up at Noel with guileless eyes and immediately shifted to eating with the fork.

Eve smiled at Noel. Perhaps a week spent at the Cokesbury town house wouldn't be so bad after all. Noel might finally get her little brother to start behaving like a gentleman. Or at least to stop picking pockets. That would be wonderful enough as it was.

Meanwhile, Noel made the rest of dinner even more wonderful with his clever remarks and his teasing. She was surprised to learn of his interest in engravings and delighted to hear that he enjoyed Mr. Beasley's work in particular. He'd been unaware of Mr. Beasley's past as a détenu, so she and Noel spent several pleasant minutes discussing the man and his family, and the works Noel particularly liked.

By the time dinner was over and the three of them were heading out to the carriage, Eve felt rather contented. Despite her fears, her time in France hadn't wiped out her memory of all of Lady Cokesbury's lessons to her and Natalie about deportment, fashion, manners, et cetera. Tonight, Eve had stepped right into what she'd learned then, like a woman pulling on a well-used coat.

Unfortunately, as they reached the carriage, she realized she'd been having such a fine time that she'd forgotten to visit the necessary before coming outside. After all the tea she'd drunk, she really needed to do so. She didn't think she could make it back to Hatton Garden.

Thrusting her head into the carriage, she told her stepmother that she'd forgotten something, then asked the footman if they could possibly hold the carriage while she went to the necessary. After assuring him that she knew where it was, she hurried into the house, glad that Noel had chosen not to accompany them home tonight, but instead to send a footman with them. How mortifying it would have been having to explain to *him* her sudden urgent need!

She'd hurried to the necessary and was trying to hurry back past the drawing room to the stairs when she heard her name mentioned. She froze. Lady Cokesbury and Noel were in the drawing room talking about her.

"It was so good to see Eve," the viscountess was saying. "Thank you for bringing her here, son. Though I daresay it wasn't just for me that you did so."

Noel didn't answer right away. "I don't know what you mean," he said stiffly.

Eve swallowed hard. She should go. She shouldn't listen. But she couldn't seem to help herself.

"Don't you?" His mother paused. "I see how you look at Eve."

"I should hope I look at her the way I'd look at any old friend of Natalie's."

Eve crept past the door, not sure she wanted to hear yet again that he saw her as an "old friend," even if the last time he'd said that was just after he'd kissed her most passionately.

"Hmm," his mother said, clearly skeptical. "Well, I'm glad she has agreed to enter the competition. Do you happen to know if Lady Margaret also means to enter this year?"

Eve froze. Who the devil was Lady Margaret?

"How could I?" he snapped. "It's not the sort of thing Margaret and I talk about. But if you want me to ask her, I will, next time I see her."

Eve's heart began to pound so loudly, she feared they might hear it. Yet she didn't move so much as a step. He'd referred to the woman by her Christian name. And although he'd done the same to Eve—and asked her to do the same to him—she still needed to know what this Margaret had done to deserve such a courtesy.

"Have you offered for Lady Margaret yet?" his mother persisted.

Eve's stomach sank, and not even his curt "No" could quell her nausea. Did he kiss "Margaret" passionately, too? Or was "Margaret" too fine and upstanding a lady to kiss?

"Don't you think you should?" his mother said. "You're not getting any younger, and you've certainly been courting her long enough."

"Good God, Mother, stay out of it," he said irritably. Then she heard the unmistakable sound of chair legs scraping the floor. "I'm going to my study. I need to sign some documents for the estate manager before I retire."

Eve practically flew down the carpeted hall to the thankfully carpeted stairs.

Still, when his mother laughed, Eve froze again near the top of the stairs.

"I daresay you'll need a good night's sleep if you're going to take young James in hand tomorrow," Lady Cokesbury remarked.

"You can say that again," he told her, sounding grumpy now.

That was Eve's cue to fly down the stairs, grateful that the footman saw her coming and opened the door before her.

But once she was out on the steps and the door closed behind her, she had to pause to gain a semblance of control over her emotions. She should have known he had some fiancée—or near-fiancée—waiting in the wings. He was "not getting any younger," as his mother said.

She was half tempted to march back inside and tell him what he could do with his kisses and his kindness to her brother and his offers to "help" her and her family. But she thought better of it. This was about Jimmy. And Maman.

And her, too, curse it! At last she had a chance to move into a better sphere, to teach lessons in embroidery perhaps, or even force her uncle to acknowledge that she deserved whatever funds Papa might have left for her. She could endure Noel's—no, *Lord Cokesbury's*—presence if that was what it took to improve her and her family's situation.

She would merely have to protect her heart in the meantime.

CHAPTER 5

Noel scowled as he wandered his study while little Jimmy wrote down the rules they'd been going over.

Three days. That was how long Eve had succeeded in ignoring him, and he couldn't stand it. Had he insulted her again somehow? Hurt her feelings? Because he would have sworn they'd parted on good terms after their dinner. Yet she was in his house and right under his nose all day, and somehow managed to be busy or absent whenever he came near her.

Not that he got many chances for that, thanks to his many obligations, one of which was young James. How the hell the lad had become so uncouth was anyone's guess, especially when his half sister was quite the opposite.

Eve had remained a lady through and through, despite the circumstances that had brought her family low. No wonder she despaired over her half brother. Still, at least the lad was finally starting to make progress.

He amended that opinion when he turned to find James slyly slipping the pencil into his pocket. "Master Archer!" Noel ground out. "What is the one thing you must never do in public or in private?"

James thrust out his lower lip, apparently realizing he'd been caught. "Steal. But I wasn't stealing the pencil! I was only borrowing it."

"For what reason?"

"Eve uses charcoal to sketch because it comes free from the dyeworks. But she'd rather use a pencil, and this is a fine one." When Noel sighed, James said, "I'll bring it back when she's done with it, I swear!"

"Give it here," Noel said with a snap of his fingers. After a sullen James put it in Noel's hand, Noel muttered, "I'll give it to your sister myself. And next time, if you want something—for her or for you—ask for it, do you understand?"

James bobbed his head.

"Why do you steal things, James?" he couldn't resist asking.

The boy shrugged. "I'm good at it."

"Obviously not that good, given that I caught you," he said dryly. "Twice, I might add."

"My friends say—"

"Your so-called friends are entertaining themselves by trying to corrupt you. They don't care if you're caught or if you shame your family." He stared hard at James. "If you're ever caught by a constable, you could be hanged. Think how your mother and sister would feel about that. I daresay Eve would rather have you alive than have a pencil to draw with."

"Yes, sir," James mumbled.

Not sure he'd made enough of an impact, he went on. "I happen to be good at shooting. But you don't see me leaning out the window and shooting at anyone who walks down the street, do you?"

James's eyes widened. "No, sir."

"That's because it's wrong to shoot people who aren't shooting at you. Just as it is wrong to steal from people who have stolen nothing from you. We all have to get along with one another, and doing unto others as you would have them do unto you is the primary tenet of a civilized society. That's why it's called the Golden Rule."

James seemed to ponder that.

Noel could only hope it made an impression on the lad. "Now, let's return to our lesson on language. What words do we refrain from using around young ladies?"

"'Refrain' means 'not'?" James asked.

Noel nodded. "It wouldn't hurt you to read a book now and then."

"I used to read books," he grumbled. "Before Papa died."

"There's an entire library in my study. Feel free to borrow any book you like."

When James's face lit up, Noel realized he might have found the perfect way to tempt James away from stealing. "Words we refrain from using near ladies, Master Archer?" he prompted again.

"Um . . ." James screwed up his face in thought. "We don't say 'damned,' 'blasted,' 'curst,' 'deuced,' or . . . or . . ."

"The one you called the queen."

"Bloody!" James cried.

Noel sighed. James certainly enjoyed cursing. So did Noel, in certain circumstances. But James mustn't curse in polite society. Best to emphasize that rule before the queen's affair. "There are many more such bad words, but these are the ones I've actually *heard* you use, in the presence of your mother, your sister, and *my* mother."

James pouted.

"Let's go on. What do you never call a young lady?"

"'Gentry mort,' 'doxy,' 'trull,' 'harlot' . . ."

The lad went on in that vein for a while. There certainly were a great many vile words for ladies, of the evening and otherwise, more than Noel had even realized.

At last, James finished with "'low-heel,' 'cat,' and 'whore.'"

"That reminds me. No 'whore' words at all. No 'whoreson' or 'whoremonger' or 'whoremaster' or any other word of that ilk."

James scowled. "It's a lot to remember."

"Not once you get used to it."

"They're just words," James protested.

"What would you do if I called you a 'dunghill'?" Noel asked, using the cant for "coward."

"I'd punch you in the face," James said, frowning.

"Exactly. Words matter, lad. Remember that." Still, Noel fought the urge to laugh at the image of James climbing atop a chair to punch him in the face.

Noel wandered over to the window. "Now write down every word you use for constables and watchmen, and we'll take a look at those. We don't want anyone thinking there's a particular reason you use cant terms for officers."

Pulling aside the curtain, he stared out to see the same young man strolling the mews who, according to his footman, had followed the Cokesbury carriage to Hatton Garden and back yesterday and the day before. He wished the footman had pointed the fellow out to him sooner, but his servant had said he couldn't be sure it was intentional until after it happened two days in a row.

Today, the chap was pretending to be waiting for someone in the mews, but that seemed unlikely. Noel knew everyone who used their mews, and it was all families with small children, not the sort a young fellow like that would be waiting around for.

Noel glanced at his pocket watch. "It's almost time for luncheon, James. Go on down to the dining room, and I'll be along in a bit. Then we'll work on your behavior at meals."

James groaned as he walked out.

Noel left the window. He must tell Eve about the man, if only to warn her she was being watched and thus must be careful not to let James off his leash, so to speak.

You're merely taking any excuse to see her.

Nonsense. This was practical. Nothing more.

He found her in the garden room down the hall. Alone, fortunately. He didn't want his mother hearing this conversation. She might worry.

Pausing in the doorway, he took the chance to watch his frustrating obsession while she didn't notice him there. Between her and Mother, they'd decided that she should submit the slippers. At the moment, her attention to her work seemed all-consuming, her needle moving with the speed of a clerk copying documents. He had to admit he admired her dedication to her craft.

Although a blush stained her cheeks, she stared him down. "I'll answer your question if you'll answer mine. Who is Lady Margaret?"

His heart faltered as he halted a scant few inches from her. He should have told her about Margaret himself, but he hadn't wanted to . . . to what? Make her hate him? And now that she'd found out somehow . . . His stomach roiled as he realized what she must think of him.

No, it didn't matter. It was probably time that he tell her. Besides, if he did, perhaps it would put a stop to this . . . mad dance of desire he kept wanting to engage in with her. "Lady Margaret is a woman I was planning to offer for."

"Was?" she asked, her tone hopeful.

He gritted his teeth, angry at himself for that monumental slip of the tongue. "*Am* planning to offer for."

She tilted up her chin. "So, why did you kiss *me* that day in Hatton Garden if you're planning to make another woman your wife?"

How was he supposed to answer that? "I don't know. That's the God's honest truth."

She swallowed hard. "Are you in love with her?"

"No." The answer came more readily than even he expected.

It certainly seemed to take *Eve* by surprise. "Then, are you . . . are you marrying her for money?"

"I don't need to marry for money, if that's what you're asking." Not anymore, anyway, although it had been a near thing once. He crossed his arms over his chest. "Besides, I'm not marrying her for anything yet. I haven't made an offer."

"But you're going to," she said shakily.

"Probably." Although every minute he spent this close to Eve weakened his resolve to do so.

A hopeless look crossed her face. "If you don't love her and don't need a fortune from her, what do you expect to get out of such a marriage?"

"Peace."

She flinched. "And I suppose I wouldn't provide you with peace?" With a furious blush, she looked beyond him. "That is . . .

A tendril of hair had slipped free of her chignon to droop down, and he fought the urge to walk over and tuck it back in. He knew he merely wanted a reason to touch that beautiful red hair of hers, but that would show how deeply he'd begun to feel for her, and she must not guess that when he still refused to act on it.

Today she wore an unusual gown of green wool, and it fit her rather loosely, making him wonder if it had once belonged to her stepmother. It was cut rather low in front, with only a fichu of some gossamer fabric hiding the swells of her breasts.

God, what he would give to have the right to tug the fichu free so he could press kisses to every inch of that lovely flesh. But he couldn't and mustn't, and that truth drove him mad.

To keep his mind from wandering any further in that realm, he asked, "How is the work coming along?"

She jumped, then glared at him. "Good heavens, you frightened me! Don't creep up on a lady like that, my lord."

That was another thing that annoyed him. She called him "my lord" with every sentence, it seemed.

"Well? How is it progressing?" he asked, probably a bit too sharply.

She returned her gaze to her needlework. "Fine."

"May I see?"

"Why, my lord?" she asked, still refusing to look at him. "Do you have suggestions?"

"Would you take them if I did?" he pressed her.

She set down her work with a look of sheer irritability. "Why are you here, Lord Cokesbury?"

He suppressed an oath. "I need to show you something." He closed the door, then walked across the room. "Come here to the window."

Gazing at him warily, she hesitated before rising and going to meet him. He pointed outside to the fellow now looking up at the town house. "Do you recognize that chap?"

She frowned. "Should I?"

"Not necessarily. But he's been following my carriage whenever it picks up you and James and takes you back home. I was hoping you might know who he is."

Examining the young man more closely, she shook her head. "I've never seen him before. Why do you think he's following us?"

"The only reason I can come up with is he's working for your uncle and trying to keep an eye on the three of you."

She blanched. "To what purpose?"

"God only knows. But your uncle is the only person I could think of with a reason for watching you. Who else would it be?"

"That's a good point. The fellow doesn't look like any of Jimmy's band of miscreant friends. He's too nicely dressed . . . and a bit too old. In fact, his clothing is what a servant might wear on his afternoon off, so that fits with the possibility that he's working for Uncle Uriah. But why would Uncle Uriah be having someone follow us about?"

Noel shrugged. "No idea. I've written to your uncle urging him to come see what his negligence has wrought on his family, but it's too early for an answer, I fear. Anyway, if he *is* the one behind this, I was hoping you'd have an opinion of what he's up to."

"I'm at a loss." She cocked her head to look at him. "Perhaps you should speak to your servants. They might know. This fellow might have questioned them."

"Good idea. But just to be sure you two are safe, I'm sending another footman with you in the carriage from now on."

"If you wish." As if that settled everything, she returned to her seat and went back to her needlework.

He told himself he should leave now. He'd done what he came for.

But he couldn't bring himself to go. Instead, he strolled over to stand behind her so he could look over her shoulder at the dancing slippers. The needlework was every bit as good as his mother's, which was the only standard he had to compare it to. Normally, he didn't attend the queen's competition. This would be a first for him, but he was determined to support her.

He narrowed his gaze on the slippers. "You changed the greenery part of the design."

"I did. I still have holly on the gown, but your mother suggested I use mistletoe on the slippers. She thinks mistletoe is rather unique in embroidery and the unusual nature of it might help me win."

"That would be a good reason to do it. I've never seen a piece that included mistletoe." He examined her new design again. "And did you make the snow light blue instead of white so it will contrast better with the white mistletoe berries?"

"Exactly." She shot him a veiled glance. "You certainly know your embroidery, sir."

"I know what's of good quality, at least. That's what happens when one's mother and sister spend every waking moment in the weeks leading up to the holidays embroidering waistcoats, stockings, handkerchiefs, and assorted other items of clothing as Christmas gifts. Not that Natalie's work was anywhere near the quality of yours—Mother was right about that, too."

"To be honest, I don't remember much about Natalie's work."

"Remind me to show you sometime the handkerchief she gave me." He frowned. "You mentioned the gown. Mrs. Beckford won't mind that the slippers no longer have holly?"

"Actually, Maman told Mrs. Beckford about the competition, and she was quite impressed I'd be seeing the queen. She suggested that I should *wear* her gown to it, if Maman and I have time to refit it for me. That way people will see the ensemble together. Then I'm to do a gown for her for Twelfth Night instead, since her family has decided to have a big celebration for that. I said we could do that in twelve days. So, she won't care one whit about me using mistletoe instead of holly."

He bent over her shoulder to snatch the slipper she'd completed off her lap so he could look at it close up. "You know, mistletoe does have one other advantage over holly."

"Pray, do enlighten me," she said sarcastically. With some muttered complaint about "arrogant gentlemen," she rose and skirted the chair to try and snatch it back from him.

He held the slipper over her head. "A man can use it to do this."

But when he bent to steal a kiss, she backed away, protesting, "Mistletoe embroidery isn't remotely the same as real mistletoe. It certainly doesn't obligate me to allow you a kiss!"

"Is that why you've been avoiding me?" he asked, advancing on her until she came up against the wall. "Because you're afraid I'll try to kiss you again?" He lowered his voice. "Or because you're afraid you'll let me?"

I didn't mean to imply . . . I shouldn't have said . . ." She drew herself up like a true Mistletoe Maiden. "Well, we both know you would never offer for *me*, given my present situation."

"That has nothing to do with it," he ground out, hating to cause her pain and dim her radiant spirit. He dared not make her *his* Mistletoe Maiden, not if he wanted to protect himself. "You're still a baron's daughter, and unlike James, your behavior is above reproach. But you're right, marriage to you would be the very opposite of peace for me."

"Because Jimmy and Mother and my uncle complicate everything?"

"Because you make me feel things."

Damn. He shouldn't have been that honest.

Her lovely eyes, as captivating as they were haunting, met his. "What's wrong with feeling things?"

He shook his head. "If you have to ask, you wouldn't understand."

"Explain it to me then."

He hesitated. Then, seizing her hand, he pressed it to his chest and lowered his voice. "Whenever I'm near you, my heart thunders. My mouth goes dry, my blood feels on fire, and all I want to do is carry you off to my bedchamber and make love to you."

When her gaze warmed, he put as much coldness into his voice as he could muster, given that she was this close to him, making him want and need and yearn. "And although I know it's only the result of my reckless desire for you, even that sort of emotion makes me uncomfortable. Such feelings lead a man to wish for too much, hope for too much . . . and then hurt too much when it all goes to hell."

"What makes you assume it would all go to hell?" She lifted her other hand to caress his cheek, provoking such pleasure in him that he shuddered.

With a curse, he released her one hand to move the other away, telling himself not to be tempted to do something he'd regret. "Because it always does." It always had for his parents, anyway. Horses and card games hadn't been the only thing his father had wasted money on, after all.

"You don't trust me with your heart," she said, making him wish she didn't read him quite so well.

"I don't trust *anyone* with my heart," he admitted. "It's been crushed one too many times, first by my feckless father who made a hundred promises he never kept, before finally getting himself killed. Then by Natalie who . . . left me in the end, too."

"That wasn't her fault," Eve said softly.

"Of course it wasn't. But the result was the same." He glanced away, unable to stand the pity in Eve's eyes. "Sometimes I think I'd have been better off continuing to treat her like a pesky little sister. Then perhaps it wouldn't have hurt quite so much to see her suffer."

"Instead, you did the noble thing and tamped down your pain," she said tenderly, "so she could have in the end what she'd always wanted—her beloved older brother around to give her solace and be there when she left this world."

He swung his gaze back to her, unaccountably angry at those words. "Don't make the mistake of thinking me noble, sweetheart." Planting one hand on the wall, he leaned in close. "I am not the gentleman you assume. I may ache to be with you and kiss you and touch you and make love to you. But if I ever do, afterward I will also do the sensible thing and marry a woman who won't make me ache ever again."

She stared into his eyes, then grabbed her mistletoe slipper from his other hand and dangled it over *his* head. "Will you?" she whispered, then stretched up to kiss his mouth.

For a moment, he was too surprised to react. But how could he not respond when the lips he'd been longing for were pressed to his? It was too much to be borne. Besides, it was a chance to show her that he meant what he said.

You just want an excuse to satisfy your needs.

Yes, he did.

Ignoring his conscience, he caught her chin in his hand and opened his mouth over hers, practically daring her to kiss him intimately. And just like the saucy woman that she was, she rose to his dare.

So, he took his chance to devour her, unable to get enough of her. Her mouth was as sweet as fruit, as tempting as a nymph's and twice as tasty. She dropped the slipper, only to wrap her arms about his neck as he gave her long, drugging kisses that fired his need higher and higher.

His hand drifted down from her chin to her throat and down farther still until it came to the fichu, which he drew out so he could unveil the tops of her breasts. Then he moved back just enough to stare at them.

They were perfect.

Even as she blushed furiously, he couldn't resist the urge to trace a line along her bodice, that damned ill-fitting bodice that gaped open just enough to tempt him. He retraced the line, but this time with his finger beneath the edge, thrilling to the fact that she did nothing to stop him, that although she gasped, she also lifted her breast into his palm.

"God help me," he whispered hoarsely as he fondled her breast through her gown, driving himself to madness. "You're so soft, sweetheart, as soft as any man could want. I shouldn't be doing this. You shouldn't be letting me."

"I *like* what you're doing," she breathed, covering his hand with hers to keep it there. "But if you're so sure we don't belong together, it shouldn't take you too much effort to end it."

The hint of challenge in her tone arrested him. Fortunately, it also jerked him right out of his haze of desire. His gaze shot to hers, and in her yearning eyes he read the truth. She meant to tempt him so thoroughly that he'd run madly into marriage with her without thought for the consequences.

And he couldn't have that. Abruptly, he drew back mid-caress, fighting to control his rushing breaths. "You're right, as usual," he choked out. "Not much . . . effort at all." *Liar.*

Disappointment filled her face. She didn't—*couldn't*—understand. He wanted her for his own. He needed her brightness to dispel the shadows in his life. And the sheer intensity of his wanting and needing her bloody well terrified him. In an unpredictable world, such desperate feelings could prove dangerous in the end. Some people did die of asthma, after all.

He refused to risk having his heart shattered again. Because if something happened to *her* after he'd made her his wife, he suspected he'd never recover.

It took every ounce of his will to leave her and head for the door. "I must see to James," he said, retreating like the coward he was. Then he left the room.

But as he headed back to his study, he prayed he could hold fast to his resolve. Because if they had many more such sensual encounters, he would have her in his bed so quickly, they wouldn't have time to think better of it.

CHAPTER 6

In a daze, Eve picked up her slipper and returned to her chair. Could Noel really feel so hopeless about the future? So afraid of what might happen that he wouldn't embrace *anyone* who might cause him pain by being so thoughtless as to die?

She sighed. It was possible. The man had always been cursedly rigid about some things. So, she must either believe he lived in fear of what might happen or believe he just didn't want *her* and was trying to spare her feelings. Yet if the latter were the case, why do it by kissing her wildly and fondling her so deliciously that she'd wanted to purr like a cat at his touch? It made no sense.

Her eyes slid closed. Lord, what heady sensations his caress had sent coursing through her. She could never have imagined such an embarrassing thing would also be so pleasurable. Oh, she'd rubbed her breast a time or two, but it hadn't begun to compare to having *him* touch her.

I am not the gentleman you assume. I may ache to be with you and kiss you and touch you and make love to you. But if I ever do, afterward I will also do the sensible thing and marry a woman who won't make me ache ever again.

He sought to live his life feeling *nothing*, curse him. How could anyone choose such a thing?

Picking up her needle, she stabbed it into the slipper, then rose to pace the room. What was she to do? She still couldn't believe he'd actually told her about Lady Margaret. That he'd somehow thought she would understand the twisted logic that said he'd be better off with a woman he didn't love than with a woman who, according to him, made him "feel things."

Did he really mean to walk away from her after this week was over? Did he really think he wouldn't worry about her or wonder what she was doing? The man was infuriating.

She shook her head. Well, no matter what he thought, she wasn't going to just stand by and watch while he threw her away out of some cursed belief that it would keep his heart safe.

But first, she must try to determine his true feelings. Because, according to Maman, it was possible for a man to desire a woman without actually caring anything for her. And if desire was the only thing Noel felt, it was better that she learn the truth now. Then she could merely ignore him for the rest of the week and do her best to win this competition without his companionship or interference.

It suddenly occurred to her that she had the perfect way to figure out the truth. All she needed was a few minutes alone with him.

Fortunately, the next morning, when his carriage arrived to pick them up, he came, too. Maman wasn't around, thank heavens, and it apparently didn't occur to Jimmy to question the viscount's sudden appearance after three days of the man letting them ride alone back and forth to his house.

Noel stood waiting to hand her in as if they did that every day, but a gust of wind carried the dyeworks steam her way before she could get in behind Jimmy, and she erupted into a fit of coughing before she could stop herself.

Although he grew rigid, he still handed her in while at the same time offering her his handkerchief. She took it and pressed it to her mouth, delighting in the tender action while trying not to notice the scent of him on the linen.

Once she sat down and got control of her cough, she said cheerily, "Good morning, my lord. How kind of you to grace us with your presence today."

His jaw tightened at her sarcasm. "You know perfectly well why

I'm here. I don't like the idea of you and Jimmy traveling alone when there's some scoundrel trailing after you."

"Where?" Jimmy cried, looking out the window. "What scoundrel?"

"It's nothing," Eve told him, then looked at Noel. "You could have sent the extra footman you spoke of. Between the two footmen and the coachman, we would have been perfectly safe."

His cool gaze met hers. "I wanted to make sure" was all he said. Then he proceeded to stare out the window.

Fine. She might as well put her plan into action. Shifting on the seat as if to adjust her skirt, she still managed to rub his ankle with hers in the process.

That certainly got his attention, for he glanced at her, a hint of alarm in his eyes. When she smiled blithely, as if she had no idea what he was reacting to, he searched her face, then returned to looking out the window.

"So," she persisted, "have you learned any more about who's following us?"

"Afraid not. The man apparently never spoke to my servants, and none of them recognized him," Noel clipped out, though he didn't turn from the window. "He wasn't nearby when I drove up this morning, so he has either found out what he needed to know or was put off by my presence."

"In which case, your presence accomplished what you wanted," she pointed out. "How kind of you to be looking out for us all the time."

That gained her a penetrating glance, as if he were trying to make out what she'd meant.

"I'm not sure why you are bothering to do so," she went on, "given that Jimmy tried to steal your wallet, but . . ."

"I owe it to my sister," he said in his deep rumble of a voice, which gave her delicious shivers whenever he used it. "You were her dearest friend."

"And she was mine. I still feel her loss deeply." *In other words, Lord Cokesbury, you are not suffering alone.*

"Then why didn't you pay a visit to our town house to see her upon your return?"

The question startled her. "First of all, we didn't even arrive in London until June. It took us that long to find passage back. Then, we visited Papa's town house, where we were rebuffed by my uncle's servants, since he was at his estate. By the time we found lodgings and Maman and I found work, the Season had ended, and I knew she'd either be married and at her husband's estate or at your family's estate in the north country. That might as well have been on the moon, since we couldn't travel that far without funds."

"Sorry," he murmured. "I keep forgetting how difficult your situation was. Still, you could have written her. Mother would have written you back."

No doubt she would have. His mother had proved to be a real-life fairy godmother to her, much like the one in Charles Perrault's fairy tale. Eve had read every one of his stories she could get her hands on while in France.

"Do you want the truth, my lord?"

He winced, as he did every time she called him "my lord." "Always."

"I was embarrassed. I didn't want to be Natalie's impoverished friend, whom she would wish to bestow her charity upon."

Jimmy piped up. "Eve doesn't like charity."

Noel smiled faintly. "I've noticed."

"I don't mind it," Jimmy said, "especially if it's food."

"That's because food is all you think about every hour of the day," Eve said.

"Not *every* hour," Jimmy grumbled.

"What do *you* think about every hour of the day?" Noel asked her.

You, unfortunately. No, she dared not say *that.* "That détenu who's sweet on me," she said blithely.

Noel scowled. "What's his name?"

"Why do you care?" she countered.

He hesitated. "I don't . . . want anyone to take advantage of you."

"I don't want that, either. Fortunately, I am perfectly able to take care of myself. And you don't have a say in it, anyway."

He looked as if he were about to comment, but they had arrived.

As soon as the carriage stopped, Jimmy jumped out and ran up the steps, but before Noel could get out, she caught him by the arm to stop him. "I need to ask you something. It won't take long."

He sat back against the seat with a sigh. "What is it?"

"You said you wanted me. So, why not just make me your mistress?"

He blinked at her, as if not sure he'd heard her right.

"You could marry this Margaret woman," she went on, "and keep me in a tidy little house somewhere you could visit me whenever you—"

"Are you out of your mind?" he growled. "How on earth could you think I'd ever want you to do that?"

Although she actually had no intention of being his mistress, she shrugged. "Men do it all the time."

"I don't care! I would never dishonor you like that. And you know quite well you'd never shame your family like that, either. Besides, that wouldn't give me peace; it would only make me need you more. I'd let my marriage suffer just for the chance to be with you, and every time I couldn't be with you, I'd be thinking of you and worrying . . ." As if realizing how much he'd admitted, he tore his gaze from her. "No, that is not the answer, for damned sure."

"Oh, very well. If you say so."

He leaped from the carriage, fury evident in every line of his face as he handed her down, then strode off without waiting for her. She, on the other hand, was exulting. If all he'd wished to do was bed her, then he certainly wasn't going about it the right way.

So, she was back to what he'd claimed—that he wanted peace and nothing more. How was she to get around that? She had to do so. No matter how exasperating the man could be, she wanted him for her own. And she began to suspect he wanted the same, even though he was too stubborn to admit it. But how was she to change his mind?

By doing whatever she must. And she had some fine ideas for *that.*

Noel couldn't believe it. The past three days had been hell. How was a man supposed to keep his wits about him when the woman he wanted was actively trying to tempt him? Because clearly that was what Eve was doing.

Be his mistress, indeed. He should have realized then that she was trying to provoke him into changing his mind about their future.

Ever since that day, she'd tempted him with all the weapons at her disposal. She laughed at his paltry jokes. She brushed up against him every chance she got. She made sure to sit next to him at dinner so she could lean close to whisper witty or engaging comments about the food or the conversation that made him laugh in spite of everything. Worse yet, it allowed her delicious citrusy scent to waft over him until he couldn't breathe without wanting her.

Sometimes she was downright outrageous in her temptations. She lifted her skirts rather higher than necessary to climb the stairs ahead of him, treating him to the awe-inspiring sight of her trim ankles and a part of her shapely calves. It made his mind wander in the ungentlemanly path of what it would be like smoothing his hands up her endless, stocking-clad legs to where the stockings ended and the soft skin was bared, so he could plunder what lay between those delightful thighs.

Her greatest triumph had come today . . . and wasn't even really hers! His mother had decided that Eve, Lady Archer, and James should all stay here tonight, since the charitable auction was tomorrow evening and there was still so much left to do to prepare.

So, now that he was in bed, he was facing a night full of tossing and turning, of imagining her in her nightdress in the room upstairs, practically right above his own bedchamber. It had been Natalie's at one time, which is probably why Mother had put her there, but still it was too close for his comfort.

He fancied he could hear Eve moving about, and it drove him mad. It was nearly midnight, and he still hadn't managed to fall asleep. With a curse, he left his bed to put a banyan on over the smallclothes he wore to bed, then headed for the door that led to his adjoining study, hoping to find some boring tome that would put him to sleep.

But when he walked in, it was to find Eve herself leaning over his desk in a flimsy nightdress and wrapper that left very little to the imagination.

He shut the door behind him, making her jump and whirl around. She blushed bright red and for a moment he wondered if that blush extended beneath her clothes.

Then she found her voice. "Wh-what are you doing here, Noel?"

"It's my study." He lifted an eyebrow. "What are *you* doing here?" *Aside from making me want to throw you down on my desk and ravish you.*

"I-I embroidered something as a little thank-you for all you've done for me and my family. I was just writing a note to go with it . . ." She held up an embroidered loop that had a tiny bell on one end of it. "You can put the loop around the fold of your wallet so that even the most accomplished thief can't get it out of your pocket without ringing the bell."

As she handed it to him, he couldn't help laughing. "Now, that is ingenious. Where did you get the bell?"

"From your mother's box of unused items."

"Ah. Well, thank you." He smiled, amazed that she'd managed not only to give him something useful, but something unique to their . . . friendship? Could he even call it that? It felt like so much more. "But you didn't need to go to all that trouble."

"It was no trouble." She started to pass him, headed for the door to the hall, when he stepped into her path.

As her gaze shot to him, he said, "I'm glad you're here. I . . . er . . . wanted to wish you good luck for the competition. In case I didn't get the chance to say it tomorrow."

She gazed at him steadily. "And are you next going to go wish your true love good luck? Your mother showed me the list of ladies submitting to the competition, and Lady Margaret's name was on it."

"Margaret is not my true love, as you well know," he said irritably.

"You picked her over me and you intend to marry her, so as far as I'm concerned, she's your true love. The result is the same, is it not? You'll be with her, and I'll still be alone."

Annoyed by that apt description, he glared at her. "You will never understand why I want a boring, commonplace marriage, will you? You don't know what it's like to watch your world be shattered repeatedly, then have to pick up the pieces of your broken heart and try to put them back together every time."

He knew he'd said the wrong thing when a scowl knit her brow, and she narrowed her gaze on him. "I don't know? *I* don't know??" She began to pace in front of him. "Perhaps I should remind you that against my will, I spent half my life in France in a détenu camp at the whim of a cursed tyrant. Then my father died, and as a consequence, I lost most of my future prospects and all of my former London friends. I returned to find that I'd even lost Natalie forever."

She halted in front of him, her anger evident in every rigid line of her face. "I've had to live in a place that constantly aggravates my asthma, watch my beloved stepmother suffer and my beloved half brother turn himself into a pickpocket, all while not being able to do a thing about it!"

He could only stare at her, taken off guard by her fit of temper, not to mention the truth behind her words. He'd driven her to that with his thoughtless remarks, which he now fervently wished he could take back.

She poked him in the chest with her finger. "So, yes, I *know* precisely what it's like to watch my world be 'shattered repeatedly' and have my heart broken into pieces, you . . . you pompous, unfeeling wretch!"

Then, to his horror, she burst into tears.

Oh, God, he'd made her cry! He'd caused it with his stupid, heedless comments, by being exactly what she'd accused him of—an unfeeling wretch.

Pulling her close, he tried to soothe her, but apparently that only made matters worse. So, when she shoved him away and headed for the door, he scooped her up in his arms and sat down in the nearest chair with her in his lap.

"Please don't cry, sweetheart," he whispered into her hair. "I can't bear it."

"Then . . . then g-go away!"

"I can't," he murmured. "I can't leave you hurting like this. Shh, shh, dearling. Don't go on so. You're breaking my heart."

"Good!" she muttered. "You d-deserve to have your h-heart broken, you . . . you . . . scoundrel!"

He did, that was for damned sure. "Yes, that's exactly what I am," he crooned, cursing himself for ten kinds of a fool as he cradled her head against his chest. "Let it out. Call me all the names you wish. I deserve every one of them, God knows."

She gazed up at him, tears glistening in her eyes. "How dare you tell me . . . How could you possibly think my pain matters any less than yours?"

"I don't think that, I swear. I'm just a fool. I'm so sorry for trampling over your feelings. I had no right." He smoothed her hair and brushed tears from her cheeks with his thumbs. "Sometimes I get so caught up in my own losses that I forget other people have them, too."

"Everybody has them, you b-bloody arse!" She clapped her hand over her mouth in horror. "Now, look what you've done! You have me cursing!"

He'd never so much as heard her use a mild oath, and now she was cursing at him. "I deserve it. Go ahead, you can say it again. It's true." Now that the storm of her tears seemed to be on the wane, he held her close, murmuring sweet words and rubbing her back, wondering helplessly what else he could do to make it better.

She curled into him, as if seeking comfort in his arms, which he didn't deserve. "I-I suppose I shouldn't call you an arse."

"Why not, when I am one sometimes?"

"Yes, but it's not ladylike to say it," she mumbled. "And I definitely sh-shouldn't have said 'bloody.' "

He couldn't help laughing at that, and she glared at him. She used the tie of her wrapper to wipe her eyes, reminding him that he had a handkerchief in the pocket of his banyan. So, of course he produced it for her, and she took it to blow her nose with.

They sat there in silence for a while more.

"Better now?" he asked as she wiped her nose with his handkerchief again.

"I probably look a fright," she said with a frown.

"You look beautiful," he said in a husky voice. "You always do."

She gazed into his eyes. "I meant what I said about everyone having losses. Everyone suffers. You're so intent on your own misery that you forget to see the people you still have. Your mother, for one. She would do anything for you."

It was true. He hated that Eve thought him so ungrateful. "I know."

She ducked her head to focus on his handkerchief in her hand. "And surely your Lady Margaret must have *some* feelings for you that—"

He kissed her then, at first to make her stop talking about Margaret, and then because he wanted to. Because three days without kissing her had been three too many. After a very long, very passionate kiss, he whispered, "She can't hold a candle to you, darling."

Then he began to kiss her in earnest, with deep, drugging kisses meant to show her how much he cared. And to his great pleasure, she leaned up into them, sliding her arms about his neck . . . crushing his hair beneath her fingers . . . surrounding him with her luscious scent that perversely made him think of clove-studded oranges hanging in the dining room at Christmas.

Realizing that if he didn't stop, he'd soon go too far, he drew back and tried to regain control of his desire for her. "Your resilience humbles me, you know. How do you do it? How do you always manage to put a cheerful face on things even when you have—"

"Nothing?" she said, anticipating the word he'd just barely kept himself from saying. "But I have wonderful things in my life. I have people still around who love me. Work I enjoy. Enough food to keep from starving, and a place to live that is larger than we had for years in Verdun." She stroked his hair. "Besides which, my family is all in good health."

"Except for your asthma," he pointed out.

"Yes, but that can be controlled with a change of my surroundings. Whenever I am tempted to despair over my lot in life, I remind myself how lucky I am to be back in London, where I can walk to parks and museums. How wonderful it is to have friends like you and your mother."

"Friends who make you cry."

She smiled. "Sometimes. But who make me laugh other times. You have as much as I do and more." She swept her hand around to indicate his study. "You have all this, and your mother, too. Only think how lucky *you* are."

A lump caught in his throat as he stared at her shining face. "Lucky, indeed," he said hoarsely, then kissed her again. But this time, he wanted more than just her mouth. He wanted to touch her, taste her, imprint her essence on him so he never felt broken-hearted again.

He wanted *her.*

CHAPTER 7

Eve sensed the change in his mood at once. So, when he slid his hand up and inside her wrapper to caress her breast through her thin nightdress, she not only let him but she reveled in it, leaned into it, silently begging him to do more.

He did. Flicking open the buttons of her nightdress, he bent her over his arm so he could take her breast in his mouth and suck, tonguing her nipple to a hard peak as she delighted in the sensations it beat through her very veins. She caught his head to hold it there while he slipped his hand inside her nightdress to fondle her other breast and thumb *that* nipple over and over until she thought she'd go mad from the pleasure of it.

She could feel the thickness of his member pressing against her bottom and knew what it meant. Her stepmother had been very clear about what happened between a man and a woman. He was aroused, and it suddenly dawned on her that she *wanted* him aroused.

Not just that, she wanted to be his. Completely. Thoroughly. After tonight, he'd probably go wed his Margaret to keep his heart safe, but she didn't want to keep hers safe. She liked that he'd remembered her even though he hadn't paid any attention to her as a girl. She loved how he'd changed himself after Natalie had fallen sick because he'd wanted to be a better brother. And she positively adored that he hadn't looked down on her stepmother and had been unfailingly patient and kind toward Jimmy. No matter what happened after, what pain it caused her, she wanted him to be her first, her only. She couldn't imagine doing this with anyone but him.

She must have undulated or something against his arousal, for with a groan, he drew back to look at her. "We have to stop, dearling, before I take you to bed the way I want to do so badly."

"Then, why stop?" she whispered.

He stared at her as if uncomprehending. "Wait, are you trying to tell me all that rot again about wanting to be my mistress?"

"No. You were right—I would never shame my family like that." She slid her hand inside his banyan to find his chest fully bare. My, my. Her Noel had quite the manly chest, didn't he? "But I want to be yours, even if just for tonight. Make me yours. Please?"

He closed his eyes as if to shut her out. "You don't know what you ask."

"I do. I want you to be the one who shows me what it's like to be with a man. Only you. Consider it your Christmas present to me." And to clarify what she meant, she rubbed her bottom over his arousal.

His eyes shot open, and he stared at her a long moment. Then with a groan, he shifted from beneath her so he could stand, but only to catch her up in his arms and stride for the open door to his bedchamber.

She blinked at him.

"I'm not going to make love to you in my study, for God's sake," he growled, as she threw her arms about his neck to hold on. "You deserve better than that. And if this is anyone's Christmas present, it's yours to *me.*"

"Then it's our present to each other," she whispered.

After carrying her into his bedchamber, he kicked the door shut behind him. "I must be out of my mind," he grumbled, as he headed for the bed. "I only went into my study in the first place for a book to put me to sleep, so I wouldn't toss and turn, thinking of you in your bed upstairs and wanting you. Clearly, that plan didn't work very well."

"I think it worked perfectly." She flashed him a teasing smile. "You won't be tossing and turning, will you?"

"There will be a certain amount of tossing and turning, I daresay. Just not the kind I anticipated." When she stretched up to brush a kiss to his lips, he deepened the kiss, but after he laid her down, he paused to look at her with a gaze so hungry, she felt it to her toes. "Are you sure about this?"

She sat up to put her legs over the edge of the bed so she could open his banyan, then press a kiss to his stomach.

"God in heaven, Eve," he rasped, shrugging his banyan off as she spread kisses up his stomach to his chest. "You are a wonder."

With both hands, he pushed her wrapper off her shoulders. When she shrugged out of it with a shy smile, he tugged her nightdress up and off of her, leaving her as naked as when she was born.

"No drawers, I see," he murmured as he stared down at her, his breath coming in quick gasps.

"Maman says it's wicked to wear drawers. Men wear them, so . . ." She ducked her head, a bit embarrassed. "I don't understand why that makes it wicked, though."

"I've heard the argument before," he said hoarsely as his eyes ate her up, "but trust me, I don't mind your lack of drawers, especially now." He bent over her to fit his hand between her legs. "What pretty red curls you have, dearling, even here," he said and slipped one of his fingers inside her down there, making her gasp. Then he brought his finger to his lips and licked. "Tasty, too," he said, eyes gleaming.

"Noel!" she cried, shocked.

When she blushed to the roots of her hair, he swept his gaze down her. "I've been wondering if you blush everywhere. Apparently, you do." He fondled her again between her legs, making her shimmy at his touch. "I like making you blush."

She tipped up her chin with what she hoped was a seductive smile. "Perhaps I can make *you* blush," she said as she unbuttoned and untied his drawers.

He chuckled. "I doubt that."

She tugged his drawers down, then swallowed hard as his substantial *verge*, as Maman had called it, sprang free. It was thick and rather dark, jutting from a nest of curls much like hers, except his were black as sin. And his *verge*, so firm and bold . . .

"Good Lord," she whispered and ran her finger along it, then laughed nervously when it bounced beneath her touch.

"Oh, you think that's funny, do you, my little seductress?" he said, then lifted her legs onto the bed so he could lay her out before him. "That's enough of your teasing. Now it's my turn to tease."

Still standing by the bed, he covered her mons with his hand and began to stroke her with such deft movements that she found herself arching up to meet his questing fingers. They delved inside her wantonly, rubbing and teasing and making her gasp with how good it felt.

"Do you like that, sweetheart?" he asked hoarsely.

"Yes . . . Oh, *yes . . .*"

Now his thumb was pressing her in a certain spot so deliciously that she could hardly stand it.

Suddenly, the clock struck midnight downstairs. He froze, as if reconsidering what they were doing, what he was doing.

Oh no, she was having none of that. Grabbing his arm, she pulled him toward her. "It's Noel's Eve, dearest," she whispered. "What better time to make me yours?"

That was all it took to have him climbing onto the bed between her legs and reaching down to fit himself inside her. If one could call it that. When he slid his . . . his *member* fully inside her, she felt . . . uncomfortable, to say the least.

But not for long. He pulled her knees up, so that she felt more comfortable, and then he began to move in slow, silken thrusts that had her grasping his arms and hanging on for dear life.

His eyes closed. "God, sweetheart, you feel so good. This is . . . undoubtedly the best . . . Christmas present I've . . . ever had."

"Is it?" she choked out. It wasn't the best *she'd* ever had.

He opened his eyes to gaze at her with that dark, knowing stare he sometimes had. "It will get better, love . . . I promise. I'll . . . make it better."

Love? Did he mean that the way it sounded?

Then he braced himself on one arm while he used his other hand to press her again where they were joined. Fire leapt inside her once more, and she grabbed his upper arms to hold on to him as he plunged in and out of her in quickening strokes.

"Ohhh . . . *Noel* . . ."

"Better . . . now?"

He'd asked her that, too, after her tears had begun to subside earlier. The sweetness of it—of his calling her "love"—made her heart soar. "Yes, my darling."

Heat leapt in his eyes. "You're mine . . . now. *Mine*, Eve."

A heady excitement coursed through her. "Yes. Oh, *yes* . . ."

He thundered into her with quickening thrusts that drove her ahead of him like a hunter chasing prey. Except she wanted to be caught. She thrilled to the idea of having him capture her . . . make her his . . . so she . . . could make him . . . hers.

Suddenly he caught her . . . in a crash of sensations so powerful that she saw stars . . . felt him shudder . . . heard him cry out her name.

"Mine . . . Noel," she whispered as she vaulted into oblivion.

For a moment, he strained against her, as if to relish every second of being inside her. Then he collapsed on top of her. She wrapped her arms around him, his weight a comfort. Bending to brush a kiss to her lips, he rolled off to lie beside her, breathing heavily.

She curled up next to him, still awash in the wonderfully intense feelings he'd brought to life within her. She'd lost her innocence, and she didn't care. Because she'd lost it to Noel, the man she loved.

Loved? Oh yes. She did love him, even with all his faults. But she wasn't sure it was wise to say it to him if he proved not to want her beyond this. She had too much pride for that. For now, it was enough to have had him in her bed.

After a moment, he turned on his side and propped his head on one hand so he could look at her. Laying his arm over her belly, he smoothed his fingers up and down her ribs.

"Are you all right?" he asked in a husky voice. "Not too much pain?"

"Only a little." She ran her hand lightly over his chest with its swirls of hair. "I believe I like my Christmas present."

He arched one eyebrow in an expression she could only call wolfish. "I certainly enjoyed mine."

Mine.

While in the throes of joining with her, he'd said she was his. But what did that mean? What did he want it to mean? She was afraid to ask, and even more afraid to know. Because if he still planned to offer for Lady Margaret, she didn't know how she could bear it.

"Eve, we need to talk," he murmured.

Oh, no, she was not staying around for that. Not now, not after this. Because once he said the words ending all her pleasure, she'd never be able to unhear them. Sitting up on the side of the bed, she found her nightdress and tugged it on, then grabbed her wrapper, pulling it on as she headed for the door.

"Wait! Where are you going?" Noel muttered, vaulting out of the bed fully naked. "Eve, for God's sake . . ."

"I have to go." Frantically, she fought to think of a reason and miraculously did. "Sometimes when Jimmy's in a strange place, he wakes up, gets frightened, and seeks me out. If I'm not in my room, he'll panic."

"Just give me a moment to—" Noel began, looking around for his clothes.

She opened the door.

"Damn it, Eve, wait!" he growled, as he found his drawers and started dragging them on.

That was the last thing she saw before she closed the door and fled up the stairs. Only once she reached her room and locked the door could she relax. He wouldn't go so far as to come up here, would he? Surely not, with Maman in the room next to hers and Jimmy across the hall.

All the same, she retreated to her bed to keep herself from running back downstairs and throwing herself into his arms. She was too vulnerable to him right now. Because if she'd stayed and he'd given her his speech about Lady Margaret and his need for a boring marriage again, she might have done something truly unladylike and punched him.

She sighed. No, she would never do such an inane thing. Which was why she'd had to run away. To avoid having her heart broken.

Tears leaked from her eyes. She was as bad as he was, wasn't she? A coward when it came to having her heart broken. Still, she didn't regret giving herself to him. She should, but she couldn't.

She only hoped that by tomorrow morning, she'd be ready to endure whatever he told her.

By the time Noel had donned his banyan and raced out into the hall, he could hear the door close upstairs and the key turn in the lock. Still, he hesitated, fighting the urge to march up there, pound on the door, and tell her he had to talk to her.

Because, truth was, he couldn't act so thoughtlessly. It would awaken the whole household, and the discussion would suddenly involve more than the two of them. Also, everyone might guess what had happened, and he wouldn't shame Eve for anything.

Besides, he needed time to plan what he meant to do. Of course, he would marry Eve. The minute he'd agreed to take her to bed, he'd known what it meant. But by then he hadn't cared, because after hearing her relate how she'd dealt with her own pain and losses, he'd realized he couldn't watch her walk out of his life. She was too precious to him.

Besides, he was in love with her.

The thought stunned him. How could that be, when he'd protected himself so carefully? He'd worked so hard to resist Eve, to keep his own heart safe. Obviously, he'd failed.

And never had failure felt so much like success. Because the idea of having Eve for his own, of spending his days and nights with her, of watching her bear his children, didn't feel nearly as alarming as it had before. It felt downright wonderful.

He could no more marry Margaret now than he could fly to the moon. But even though he'd never made a formal offer to Margaret, he did owe her something of an explanation. Margaret had been expecting an offer. It would be callous to let that continue.

Wandering back to the bed, he saw the blood on the sheets and groaned. Not that it surprised him all that much—he'd been sure Eve was an innocent, even when she was playing the seductress. But it just reminded him he'd been a fool not to tell her how he felt about her as soon as they'd finished making love.

He should have said something sooner. Removing the sheet from the bed, he threw it into the fire. At least he could preserve her reputation. Then tomorrow, he would offer her marriage, even if he had to do it at the breakfast table, in front of everyone. One way or the other, he'd make sure she knew he meant to marry her.

Only after he'd decided that, was he able to climb under the covers and sleep.

He awoke to the scratching at the servant's door that signaled the entrance of his valet, who came in with a cheery smile and a tray containing coffee and a newspaper. "Good morning, my lord."

"Good morning. Are the ladies up yet?"

He couldn't see Eve soon enough.

"They are, but they're working in the schoolroom upstairs—something about adding final touches to Miss Archer's gown to match her slippers. They asked that you and young Master James not bother them. I told them that you were taking Master James to the tailor this morning at eleven, anyway, to have any necessary alterations made to his clothing for this evening."

"Damn, I forgot about that." A glance at the clock told him he'd be late if he didn't hurry.

"Of course, Mrs. Archer yet again voiced her objections to having you take that responsibility on yourself, but the viscountess explained why it was necessary to present young Master James as looking more gentlemanly, and she and Miss Archer acquiesced."

He wasn't sure what that meant for his own chances with Eve, but it couldn't hurt, surely. Hastily, he got dressed and headed downstairs, only to be met by James at the stairs.

"I get my new clothes today, don't I?" the lad asked.

"You do." Noel checked his watch. "And we need to go this minute, I'm afraid."

The trip to the tailor took longer than he'd anticipated, since a few alterations had been required, and they'd had to wait for them. By the time they returned to the town house, the ladies had gone over to St. James's Palace where the competition was being held, so they could help the ladies from Mrs. Pawsey's School set things up and decorate. His butler told him they would return home in time to dress for the evening.

Frustrated by his present inability to gain a moment alone with Eve, he asked, "Do you know when?"

"They didn't say, my lord."

"Then I'll go join them at St. James's Palace."

"You can't, my lord!" his butler cried as Noel turned for the door.

Noel glowered at him. "Why not?"

"Because a man from Mr. Hall's office is awaiting you most impatiently. He refuses to leave until he speaks to you."

Mr. Hall was his attorney. "Fine," Noel said, "I'll get rid of him." He had to talk to Eve before she hardened her heart against him. He couldn't bear one more moment having her think he might still be planning to marry Margaret.

When Noel walked into the drawing room, the fellow awaiting him said, "Mr. Hall has sent me to fetch you, my lord."

"What for? I have another obligation that—"

"Forgive me, sir, but Miss Archer's uncle has come to London. And he is demanding to speak to *you*. But he asked that you not involve Miss Archer and her family just yet."

That brought Noel up short. Then it fired his temper. After everything the Archers had been through . . . "I believe Miss Archer, at the very least, should be included in this discussion." And why the devil had the man chosen this very moment to do this?

"He says he will only speak to you."

Noel sighed. It wasn't as if he could refuse. Eve and her family had been waiting for this, and he meant to make sure they got what they needed.

"Very well." He gritted his teeth. "But you'll have to wait while I dress for my other commitment this evening." No matter what, he was *not* going to miss Eve's appearance tonight. "It involves the queen."

"Of England?" the man said, incredulous.

"What other queen would I be talking about?" he snapped before hurrying up the stairs.

Thankfully, his valet already had his clothes laid out for the night. Normally, he would wait until the last minute to put on such finery, but he dared not. He didn't know how long this discussion would take. Besides, it couldn't hurt to cow Eve's uncle by appearing in clothing only reserved for appearing before royalty.

Once attired, he arranged with his butler to have young James fed and dressed in his new clothes while the lad was waiting for the ladies to return. "If I'm not back by the time they need to leave for St. James's Palace, give this to Eve." He handed his butler a handkerchief. "Tell her it was Natalie's. That it's for luck. And tell her I'll be there as soon as I can."

His butler nodded, though he clearly had questions.

Even if Noel would have answered them, he couldn't stay for them. It was time to go meet Eve's villainous uncle.

Chapter 8

Eve, her stepmother, and Lady Cokesbury had gathered in the foyer of Cokesbury Place in their finest attire, watching for Noel. Earlier, when they'd come home to dress, it was to find that Noel had gone off to see his attorney for who knew what reason. He still hadn't returned. He'd even instructed the butler to tell them not to wait if they were ready to go to the palace before he got back.

They didn't have much time, though. All ladies participating in the competition were to be there half an hour early to lay out their submissions. Noel *knew* that.

Eve sighed. Remembering how she'd fled Noel just last night, she winced. She'd been a coward, and now she was paying for it. She hadn't seen him all day, and she didn't know if his sudden defection boded ill.

Not that it mattered. He would do as he pleased, and she would just have to endure whatever that was. Although if he asked her to marry him . . .

Surely that was a dream.

Jimmy raced down the stairs in front of Noel's valet, coming to a halt in front of them.

"Why, aren't you just the *handsomest* young man," Lady Cokesbury told Jimmy.

Jimmy gave a courtly bow. "Thank you, Your Ladyship."

"Oh, and he even *sounds* like a little gentleman, doesn't he?" Maman said, brushing tears from her eyes. "Your son has worked a miracle on the lad, Lady Cokesbury."

Eve had to wipe a tear from her own eye. Who would have guessed Jimmy could ever carry off such attire and good manners? Apparently, Noel had.

"His Lordship even gave me one of his handkerchiefs to carry!" Jimmy said. "It's really nice and soft." Taking it out of his pocket, he demanded that his mother and Eve feel it. Neither of them had the heart to tell him that most gentlemen's handkerchiefs were "nice and soft."

The butler approached her. "That reminds me, Miss Archer. His Lordship gave me a handkerchief for *you*, too."

"Really?" She couldn't imagine why.

"He said to tell you that it had been Miss Davenant's. That it was for luck."

Natalie's embroidered handkerchief. He'd given her the handkerchief of the sister he still mourned? That was so unbearably sweet that tears stung her eyes. She blinked them away. It was hard not to see that as a hopeful sign.

"I fear we cannot wait for Noel any longer," his mother said. "Shall we go now, ladies? And gentleman?"

While Jimmy preened at that, the ladies reluctantly agreed they'd best return to the palace. Carrying Eve's embroidered slippers in a cloth bag, they climbed into the carriage. But Eve couldn't shake her worry that something was wrong to make him so late.

She must not have been the only one worrying. Everyone but Jimmy was silent on the way to St. James's Palace. He chattered on about what going to a tailor was like and how he couldn't wait to see the queen. They indulged him by smiling and pretending to be interested the whole way to the palace. Fortunately, it wasn't far from Mayfair.

As soon as they arrived, they entered the large room designated for displaying the embroidered items. They'd all spent the afternoon placing sprigs of holly on tables, hanging kissing boughs from the ceiling, and festooning evergreen branches about the room. It looked and smelled like Christmas, making Eve smile.

They headed for where they knew Eve's item was supposed to be displayed. They had almost reached her spot when she heard Lady Cokesbury groan beside her, and she looked up to see Noel in the midst of a discussion with an elegantly dressed blonde woman.

Eve caught her breath as she glanced at Lady Cokesbury. "Is that . . . Lady Margaret?"

The viscountess's gaze met hers. "You know about her?"

"Yes. Noel is planning on making her an offer of marriage."

"Not anymore, I daresay," Lady Cokesbury remarked as she nodded to the pair and broke into a smile.

Eve followed her gaze. The two were now in a heated argument. Noel was stabbing his finger at the item on the table between them. Then he stalked away from her, his expression resolute.

Meanwhile, behind him Lady Margaret caught sight of Eve with Noel's mother. The smug look that the woman shot Eve would have withered any ordinary woman.

It made Eve despair.

Noel spotted them and strode toward them at once. Oh, how delicious he looked in his evening finery. Oh, how she hated that she cared so much.

When he reached them, his mother asked, "What the devil was so important that you had to go to your attorney's today, of all days?"

"I'll get to that in a moment. I came straight to the palace, hoping I might catch all of you before you left to go home and dress. Apparently, I'm running later than I thought." He turned to Eve. "But at least I now know who's been following you and James."

"It's my uncle, isn't it?" Eve asked. "He had one of his servants doing it. Is that why you went to your attorney's?"

"No. Yes." He ran a hand through his hair. "It wasn't your uncle's man following you. It was Lady Margaret. Or rather, her servant."

"She told you that?" his mother said incredulously.

"She didn't have to." He glanced at Eve. "The minute I saw her submission I knew. The bloody woman stole your design for the slippers."

"You said 'bloody'!" Jimmy cried. "In front of ladies, too, and you're not supposed to!"

"Quiet!" he and Eve said together.

Jimmy lapsed into a sullen silence.

"What do you mean?" Eve asked.

"I can only guess she heard from one of our servants about your recent appearance at Cokesbury Place. Then she must have set her own servant to following you, and the chap found your drawings on the dyeworks wall. He copied them and gave them to her. That's the only explanation I have for why her submission is a pair of slippers embroidered exactly the way your old design was drawn—with holly leaves."

"The devil you say!" Lady Cokesbury exclaimed.

"Her embroidery isn't nearly as intricate or accomplished as yours, of course," Noel told Eve, "but when I pointed out that I would inform the queen about her copying your design, she knew she was caught. Then she said she would just claim that *you* had copied *hers*. She is certain that the queen would never believe 'a nobody who lives next to a dyeworks in Hatton Garden.' She thinks to convince Her Majesty that I've been taken in by some 'grasping harpy' and seems to believe that saying such a thing will somehow prompt me to return to *her*."

"That unconscionable, lying wretch!" Maman exclaimed.

"My sentiments exactly," Noel said. He looked at her stepmother and his mother. "But I think we can salvage this. There's still enough time that I can go home and bring back one of Eve's other pieces. We can even use Mother's apron as the submission. The queen is always late anyway, or so Mother says, so—"

"No," Eve said quietly.

He blinked at her. "What do you mean, no?"

She steadied her shoulders. "These slippers are the best thing I've ever done. I'm not submitting something else."

"And surely, son," his mother added, "the queen will realize I would never champion a thief and a liar. If I speak on Eve's behalf—"

"Look," Noel told his mother, "if the queen realizes that two women have very similar submissions and you champion Eve, Margaret will merely use that to blacken *your* reputation."

Oh, Lord, Eve hadn't thought that possible. She would cut off her hand before she'd let his mother suffer.

"Let her just try," Lady Cokesbury said stoutly. "The queen knows my character. We may not be intimates, but—"

"Damn it, Mother, this is more important than any of you realize!" When she flinched, Noel groaned. "You see . . . well . . . I didn't just go to meet with my attorney. I went to meet Eve's uncle, who summoned me to my attorney's office. And I have invited him here tonight."

That momentarily stunned everyone to silence.

"He agreed to come?" Eve finally asked, her heart in her throat.

"Only because I insisted. Apparently, he's been very ill for the past several months, too ill even to come to London to look in on all of you. He admits he should have sent for you, Eve, at the very least, but his servants kept the information about your situation from him for fear it would impede his recovery."

He grabbed Eve's hands, making her heart leap in her chest. "His attorney has had a man following you, so discreetly that none of us noticed. But the fellow reported to your uncle of James's pickpocketing and your mother's work as a seamstress. Those things are what convinced him that your stepmother couldn't possibly be worthy of being Lady Archer and that James should certainly never become baron. He still thinks your father was taken in by a schemer. He has come to London to determine the truth for himself."

Eve could already tell where this was headed, and her heart sank even further.

"I told him that once he saw how ladylike and accomplished you are, some of which is due to your stepmother's guidance, he would realize that your father married Lady Archer for a good reason. So, if he comes tonight and thinks that you have stolen some other lady's design—"

"But I haven't!" Eve said.

"It won't matter to him! He'll assume that it's under your stepmother's influence that you've done so. He already means to separate you from her in any way he can. I convinced him that your family is not what he thinks, but if he sees otherwise . . ."

Why was he pushing this? Why not just let the two ladies both put their slippers out, and see what happened?

She could think of only one reason, especially in light of Lady

Margaret's smug look. She pulled her hands free of his, feeling all her hopes die. "You're afraid that your future wife's thievery will be exposed if both sets of slippers are submitted. It's not me you're protecting. It's her." The woman who would give him the peace he craved.

The bloody woman stole your design for the slippers.

She swallowed. Had he meant to call her a "bloody woman"? And if so, why was he fighting so hard to have Lady Margaret present her counterfeit slippers and Eve *not* to present her own?

"You can't possibly believe that," he murmured with a stricken expression. He searched her face. "May I talk to you privately? Please?"

With a terse nod, she took the arm he offered. But they had no sooner ventured out of hearing of her family and his mother than she said, "If you're merely going to keep arguing for me standing down to allow Lady Margaret to get away with . . ." She caught her breath on a sob.

"Damn it," he muttered under his breath and dragged her into an empty room nearby, then shut the door. He caught her head in his hands and kissed her with a thoroughness that fired her blood. When he drew back, he said, "I shouldn't even have let you leave my room last night before I had the chance to say how I felt. I don't care about Lady Margaret, especially not now. It's *you* that I love, you that I want as my wife, you that—"

"You love me?" she whispered, hope flickering to life again in her chest.

"Are you daft?" He scattered kisses over her cheeks and nose and forehead. "Of course I love you! Do you think I make love to respectable females every day? I assure you, I do not."

She dropped her gaze from his. "You said you wanted peace. You said you could never find it with me, only with her. As recently as last night, you told me, 'I want a boring, commonplace marriage.' "

He groaned. "I said a lot of idiotic things last night in my attempt not to risk my heart. But that was pointless. Because I lost a piece of my heart the first time I saw you chastise your pickpocket brother. I lost another when you called me 'noble' for being by my sister's side at the end. By the time you gave me a speech about how many good things I still have in my life, my heart was wholly yours. It will always be yours."

Her own heart soared to hear it. At last, she had him for her own. He truly was hers.

He brushed a kiss over her lips. "Marry me, my dear, sweet love. And I will spend the rest of my life trying to convince you to love *me.*"

Tears of joy stung her eyes. "No convincing necessary, I assure you. You may have lost your heart to me, but you *stole* mine. I know you did it deliberately, too, you wicked fellow." She gave a giddy laugh. "I was probably quite foolish to let you do so, but you proved a far more adept thief than Jimmy."

She stroked his cheek. "With every kindness you showed me and my family, you stole my heart a little more, so slowly that by the time I realized you had it in your grasp, it was too late to snatch it back. So, yes, I suppose I must marry you, if only to retrieve my heart."

"I'll never give it back," he warned.

"I'll never give yours back," she countered.

"Good," they said in unison, then laughed.

They kissed for a long moment. Then Noel drew back with a sigh. "I suppose we still have to decide what to do about your submission."

"Will it embarrass you too much if I brazen it out with Lady Margaret?"

"It won't embarrass me at all. Look, I'll admit I was utterly taken in by her ladylike demeanor and quiet ways. It never dawned on me that beneath that façade was a woman capable of such vicious behavior toward any lady who captured my attention. But apparently, that truly is her character. I wouldn't have you harmed by her for all the gold in the Bank of England."

"And I won't put my second-best work in the place of my best simply so my uncle can be convinced to believe in me and Maman and Jimmy. I certainly won't do it to avoid a confrontation with Lady Margaret." Perhaps jealousy was riding her to do something disastrous, but she couldn't let the woman get away with her treachery. "Still, I don't want to hurt your mother—"

"You won't. Mother is right. The queen has enormous respect for her. All right, dearling. We'll do it your way. At least once we marry, I can take care of the three of you. We won't need your uncle anyway."

She sighed. "No, that's not right, either. James is Papa's rightful heir. I shall just have to convince my uncle of that. Somehow."

"He does still seem to have soft feelings for his niece. He remembers the same tart-tongued thirteen-year-old that I do. If it weren't for his misgivings about your stepmother and half brother, he would probably cart you off with him."

"Speaking of my uncle," she said, "although we could probably stay in here happily for the next hour or so, we'd best get back. Especially if my uncle is about to show up any minute."

"True."

And with that, they returned to the room where the competition was being held.

Chapter 9

When Noel and Eve emerged from the room, Noel glanced toward his mother and her stepmother and asked Eve, "Where's James?"

Eve scanned the area near her stepmother. "I don't see him."

Noel gazed all around the room.

Suddenly, he noticed James near the double doors from the foyer. An older gentleman, whom Noel recognized instantly as Eve's uncle, passed near James and then inexplicably seemed to drop his coin-heavy purse on the floor very near to James.

When Noel groaned, Eve followed his gaze to where James was picking up the purse.

"Your uncle has laid a trap for young James, I'm afraid," Noel said.

And the lad was just a bit too far away for either of them to do anything about it, although they hastened toward him anyway.

Before they could even reach Eve's uncle, much less James, they saw the boy tug on the older gentleman's coat. "I beg your pardon, sir," James said and held out the man's purse. "But I believe you dropped this."

Noel froze and pulled Eve to a halt beside him. Could James really be doing what Noel thought he was?

Eve's uncle turned to stare down at James, then at the purse in James's hand. "Why, thank you, young man. Very helpful of you." He opened the purse, checked it thoroughly, then smiled at James. "And what is your name, lad?"

"James William Archer, sir."

Noel's heart swelled with pride to see young James behaving so well with a man he couldn't possibly know.

"Are you one of the Archers from York?" Eve's uncle asked slyly.

"No, sir. My family is from Wiltshire. Never been to Wiltshire myself, on account of I was born in France, and we just arrived in England seven months ago. But my father was Baron William Archer before he died." He straightened to thrust his chest out proudly. "I'm his son."

"And heir," Eve's uncle said coolly.

"Yes, sir. Or so my mother and sister tell me."

"Are they around here?" he asked.

Eve hurried up to him. "Good evening, Uncle Uriah."

Her uncle blinked, then teared up. "Look at you, dearie. You've grown up!"

Noel saw tears filling her eyes, too. "I have indeed, Uncle." Then, like the sweet, forgiving woman she was, she hugged him. "It's so good to see you again. You remind me so much of Papa."

"You remind me of your mother," her uncle said, chucking her under the chin. "You have her eyes."

"I will have to trust you on that." Eve laid her hand on James's shoulder. "I see you've met my half brother."

"I have." Her uncle actually ruffled the lad's hair, which James clearly did not appreciate, judging from his grimace. "What a fine young gentleman he is."

"Most of the time," she said, clearly fighting a laugh.

James stared up at the man. "You're our uncle?"

"Yes, lad." He glanced around. "Where is your mother?"

"Over there with my mother," Noel said, walking up beside Eve. "They are both here to support her for this. Shall we introduce you, sir?"

"By all means," the older fellow said.

Once they reached the two ladies, Noel performed the introductions, keeping a close eye on Mr. Archer's reactions the whole time. As the two women began to explain why they were there at the embroidery competition, Noel noticed that Mr. Archer kept flashing looks at Lady Archer, as if trying to assess her.

When the conversation lagged, it occurred to him that he hadn't yet announced his and Eve's news. "By the way, everyone, I should have mentioned that Miss Archer has just made me the happiest of men and has consented to be my wife."

"I knew it!" his mother said. "Oh, son, I am so happy for you both. And Natalie would be delighted. I only hate that she couldn't be here to see it."

Lady Archer was smiling and crying at the same time. "I am so pleased, *monsieur*, to welcome you to the family."

"To *our* family," Mr. Archer said, giving Noel hope that in time the man would begin to recognize how wonderful all the Archers were. "Although you and I, sir, must have that conversation about settlements that you promised me this morning."

Eve's gaze swung to Noel. "You told him you were planning to marry me before you even saw me today?"

"I told him I meant to offer. But I couldn't be sure of your answer, of course."

"Oh, Noel," she whispered. "I love you so much."

Clearly, that had swept away any apprehension she might still have had that he'd been planning to offer for Margaret even after last night. "I love you, too, dearling." When he heard James snort, he gazed down at the young man. "Do you have an objection, lad?"

"Why do you have to be so mushy about it?" James muttered.

Everyone laughed.

"Your day will come," Noel said. "Mark my words."

"I don't like girls. Except for Eve and Mother and Lady Cokesbury, but they're ladies."

"They certainly are," Eve's uncle said, with a furtive glance at Lady Archer that had her blushing.

Before they could get further into the discussion, however, a woman at the front of the room clapped her hands for silence.

"We would like to welcome all of you to our embroidery display on behalf of Mrs. Pawsey's School for Embroidering Females, which provides worthy young women with training in being professional embroiderers. I am Mrs. Harriet Pawsey Machill, owner of the present school. The ladies exhibiting their work are women with more than a passing interest in embroidery. We're very happy to welcome all of the ladies and their families."

Polite applause sounded in the room.

"As you know, our judge of the work today is our patroness, an accomplished needlewoman and a very special lady in her own right. I give you Her Majesty Charlotte, the Queen Consort of the United Kingdom."

That brought more enthusiastic applause. The queen then said a few words about embroidery and its importance to women. Then Queen Charlotte began to stroll up and down the tables, sometimes pausing to ask the embroiderer about the work itself or to greet women she obviously knew personally or had met before. Mrs. Machill walked beside her, writing down notes that the queen dictated.

At Noel's side behind the table, Eve was clearly tense. Unfortunately, the path the queen had chosen would take her past Margaret before she passed Eve. It couldn't be helped, but Noel knew that was the cause of Eve's nervousness. All he could do to help was give her gloved hand a quick, furtive squeeze.

When the queen paused at Margaret's table to examine her slippers more thoroughly, Noel groaned. How he wished he could whisk Eve out of here and away to someplace bright and cheery, where she could be reminded that there were good people in the world, people nothing like Lady Margaret, with her vindictiveness and her thievery.

How he wished he had never considered making Margaret his wife. But he'd been blinded by the superficial trappings of her birth, beauty, and station. Sadly, Eve had proven to have more ladylike manners and mien in one thumb than Margaret had in her entire body. More importantly, Eve's sweetness and generosity, her very love of life, shone in everything she did, whereas Margaret's underlying pettiness would always mar her for anyone she met.

The queen continued to glide down the rows of tables until she came to Eve's. She paused to gaze at the design on the slippers. Then she picked up one of the slippers and examined it more closely. She whispered something to Mrs. Machill, who hurried back to Margaret's table and came back with Margaret in tow and one of Margaret's slippers in hand.

Now that the moment was upon her, Margaret didn't seem quite so keen to brazen things out, for her skin was flushed and she avoided Noel's gaze, not to mention the queen's. No doubt she'd expected Eve to bow out and leave the field to *her.*

Clearly, she had no idea whom she was dealing with. Noel fought to keep from smiling.

The Queen compared the two slippers, then gazed at Eve. "Tell me, where did you find this design?"

"It's my own, Your Majesty."

"Do you have drawings with you to show it?"

"No, Your Majesty. I drew it on a wall. Although my original design had holly instead of mistletoe."

"You mean, like the design on this?" She held up Margaret's slipper.

"Yes, Your Majesty." She moved back from the table. "And the design on *this.*" And with that, she lifted her skirts just enough so the queen could see that Eve had done some extra embroidery to the gown—mistletoe woven with the holly leaves and berries to make the slippers match the gown.

That must have been what Eve and the others had been working on this morning. But he hadn't noticed the extra design elements on her gown until now, too caught up in trying to force her into relinquishing the field to Margaret.

He should have known better. This was the ladies' realm. They knew what they were doing. There was no way in hell Margaret could argue that her design was her own when Eve had a whole dress done with it that combined both mistletoe and holly.

"And this design is on a wall at . . ." the queen prompted.

"Where we live in Hatton Garden, Your Majesty," Eve said stiffly, as if daring the queen to criticize her for it. "It's on the dyeworks wall. It's still there, as far as I know."

The queen shot Margaret a cold glance. "Is it, indeed? So, anyone who happens by can see it?"

"Yes, Your Majesty," Eve replied. "I like designs writ large to make them easier to see."

Thankfully, Lady Archer didn't so much as snort at that.

"I've seen the design myself, Your Majesty," Noel put in. He only hoped he wasn't making matters worse. "Upon my honor, it's there."

"I'm sure it is," the queen said dryly, then turned to Margaret. "You may go, Lady Margaret." She held out the slipper with two fingers as if she found it loathsome. "And take this with you."

"Yes, Your Majesty," Margaret said, clearly relieved not to be receiving a dressing down for her obvious cheating.

The queen returned her attention to him. "Really, Lord Cokesbury, you do not have to confirm the matter of the design on the wall. I can send a footman to do that if I wish. Besides, your championing of Miss Archer is somewhat colored by your obvious interest in her, so I wouldn't just take your word for it, in any case. And am I correct that the gossip saying you are about to make an offer of marriage to Lady Margaret is no longer . . . accurate?"

He swallowed. "You are correct indeed, Your Majesty."

"And am I also correct that your interest in Miss Archer has something to do with that?"

He bit back a smile. "That is also correct, madam. I have made an offer of marriage to Miss Archer, and she has accepted."

"That is one mystery solved, at least." She returned her attention to Eve. "Come out here, my dear, so I can better see your gown. Lord Cokesbury, if you will do the honors—"

At once, he separated the tables so Eve could go through. The queen spent several moments examining the truly amazing embroidery that went all around the hem, with the Father Christmas design at the center of the front.

"How long did this take you?" she asked Eve.

"Three weeks. But I worked on it several hours a day and at night, too."

"No need to be modest with me, my dear," the queen said. "It's astonishing. Don't you think so, Harriet?"

"It's even better than anything my aunt could have done."

Her Majesty sighed. "Such a pity that you are marrying His Lordship, Miss Archer. Harriet and I could give you more work than you could possibly handle, and pay you well for it, too."

"Forgive me, Your Majesty," Mr. Archer said, sounding peeved, "but my niece is a gentlewoman. Even if she did not marry, she would not need 'work.' I would see to it that she was supported."

The queen stared him down. "I should hope so. From everything I've heard, you have been lax in that respect."

Good God, did she know of what had been going on? Or had she been informed of it by someone?

He caught a look passing between his mother and the queen. Ah, yes. Mother had obviously had a hand in informing the queen of the Archers' situation.

"I-I was ill," Eve's uncle said. "But I will make sure it's taken care of from now on."

"See that you do." Her Majesty turned to James. "And who is this fellow gawking at me from behind his mother's skirts?"

Eve's mother thrust James forward. "My son, James William Archer, Your Majesty."

"I'm supposed to be the Baron Archer, Your Majesty," James said sullenly.

But before Noel could even chide the boy, the queen said, eyes twinkling, "Yes, you are." She leveled her gaze on Uriah Archer again. "You'll see to it that the lad also receives his proper due, won't you?"

Mr. Archer colored. "I will, Your Majesty."

Meanwhile, James was staring up at the queen in awe. "You're very pretty, Your Majesty." The poor lad must be nervous. Whenever James got nervous, he blurted out the first thing that leapt into his mind.

The queen laughed. "And you, sir, are a rascal."

"I'm trying not to be," James said. "Noel—I mean, Lord Cokesbury—has been helping me."

"I'm not so sure Lord Cokesbury is any less of a rascal than you are, Master Archer," the queen quipped. "What do you think, Miss Archer?"

"I think they are both charming rascals, Your Majesty. My brother only slightly less so than my fiancé."

"I can well imagine." Queen Charlotte sobered. "I must continue. But thank you for submitting your lovely work to this endeavor."

Eve curtsied exactly as Noel's mother had taught her to do, and the queen moved on.

It wasn't much later that Queen Charlotte and Mrs. Machill came to the end of the tables. Then followed some discussion between the two ladies while those at the tables whispered furtively among themselves.

At last, Mrs. Machill called for the attention of everyone. The queen gushed over how many of the submissions were stellar and how proud she was of the quality of embroidery amongst ladies in a time when it was declining in some circles. Then she announced the winner.

It was no surprise, at least to any of their party, when she named Eve's submission—The Mistletoe Slippers.

Without so much as a look of triumph in Margaret's direction, Eve walked forward to accept her certificate and hand the slippers to the queen. After the applause died down and the entrants began to form small groups while waiting for the auction of the rest of the items to begin, Noel, his mother, and Eve's family were allowed to go to the front where Eve stood watching the queen try on the slippers.

"Nearly a perfect fit!" the queen said. "I will have to add a bit of padding, but I can wear them, which is what I'd much prefer. Displays are so cold and impersonal." As she removed the slippers and handed them off to one of her ladies, before putting on her own again, she said to Eve, "I do have one question for you about your embroidery. Why did you change your design on the slippers from holly to mistletoe?"

Eve paused, as if weighing her words. "When I first drew the design, I thought only of celebrating Christmas. At that time, I didn't even know of this embroidery exhibition. But once I learned of it, after my acquaintance with Lord Cokesbury grew into something deeper, I did it in honor of love—my love for my fiancé and your love for the king. I have heard that the two of you have always been deeply in love." She shot Noel a shy glance. "I only hope that our love lasts as long as yours has."

Clearly, the queen liked that answer, for she smiled and patted Eve's arm before she was hurried off by the ladies, who were eager to protect her from having too many other people accost her.

"Well done, Eve," Noel's mother said. "I couldn't have given a better answer myself."

As she walked off to speak to a friend she'd just spotted, Noel murmured, "That's not the reason you gave *me* for doing it. You said you were doing it to win."

"That is *not* what I said." She smiled mischievously. "I *said* that your mother suggested I do it for that reason."

With a frown, he thought back over their conversation and realized she was right. "So, you weren't doing it to win?"

"Oh, I was," she said lightly. "I was doing it to win *you.*"

"I should have known. Your campaign was quite effective."

She suddenly looked anxious. "Does it bother you that I was so . . . determined?"

"Not one whit, dearling. You showed me that my plan for the future was decidedly flawed. Because it's impossible to avoid turmoil in one's life. And sometimes turmoil leads to changes that quite improve one's chance of happiness."

"Turmoil like our meeting each other in the street?"

"Exactly. Leading to changes like our falling in love." He took her hand and kissed it, wishing they were alone. "Because of you, my life will now be full of changes . . . Jimmy gaining his title, you becoming the grand dame of embroidery, us having children together . . ."

"You becoming a little more grateful for the good things in your life?" she said softly.

"A lot more grateful. Especially when the best thing in my life is you."

Her eyes sparkled. "Where is that mistletoe slipper when we need it?"

"We don't need it." He pointed overhead.

They were standing under a kissing bough.

"In that case . . ." Eve said with a delightful laugh, then stretched up to give him a kiss on the lips.

She was *his* Mistletoe Maiden at last.

Author's Note

Although the queen's competition was my own invention, Queen Charlotte was every bit the champion of women's crafts that I depicted. Mrs. Pawsey's School for Embroidering Females began as Mrs. Phoebe Wright's Celebrated Establishment in 1772 after Queen Charlotte wanted to place some indigent girls in a situation where they could learn a useful skill. Since needlecraft was a particular love of hers, she turned to Mrs. Wright's embroidery shop for that, and a school was born. Queen Charlotte subsidized the school to the tune of five hundred pounds a year from 1772 on. What's more, she often went to the school to observe the girls and provide encouragement.

When Mrs. Wright died six years later, her niece Nancy Pawsey took over the business and the school and ran it until her own death in 1814, when her daughter, Harriet, took it over. But after the queen's death in 1818, the annual subsidy ended, and the school did, too. So, while I did fudge things a bit by inventing the competition, all the rest of it already existed!

The Cinderella Challenge

Mary Jo Putney

CHAPTER 1

Chatham, Kent 1790
Fourteen Years Ago

On market days, sellers often stayed open late to serve workers leaving the nearby Chatham Royal Navy Dockyard. Shivering from hunger and the cold wind blowing off the nearby River Medway, Casey studied the people buying food at the stalls, looking for the best one to approach.

Dressed as a little boy and with a hat covering her raggedly short hair, no one suspected she was female. It was safer this way, especially since she preferred asking women, usually more sympathetic to scrawny children like her.

A middle-aged woman struggling with two bulging bags of food looked like she needed help. Casey approached and asked shyly, "Do you need a hand, ma'am?"

The woman snapped, "Away with you, lad! You'll not be stealing my family's supper!"

Casey cringed at the woman's virulence and backed away, her face flushed. But she was desperately hungry, so she looked for another prospect. The crowd of shoppers was thinning and some stalls were closing, so there were fewer choices.

Ah, that elderly man buying potatoes and onions and dropping them into a worn canvas bag. He had a cane hooked over his arm, so maybe he'd be grateful for assistance.

Approaching warily, she asked, "Sir, do you need help carrying your market bag?"

He turned to look at her, and his pale blue eyes had a power that seemed to scour her soul. She froze, wondering if she should flee.

But his voice was kind when he replied, "Aye, a bit of help would be useful." He handed her the bag, which was heavier than she expected.

She hesitated and studied his energy again. Yes, he was safe as well as kind. Gripping the bag with both hands, she followed him down the street. It was almost full dark, and they walked several blocks before reaching a small cottage.

The man paused to unlock the door before turning to her. "You look like you could use a hot meal. If you come inside, I can give you soup and toasted bread."

Hot soup and bread! The thought was almost too much for her. She briefly weighed her hunger against her sense of the man before saying, "I'd very much like that, sir."

He opened the door and led her into a simple kitchen. A table, two chairs, several shelves containing utensils and simple food containers. Best of all, it was welcoming. Seeing the dim glow of hot coals on the hearth, she asked, "Shall I stir up the fire, sir?"

"Yes, please. My knees aren't what they once were."

She knelt by the banked fire and stirred it, adding more coal from the bucket and using the bellows to increase the heat. "I'm called Casey, sir."

"A pleasure to meet you, Casey. I'm James Harris, usually known as Jamie, and I work in the dockyard office." He lit a lantern, then swung a kettle over the fire. "Lentil soup with vegetables and a bit of sausage. It will take a few minutes to warm up. Would you like to toast some bread?"

She swallowed hard. "I would, sir."

He unwrapped half a loaf of bread and cut several slices. "There's a toasting fork hanging by the fire. Feel free to eat the first piece of bread before you toast any."

"Thank you, Mr. Harris." She wolfed down the first piece. It tasted so *good*!

She began toasting other slices. While the kitchen warmed, Mr. Harris poured two mugs of ale and set them on the small table. He said mildly, "It's usual to remove one's hat when dining."

She froze a moment, then reluctantly removed her hat. Her host blinked before saying, "Your hair is a very pretty blond, but distinctive. Is that why you want to hide it, so you won't be noticed?"

Biting her lip, she nodded.

"I know a simple hair coloring that will make your hair look an unmemorable brown," he said.

"I'd like that," she said in an almost inaudible voice.

"It's easily done." Since the soup was warm, he ladled out two full bowls and they settled on opposite sides of the table.

She'd never in her life tasted anything better than his lentil soup.

When she finished her bowl and three pieces of toast, Mr. Harris said. "If you'd like more, lass, help yourself."

She froze like a frightened rabbit.

Seeing her reaction, he said softly, "You're a young girl, and gifted. I'd wager you were thrown out of your home."

Her voice was a croak. "H-how did you know?"

"I'm also gifted. As you've learned, many people resent those of us who have abilities they don't understand. I was driven from my home when I was even younger than you are now," he replied calmly. "I've helped others like you. My house is a sanctuary for as long as you wish to stay."

As tears stung her eyes, she reached across the table and clutched his thin right hand in both of hers, sensing years of kindness and safety ahead of her. "Thank you, Mr. Harris," she whispered. "And God bless you!"

CHAPTER 2

London
November 1804

A gust of wintry wind blew Cameron Tremayne into his family home, along with a few whirling flakes of snow. He had just removed his coat when his foster mother, Gwyn, the Countess Tremayne, appeared from the drawing room. "Perfect timing, Cam! A nice luncheon will be served in a quarter of an hour."

"That will give me just enough time to report to Rhys. Is he in his study?"

"Yes, and he'll be glad to see you." Gwyn bent and scooped up a large brown tabby cat that had just appeared to see who had arrived. She handed the tabby to Cameron. "You look cold. Have a nice warm cat."

He chuckled. "Thank you for sharing your warmth, Lord Stripes." He draped the purring cat over his shoulder and petted it as he made his way through the house to his foster father's study.

The study was well lit and warmed by a cheery fire. Rhys, Lord Tremayne, was reading a document with furrowed brows. He and Gwyn were both gifted, and together they had fostered a number of gifted children who had been discarded by their families, adding them to their three natural children.

All were combined into the Tribe of Tremayne, loved and supported equally. Cam considered Rhys and Gwyn the finest people he'd ever known, and he gave thanks regularly that they had taken him in when *he* was one such small, desperate child.

Rhys rose with a smile and clasped Cam's offered hand, then scritched Lord Stripes's neck before sitting again. "You're back sooner than I expected! Does that mean your mission went well?"

As Cam settled into a chair opposite his father's desk, the cat flowed down onto the floor and curled up in front of the fire. Wise creature.

"Here's the official report," Cam said as he pulled a folded document from inside his coat and handed it over the desk. "There was no French involvement, only homegrown British thieves. They've been dealt with."

The report was required because Rhys was not only father to the Tribe of Tremayne, but head of the gifted department of the Home Office. His agents worked to protect Britain from threats both domestic and foreign. With war recently resumed against France, a number of Cam's missions involved potential threats by French agents.

"Good work, Cameron." After Rhys had scanned the report, he set it aside and handed a letter over the desk. "This just arrived an hour ago. What do you think?"

Cameron was very good at reading the energy on objects, and this one gave him a sharp tingle, which was unusual for paper. The note inside was written in a clear, educated hand. He frowned as he read the message.

Dear Lord Tremayne

My name is Casey Harris and I'm a clerk in the Inspector General's office at the Chatham Royal Navy Dockyard. I have recently heard things suggesting threats against Sir Samuel Bentham, the Inspector General, but I was unsure what to do about them. I had been told once that if I became aware of any potential threat, it would be wise to contact Lord Tremayne at the Home Office. I hope that if the threat is real, you can do something to prevent a disastrous outcome.

Respectfully yours,
Casey Harris

Cameron frowned as he read and reread the message. "I'm not sure if the danger is real, but Mr. Harris certainly believes that it is."

"What else do you sense about him?"

Cam cleared his mind and sank more deeply into the energy of the letter writer.

"Mr. Harris is young and deeply reserved, and there is something very elusive in his nature that makes him hard to analyze. He lost the man he was closest to two or three years ago and has been very alone ever since."

"His father?" Rhys asked.

Cam shook his head. "Not his actual father, I think, but someone who held that place in his life." A man like Rhys, in fact. Cam didn't want to even think of the terrible future day when he would lose Rhys or Gwyn.

"What else do you sense?"

"I think Mr. Harris fears that the threat could come from the people around Sir Samuel, which is why he's been reluctant to speak of this to his coworkers," Cam said slowly. "He believes that talking to his colleagues might increase the danger to himself as well as Sir Samuel."

"He's wise to be cautious. Sir Samuel Bentham is the most brilliant naval engineer and architect in Britain," Rhys said, frowning. "His inventions have done much to keep Britain's navy powerful, but he's said to be a difficult man. There are many who resent him. His loss would be a great blow to Britain."

"I'm guessing that you're about to suggest that I visit Chatham."

"I have a feeling that you're the best person to send."

"And when a Tremayne says that he 'has a feeling,' that ends the discussion," Cam said with amusement.

"Exactly so," Rhys said. "You've just returned from one mission. Would you be willing to travel down to Chatham tomorrow for another?"

Cam considered, and realized that like Rhys, he had a feeling that this was something he should do for a number of reasons, not all of them clear. He glanced out the window at the pale winter light as he thought about what he'd sensed in the letter. "The matter feels urgent. If I leave now, I can reach Chatham by tonight."

"Good." Rhys nodded, then transformed again into Cam's father. "Be sure to have something to eat before you leave."

"Yes, sir," Cam said with a grin.

Chapter 3

Casey shivered as she walked home from the dockyard to the small cottage that Jamie Harris had left her when he died two years earlier. This dark, bitterly cold night reminded her of the first time she'd met him and found the love and acceptance she'd yearned for. He'd educated her about being gifted and later found her a position in one of the dockyard offices. She'd been devastated when he died. He left her all his modest possessions after she'd nursed him through his final illness, but she would rather have had him still alive.

They'd agreed that it was safest for her to continue dressing as a male since it gave her more freedom and security. Since she was tall for a female and had a slim build, she'd had no problem maintaining her male masquerade, though sometimes she wondered wistfully what it would be like to live her life as a young lady.

But she always shut those thoughts down quickly, since she couldn't imagine how that would ever be possible. She'd be discharged from her job immediately if her superiors realized she was female, and she had no other way to earn a living.

But on dark nights like this, she sometimes wondered what the point of survival was. She was painfully alone, unable to have anything more than distant acquaintance with her male coworkers and neighbors, unable to be a female among females.

She was nearing her cottage when she felt a sudden jolt of fear. She'd been on edge ever since she'd written the Home Office with her concerns for Sir Samuel Bentham's safety, but this fear was sharp and immediate.

Usually she tamped down on her awareness of her surroundings because it was too distracting, but now she turned her senses up to full power. She was not alone. Not far behind her was a man who smelled of fish, and she could feel that his intentions were murderous. Farther away, another man was quietly walking the street, but she had no clear sense of him other than that he wasn't a danger.

She debated running away and calling for help, but at this hour most people would be having their evening meal, and the sounds of the wind and the nearby river made it unlikely she'd be heard. Her best hope of safety was in her own cottage, which was only a few steps away.

Bolting at full speed, she dug her key from her pocket. Up the few steps in one leap, insert the key into the lock . . .

Brutal hands seized her and jerked her backwards down the steps. Her cry for help was smothered as her assailant clamped a rough hand over her mouth. She struggled and tried to kick back, but couldn't break free of his grip.

She bit his hand viciously. He swore and loosened his hold on her mouth enough for her to call out a strangled, "*HELP!*"

He swore again but didn't release her. She realized with icy certainty that he was going to pull out a knife and kill her.

As she made a last desperate attempt to wrench herself free, a shocked male voice barked, "What the devil?"

It was the man who had been farther away. The fog had thinned enough for her to see a tall figure racing toward the fight. The fishy man released Casey and swung toward the stranger, his raised right hand holding a gleaming blade.

No! Unable to watch her attacker murder a stranger, Casey swung her booted right foot with lethal precision to smash into the fishy man's crotch. He howled horribly, but his knife still slashed the stranger's arm. It wasn't enough to stop his target, however, who spun away before landing a hard punch on the first man's jaw.

Radiating rage, her assailant stumbled backward, then turned and disappeared into the night at a lurching run. Casey sensed that her rescuer was torn between pursuing the attacker and checking on her. "Are you all right?" he asked swiftly.

Shaken, she struggled for breath. "I'm not injured, but he stabbed you, didn't he?"

"So he did," the man said with a hiss of pain.

"Come inside so we can see the damage." Hands shaking, Casey unlocked the door and led them both inside. She turned to see that her rescuer was a well-dressed man perhaps a few years older than she was. He had a satchel slung over his shoulder, an air of competence, and seemed unfazed by what could have been a fatal encounter. He was also remarkably good-looking, with wavy brown hair and interested blue eyes.

"You'd best take your coat off so we can get a look at the wound," she said.

"I don't think it's serious," he said as he set his satchel on the floor and cautiously tugged off the coat before sitting in one of the kitchen chairs. "But rather messy."

Frowning at the amount of blood, she rolled up his left sleeve, then carefully cleaned the long gash and sprinkled basilicum powder over it to reduce the chance of infection. She tore up a worn but clean towel to improvise a bandage. "My thanks, sir. I'm Casey Harris and I don't know what would have happened if you hadn't come along."

His gaze moved to her face. "Then you're the man I was looking for. I'm Cameron Tremayne. I'm here because you wrote a letter to the Home Office."

She caught her breath. She'd written that letter because she could think of nothing else to do, but she hadn't expected such a prompt response. "So you know I've been concerned and unsure of whom to trust."

"Sir Samuel Bentham's life is well worth worrying about." He sucked in his breath when she tightened the bandage. "Why have you been concerned?"

She ducked her head as she wondered what to say. "It doesn't sound like much when I try to explain. A few overheard words." She hesitated. "And . . . a bad feeling."

"Since you're gifted, feelings matter."

She froze and stepped back. "Why do you think I'm gifted?"

Cameron arched his brows. "You wrote to the gifted branch of the Home Office."

"I didn't know that! My cousin, Jamie Harris, had told me that I could write to Lord Tremayne at the Home Office if there was trouble and I didn't know where else to turn." She bit her lip. "I wonder if he had a feeling that I might need such help."

"Quite possibly, since I gather he was gifted also."

"You sound so casual about that," she said cautiously. "Many people despise those who are gifted."

"You seem surprised," Cameron replied quietly. "Were you rejected by your family?" He studied her with a gaze that felt as if he was seeing through to her soul. She felt lightning-struck and didn't know if what she felt was fear or hope.

She slammed the feelings down for later investigation because they were too intense to deal with right now, focusing instead on securing his bandage. "Yes. I almost starved before Jamie took me in. We weren't really cousins, but . . . we became family to each other. He died two years ago."

"I'm sorry for your loss," he said, his voice soft. "You don't know any other people who are gifted?"

"None that will admit it," she said dryly.

"Gifts are not uncommon, but many people prefer not to disclose that they have them," he agreed.

"I assume you're also gifted . . . though I doubt you were thrown out of your home," she said, unable to keep envy from her voice.

"Yes, I'm gifted, but I was indeed thrown out of my home." Cameron grimaced. "My real father tossed me into a river and shouted that he hoped I drowned. I was four years old."

Casey gasped. "How horrible! How did you survive?"

"I flailed around and managed to stay afloat long enough to be pulled out of the water by a farmhand. The Tremayne family estate was nearby, and the farmhand knew the Tremaynes were gifted, so he took me there. I was terrified and hid in dark corners until my foster sister Tamsyn lured me out with cream cakes." He grinned.

"She chose her bait well. It wasn't long until I ventured out of hiding and joined the family."

Fascinated and impressed, Casey asked, "You took the name Tremayne?"

He nodded. "Lord and Lady Tremayne have three legitimate children and ten fosters like me, but we are all family." His voice dropped to a whisper. "I give thanks daily for the Tremaynes. As you surely do for Jamie Harris."

She nodded, her throat tight. Turning to practicality, she said, "I have potato leek soup on the hob. It's a simple meal, but if you're hungry, it won't take long to heat up."

"I'd like that." Realizing she'd finished, he carefully pulled his bloodstained sleeve down over the crude bandage. "I suspect that your concerns for Sir Samuel are well founded and that's why that brute tried to kill you, so I'm going to be your house guest and guard until we sort the danger out."

"You believe me just like that?" she said, startled.

"It's part of being gifted," he explained. "One of my talents is evaluating how serious risks are. As soon as I read your letter, I knew your concerns merited immediate investigation."

Unnerved, she bent to add coal to the fire, then swung the pot of soup over the heat. A house guest? This man who was alarmingly attractive? "You really think it's necessary for you to stay here?"

Gaze serious, he said, "Given how close you came to being murdered tonight, I'd say yes, it's necessary."

She shivered at his words. It was hard to argue with them, but having him under her roof would make it difficult for her to conceal her gender. "If you stay here you might be in danger also."

"Perhaps, but luckily I'm good at sensing danger, or you might be dead now."

She winced at a swift memory of that slashing knife. "You might be right." She rose and poured two glasses of ale, then sliced bread for toasting. "I'm used to a quiet life. You're sure that man wasn't a mad random stranger?"

"I am." His voice was gentle. "It can be hard to accept that you're a target for violence, but these are difficult times." He took a sip of the cool, tangy ale and gave a nod of satisfaction. "The

Chatham dockyard and Sir Samuel are both very important to Britain now that we're at war again. There have been serious threats at other dockyards as well, recently."

She was about to ask about the other threats when a sleek black shape materialized from the shadows and leaped onto the table next to her guest. "Sorry, Mr. Tremayne!" she exclaimed. "Gentleman Jack is always curious."

"Please call me Cameron, or Cam." He scratched the cat's neck. "He's not a problem. Cats are always welcome in Tremayne homes. I suppose he's Gentleman Jack because he's fashionably attired in black with white whiskers and feet?"

Casey smiled. "Exactly. He showed up not long before Jamie died and kept him good company while I was at work." She stroked Jack's back fondly and was rewarded by a rumbling purr. "I was honored that he stayed with me after Jamie was gone." The cat had been a bright spot in a dark time, and he'd become her valued companion.

Cameron took another sip of the ale, then reached down into his satchel and produced a small notebook and a pencil. "Can you describe some of the incidents that have concerned you? They may not seem like much, but writing things down can sometimes show patterns."

As the soup began to simmer, Casey toasted several pieces of bread over the fire and thought about what to say. "Sir Samuel is a genius of naval engineering and efficiency, and he can be impatient with lesser minds. Efficiency means fewer jobs, so some of the men who work at Chatham really resent him."

Cameron nodded. "And dockyards can be dangerous places. Have there been any suspicious incidents?"

"He was crossing the main road that runs through the yard when the harness for a team of horses drawing a heavy wagon broke and the horses bolted. They almost ran Sir Samuel down."

"It could've been an accident, or it might have been a deliberate attempt to injure or kill Sir Samuel, though a chancy one," Cameron said thoughtfully. "Have there been other reasons to feel concern?"

"A fortnight ago, he was checking the progress of a new slipway when he fell into the water and there was some trouble getting him out. He said someone had pushed him but there were a number of people jostling around, so it could have been an accident."

"Perhaps, or perhaps not. Have there been any other dangerous incidents?"

"Not that I know of," she said hesitantly. "But last week I overheard two of the senior men in the office talking in low voices in the next room. One said angrily that he couldn't endure 'bloody Bentham' any longer, and the other man said, 'Not long now until he's gone,' " she said. "But I haven't heard anything conclusive."

"Could you identify the men who spoke?" Cameron asked.

She shook her head. "I could guess, but I'm not certain. There was too much other noise in the office."

"What does your intuition tell you?" he said seriously. "Your gifts."

She hadn't thought to use her abilities to analyze this kind of problem, so she closed her eyes and tried to listen to what her intuition said. When she opened her eyes again, she said slowly, "When Sir Samuel is in the office, I can feel anger and resentment coming from some of the other employees. Not all of them. Most of us respect his abilities and value what he's accomplished. But he is not an easy man, so there is also anger from some."

"That sounds exactly right. It's very fortunate that you contacted the Home Office when you did." His gaze holding hers, Cameron asked mildly, "Casey, do you prefer to masquerade as a young man because that's how you think of yourself, or because it's safer?"

CHAPTER 4

Casey's face turned chalk white and her hand jerked, spilling ale across the table as she stared at Cameron in horror. Her throat worked before she managed a reply. "How . . . how did you know?"

"As soon as I read the letter you sent to the Home Office, I intuited that there was something . . . hidden about you," he explained. "My intuition kept working and suddenly I was sure. Now that I know your situation, I understand you have powerful reasons to conceal your true self."

Voice shaking, she said, "When I was thrown out of my home, I knew I'd be much safer as a nondescript little boy than as a young girl."

Cam suppressed a shudder at the thought of all the horrific fates that might befall a vulnerable little girl. "You were very wise. Since Jamie was also gifted, I assume he identified you very quickly."

She nodded, her face less pale. "As I told you, we . . . needed each other. I learned so much about being gifted from him. As a child I'd been well educated in writing, numbers, and other skills, so when I got older he was able to find me a position in his office at the dockyard. Until now, I don't believe anyone has suspected my true gender."

"Probably because no one thought that a capable young clerk would be anything other than male," Cam said dryly.

She made a face. "Luckily I didn't grow into an obviously curvy young female. That would have been difficult to conceal. As it is, with some binding on my chest, I look sufficiently male." Her face colored. "It's so strange to be talking like this with someone other than Jamie!"

"Is it uncomfortable to discuss this with me?"

"Odd . . ." she said slowly. "But not uncomfortable. You're very easy to talk to and, like Jamie, you feel safe." Her voice dropped to a whisper. "I've not been able to speak freely to anyone for too long."

The poignancy of that caught at his heart as he tried to imagine how incredibly isolated she'd been since Jamie had died. Ever since Cameron had been taken into the large and loving Tremayne family, there had always been someone he could talk to, play with, work with, and hug if he was in the mood. His sisters were an affectionate lot. He'd been blessed. Casey had been lucky to have found a man who became family, but ever since she'd lost him . . . The thought made him cringe.

"Is Casey your real name?"

"I was christened Cassandra at my mother's insistence and called Cassie." She shook her head. "Perhaps she sensed that I would know things I shouldn't."

Hearing the grief in her voice, Cameron asked softly, "She's gone now?"

Casey swallowed hard. "She died when I was ten. She was the one who made sure I was well educated. She—kept me out of my father's way. Less than a year after she died, he threw me out the evening after I accidentally told his fellow card players how he was cheating. I thought it was obvious and part of the way the games were played. I didn't know."

Cam winced. Most discarded gifted children had similar stories of how their talents enraged their families. "I'm sorry. But you found a wonderful foster father and have developed into a remarkable young woman. And unlike the Cassandra from myth, I believe you."

"Jamie taught me how to survive," she said, her silvery blue eyes bleak. "But I can't even imagine what my future might hold."

"Have you ever wished to live your life as a female?" he asked. "To wear silk skirts and dance at balls and flirt with young men?"

She sighed, her expression uncertain. "I sometimes think about it, but I can't imagine how it might happen. All I know is how to be a male clerk, and at the moment, all my thoughts are on ensuring that Sir Samuel is safe and able to continue making the Royal Navy the finest in Europe. Britain needs him."

"Indeed it does." Cameron's brows drew together as he considered what to do next. "Will you take my hand? Together we might have a clearer idea of what must be done."

He held out his hand. Warily, Casey clasped it—and energy flared around them like an invisible lightning bolt. She gasped and dropped his hand as if it was on fire. He didn't blame her.

He had to draw a deep breath as he steadied himself. He had sensed profound danger. And under that was a light, clear note that said, *This one!*

He buried the second message as too confusing to think about yet, and concentrated on the warning. "I have a very clear sense that Sir Samuel is threatened. Did you feel it also?"

She swallowed before saying, "Yes. Danger, and very soon, I think."

"If I go to the dockyard in the morning and talk to Sir Samuel about the threat to his safety, how is he likely to react?"

"He'll most likely brush you and your words off and turn back to his work," Casey said with a sigh.

"Does he think he's immortal?" Cameron asked dryly.

"Quite possibly. But since you're from the Home Office, perhaps he'll listen to you. I hope so." Casey smothered a yawn. "I'm sorry! It's been a tiring day." She looked at Cam uncertainly. "You still think it's necessary to stay here to protect me?"

"I most certainly do." He smiled reassuringly. "Don't worry, the first thing a Tremayne son learns is to respect all females and never, never do anything to make one feel uneasy. I'm quite harmless."

"Except when engaging with murderous attackers, for which I'm profoundly grateful." She collected the used dishes and moved them to the kitchen area for washing. "There are two small bedrooms. You can use the one that was Jamie's."

"I'd like that." It would give him a chance to feel Jamie's energy.

He wanted to know anything that would help him understand Casey better.

Casey, Cassie. She looked like a Casey to him. The name was rare and special, as she was.

She began cleaning the dishes with brisk, efficient movements. Cameron had always been fond of women, starting with his varied, clever, and mischievous sisters. Now that he'd confirmed that Casey was one, he couldn't help but admire her grace, and wonder what she would look like if she were dressed as a young lady.

This one! Again, he buried the thought. He was sure she'd be slimly feminine and alluring. Beyond that—he'd wait and see. For now he was her protector. Anything more must wait.

There were two doors in the wall behind the kitchen and living area. Casey led him to the left-hand door and opened it to reveal a painfully neat room with a crisply made-up bed, a comfortable chair, and two shelves of well-worn books.

Cameron opened his senses. "I can feel Jamie's energy here. His kindness, his humor, his wit."

Casey bit her lip. "Yes. I like to sit here in the evenings with Gentleman Jack. We both miss him."

"He'll always be part of you. But think about what you might like for your future. Gifted people help each other, so we Tremaynes can help you toward what you want."

She gave him a startled look. "I don't even know what I would like that's different from what I have! I have work I'm good at and a peaceful home. That's been enough for me."

"And you have a fine cat." Cameron bent to scratch the dark furry neck and was rewarded with a purr. "There's no hurry. First we must deal with the threats to Sir Samuel Bentham. Then we can discuss your possible futures."

"Possible futures. I can barely imagine a different life." She shook her head, her expression unreadable. "Good night, Cameron Tremayne. I hope you sleep well."

She quietly closed the door after she and Gentleman Jack left the room. As Cameron stripped off his outer garments and prepared to go to bed, he wondered what kind of life Casey would want if she had a choice. Living as a young man had been a practical decision that gave her safety and a livelihood, but after years of living with male freedoms and choices, she might feel constrained if she had the chance to live a female life.

His sisters seemed quite comfortable with their lives, but they were an independent lot. Once the threat to Sir Samuel Bentham was resolved, he needed to persuade Casey to visit Tremayne House in London. Meeting the Tremayne females would give her an idea of the possibilities.

Casey managed to hold herself together until she retreated to her bedroom, but then she sagged onto the side of her bed, shaking at all the changes in her world. Gentleman Jack jumped on her lap and bumped her chin with his head comfortingly. He'd always been good at sensing moods. She stroked his sleek coat, grateful for the warmth of his familiar purr.

Cameron Tremayne had seen her for what she was, accepted her, and suggested that a different kind of life was possible. It had been many years since she'd thought of herself as female. Her safety and her livelihood required that she act, dress, and think of herself as male. She'd suppressed any sense of her own femininity.

Now she wondered what it would be like to wear a silken gown with skirts that fluttered around her ankles. To laugh with female friends who accepted her as one of them.

To have an attractive man look at her with admiration.

To be kissed by him . . .

She swallowed hard. Before her mother had died, Casey had had female friends. As little girls, they'd laughed and played together and sometimes talked about that distant day when they'd marry. Sometimes they speculated about what they'd want in that future husband.

All such behavior had ended after her mother died and her father threw her out of the house. She'd renounced it in order to survive. Jamie had been her whole family, giving her love and protection. For years she'd worked with men every day and had casual friendships with most of them, but she'd had almost no contact with other women.

Yet, after her conversation with Cameron Tremayne, she suddenly felt her suppressed femininity churning inside of her. Despairingly, she recognized that she didn't know what to do with it.

She didn't even know if she wanted it. Men had so many advantages in the world, particularly when it came to independence and employment.

She admitted that she was very aware of Cameron Tremayne as a man. He was strong, kind, and good company, and she would like him to see her as a woman.

But with the iron discipline she'd mastered to survive, she suppressed all thoughts of reclaiming her female identity. First she and Cameron must ensure the safety of Sir Samuel Bentham.

Then, perhaps, she could learn to be a woman.

CHAPTER 5

Cameron seldom had trouble falling asleep, especially not after a long day of travel, but on this night he was too restless to relax. He was fascinated by his unexpected hostess. Under the appearance of a quiet, unremarkable young man lay a strong, brave young woman. It was deeply unfair that she'd had to disguise her own nature in order to be safe. And while she might be content with her life as it was, he couldn't help thinking she'd look lovely in a ball gown. Even more, he wondered how it would feel to hold her in his arms as they danced together.

He fell asleep on that thought, then rose early the next morning and put water on to heat over the kitchen fire. He'd already dressed and shaved and tea was steeping by the time Casey and Gentleman Jack emerged from her bedroom. Neatly dressed in her male office clerk clothing, she was convincing as a young man who was easy to overlook.

"Tea!" she said happily. "You have your uses, Mr. Tremayne."

"All members of the Tribe of Tremayne are raised to be able to take care of ourselves," Cam explained as he handed her a steaming cup of tea.

Casey accepted the cup and gave a pleased sigh after sipping it. Then she opened a small cabinet that held a pitcher of cream. She poured some for the cat, then removed a partial loaf of bread from the cabinet and began cutting pieces. "Breakfast is simple here. Besides tea, I just toast bread and spread honey or preserves on it. Will that suit you?"

"That will be fine." He'd always been good at adapting.

After they'd eaten, Casey asked, "What are your plans for investigating possible threats to Sir Samuel?"

"Very straightforward," Cam said. "I'll go over to the yard to see if I can find him. I hope my Home Office credentials will persuade him to give me a hearing so I can discuss possible threats to his life."

"If he's in his office, he'll likely see you just long enough to dismiss your warning," Casey said with a sigh. "Assuming that he's even in his office. He often roams around the yard."

"Are all the offices in one building?"

"Yes. There are several large rooms for clerks and individual offices for the senior officials, like Sir Samuel and Mr. Seppings, who is the new master shipwright. Mr. Seppings will be working with iron along with Sir Samuel, who has commissioned a new and much larger smithy. They both think that iron is the future of shipbuilding."

"I agree with them. Iron will make larger ships possible," Cameron said. "If Sir Samuel isn't in his office when I go over this morning, I'll run him down eventually."

"It's a large shipyard," she said doubtfully.

"I'm good at finding things." Cameron considered. "I'm thinking of introducing myself as another cousin of yours. Would your superior allow you to give me a tour of the yard if I'm hunting for Sir Samuel?"

"I think so. Mr. Norman approves of me because I do my work well and don't cause trouble." She glanced at the simple clock on the mantel and frowned. "Except for today, it seems. I'm going to be late."

Cameron stood. "If you don't mind riding pillion, we can take my horse, which will be quicker than walking. He's at the livery stable just around the corner."

"Thank you. I'd rather not be late." She reached for her coat, which hung on a peg by the door.

As he opened the door, he asked, "Do you ever tire of always doing the right thing?"

She made a face. "I used to, but I've forgotten how to misbehave!"

"That can be cured," he said with a smile.

After a startled moment, she smiled. "I suspect you're good at persuading your sisters to mischief."

"That's entirely possible," he admitted as he stepped outside. It was a gray morning with a sharp wind blowing off the river.

After she locked the door, they walked briskly down the street and around the corner to the livery stable. Cameron arranged to board the horse for the next several days, then disappeared inside the hay-scented building to retrieve his mount.

Casey followed as he saddled his horse, a leggy and unbeautiful chestnut. "I assume you didn't buy him to impress other riders in the park."

Cameron laughed as he swiftly saddled his mount. "Arthur sneers at park-sauntering horses. He's built for speed and stamina. I bought him at a horse fair when he was just an unpromising looking colt, but I had a feeling about him."

She patted Arthur's neck. "And for gifted people, feelings matter."

Her companion chuckled. "Exactly." He led Arthur outside and swung into the saddle. Looking down at Casey, he said, "I should have asked if you have experience with horses. Will you be all right balancing behind the saddle?"

She nodded. "I loved riding and had my own pony before I was thrown out of my home." She sighed. "I missed my pony far more than my home, actually."

Eyes sympathetic, Cam extended his hand to her. She clasped it and he easily pulled her up so she could settle behind him on Arthur's rump. Since she wore trousers she was able to ride astride, but even so she realized that she'd have to hold on to Cameron in order to stay on the horse.

She tentatively set her hands on his waist and he set Arthur off toward the dockyard. Her grasp tightened as they began moving. Cameron had a firm, strong, masculine body, and she admitted that she liked having an excuse to touch him.

He called over his shoulder, "Are you managing well?"

"Yes! I love being on a horse again." Riding was one of the many things she'd lost when her father had cast her off. She'd buried that pleasure along with all the difficult memories of her childhood. It was good to remember it now.

"I presume I'll have to check in with the yard's gate guards," Cameron said. "It's been a while since I visited, but I remember that the yard is huge."

"Even larger than you remember," she said. "Now that the war has resumed, the navy needs new ships as fast as we can build them, and Chatham is the largest shipbuilder in Britain."

"Can you sense if Sir Samuel is in his office?"

She liked that he was gently encouraging her to test her abilities. She closed her eyes, which made her even more aware of the fact that she was holding on to him, and tried to focus on Sir Samuel, holding an image of him in her mind. "I don't think he is," she said uncertainly.

"We'll know soon."

It was a short ride to the dockyard, whose solid buildings spread for over a mile along the River Medway. Clusters of masts rose from the water like a stark wintry forest. As Casey had said, when they reached the impressive main gate the guards recognized her, and Cameron's Home Office credentials got him admitted easily.

As they rode onto the main road that ran the length of the dockyard, Cam said, "Now for your office building. Is it close enough to walk, or should we ride?"

She made a face. "With this icy wind off the river, better to ride."

It took only a few minutes to reach the building that contained all the offices. As they approached, he asked, "If Sir Samuel isn't there, do you know where he might be?"

"Somewhere in the yard, I think, but I'm not sure where."

Cam laid his left hand over hers where it clasped his waist. "Does sharing energy help?"

She gasped at the warmth and sense of power that swept through her. After reveling in that for a few moments, she focused her attention on Sir Samuel again. The image in her mind immediately sharpened. "He's definitely not in the office. He's in . . . the smithy, I think. He's been spending time there because he's commissioned a much larger smithy to be built for the iron ships that will be coming soon."

"Very good!" Cameron said. "Can you sense anything more about him?"

She gave a sudden gasp and her grip on Cameron's waist tightened. "His life is in danger *right now*!"

She felt a shift in Cameron's energy and realized that her easygoing companion had transformed into a warrior. "Which way to the smithy?" he snapped.

"Straight ahead and then right on the second cross street!"

"Hold on!" He kicked his mount into a fast canter and they began racing down the yard's main road. She almost slid off when he accelerated, but she managed to keep her seat by grabbing harder at his waist and locking her legs around the horse.

He expertly dodged wagons and workers until she raised her voice and said, "This next right turn!"

He obeyed, slowing because the street was narrower and more crowded. As they neared the end of the cross street, she said, "That long building ahead is the smithy."

"Is he in there?"

Closing her eyes, she did her best to focus. The smithy looked like a collection of separate buildings that had been added on, one after another. *Sir Samuel?*

Yes! "He's at the far left end of the building." She gasped as her intuition told her more. "I think there's going to be an explosion!"

Cameron swore and pivoted to the left, pulling his mount to a halt by the far end of the sprawling building. "Off!" he ordered.

He swung from the saddle, then reached up his hand to help her down. As soon as her feet touched the ground, a deep boom erupted from the end of the last section of the smithy. The windows blew out with a shattering of glass, and flames began flaring inside.

Casey was blasted from her feet by the force of the explosion. Her breathing choked when something large and heavy landed on her. It took a moment for her shaken wits to realize that it wasn't a piece of wall but a powerful male body protecting her from the debris falling all around them.

As the air cleared, Cameron rolled off her. "Are you all right?" he asked urgently.

She began coughing from the dust she'd inhaled. "Not. Hurt," she managed to gasp.

He stood and offered a hand to help her to her feet, but his stark gaze was on the ravaged building. "We were too late," he said bleakly.

She closed her eyes and focused her attention on Sir Samuel Bentham. "I believe he's still alive! There, I think." She pointed to the area just to the right of the greatest damage.

"Stay here!" he ordered as he bolted toward the door nearest the blasted section of the building.

Casey followed him toward the shattered building, calling, "But I think I can find him inside!"

"Very well, but be careful!" The door was half off its hinges. Cameron wrenched it open. "Pull your scarf over your mouth." Yanking his cravat over the lower part of his face, he bent and charged into the damaged building.

Grimly she obeyed and followed him into a scorching chaos of smoke and fire that stung her eyes and choked her breathing. Blinking to clear her vision, she tried to decide which way. No, normal vision wasn't the way to locate him. She closed her eyes and reached out with her senses to find him.

It took only a moment to sense where Sir Samuel was. She tugged at Cameron's arm and pointed ahead to the left. Only a dozen steps forward, they discovered his crumpled body. There were no obvious injuries, but he was unconscious. Cameron bent and caught the older man under the arms so he could drag him outside.

Casey was going to lift Sir Samuel's feet until she saw a small figure sprawled on the floor to her right. Just a boy, probably an apprentice smith. Eyes stinging, she turned back and caught him under the arms as Cameron had done with Sir Samuel and began hauling the boy to the door. The fire was scorching her right side, and she sensed that this whole section of the smithy was about to collapse.

The door was a lighter rectangle ahead. Cameron had managed to get Sir Samuel outside. She felt on the verge of collapse but grimly continued forward. Step by step. Just a few feet more . . .

She was in the doorway when the building exploded around her. The force of it blasted Casey and the boy out into the yard.

As she lost consciousness, she realized that her clothing was on fire, and she wished despairingly that she remembered how to pray.

CHAPTER 6

Cameron knelt beside Sir Samuel, checking for injuries. His breathing was steady though his clothing was scorched, but his upper left sleeve was saturated with blood. Frowning, Cam used his pocket knife to hack off most of the sleeve at the shoulder so he could examine the damage. The laceration was deep and potentially dangerous, so he used the cut-off shirt sleeve to tie a tight bandage over the wound.

Hearing a second explosion, he looked up to see that Casey had been hurled through the door along with the boy she'd been bringing out—and that her clothing was on fire. He found himself screaming the word *NO!* He couldn't lose her now when he'd just found her!

Heart pounding, he leaped to his feet, but by this time the fire and explosions had brought other workers running. Two men pulled Casey and the boy away from the building.

One of the men began tearing off her burning garments. In a matter of moments, her coat and vest and shirt were off—revealing much of her bare female body. Gasps of shock rose from the gathered men. Someone said disbelievingly, "He's a girl!"

Locking down the fierceness of his emotions, Cam shoved his

way through the men surrounding Casey. Dazed and horrified, she tried to cover her bare breasts. Another man had joined the group, and he stared down at her with appalled disbelief. "Mr. Harris?"

She looked up at him, her face turning ash white. "Mr. Norman!"

Cameron dragged off his coat and dropped to his knees so he could wrap the garment around her. Luckily she didn't seem to have any serious burns, but her expression was devastated as he lifted her in his arms.

As she hid her face against his shoulder, Mr. Norman stammered, "That was very brave, Mr. Harris. *Miss Harris*. But you can't possibly continue working for me!"

She began sobbing silently, her face hidden. "I'm sorry," she managed to say.

"You have nothing to be sorry for," Cameron said sharply. "The problem is a world that doesn't accept the talents of women."

Mr. Norman frowned. "Who are you?"

A man said with a sneer, "I'm guessing he's her lover."

If Cam hadn't been holding Casey, he would have been tempted to knock the man out, but Casey was more important. "I'm her cousin Cameron Tremayne, and I'm with the Home Office," he said forcefully. "I came here because she told us she was worried about threats against Sir Samuel. As you see, she was right to be concerned."

His expression confused and unhappy, Mr. Norman said, "He—*she* has been one of the best clerks I've ever had. She'll be missed."

Cameron cut through the gathering crowd to reach his horse. He asked Casey, "Can you stand while I mount Arthur?"

She nodded, so he slid her down till her feet touched the ground. She was shaking but managed to stay upright while he mounted. Then he offered his hand and lifted her so that she was sitting on his lap. She burrowed against him after he tucked his coat more closely around her. Turning his mount, Cam headed back to the main road that led out of the dockyard. With one arm supporting Casey, he traveled slowly to keep her secure.

Once more, his mind whispered, *This one!*

Though he knew this wasn't the time to think about that, he couldn't resist brushing a weightless kiss on the top of her head.

She was such an intoxicating blend of courage and vulnerability, he didn't know whether to kiss her or protect her. But for now, he knew what she needed was protection.

She said in a raw whisper, "My life is over."

"It has changed irrevocably, but it isn't over," he replied seriously. "Your future will be full of fascinating and sometimes frightening new possibilities. I'm going to take you to Tremayne House in London, where you'll be able to come to terms with all the changes you're experiencing. You'll be able to become the person you were meant to be."

She sighed, but her voice was steady when she replied, "I have no idea who that person is or should be."

"It will take time for you to find that out," he said. "Luckily, gifted people are usually very resilient. You will survive and flourish."

"I hope you're right," she said bleakly. "Are you taking me home now?"

"Yes, you can rest while I take Arthur to the livery stable and arrange for a carriage to take us to London tomorrow."

She straightened up in his lap and yanked his coat around her shoulders. "I'm not leaving Gentleman Jack behind!"

"Of course not," he said reassuringly. "He's family. There's a cook shop next to the livery stable, so I'll bring back food for all three of us."

The rest of their ride was silent as he thought, and she tried not to think.

Chapter 7

Once they returned to her cottage, Casey curled up in one of the two upholstered chairs with Gentleman Jack on her lap. Cameron quietly built up the fire and set water to heat over it for tea, then said, "I'll take Arthur to the livery now and then pick up the food. Is there a key I can use to lock the door?"

In the past she hadn't always felt the need to lock the door. "There's one hanging under the coat to the left of the door."

She heard the rasp of the key as he locked the door behind him, then closed her eyes and wondered what would have happened if she hadn't written to the Home Office. Very likely Sir Samuel Bentham would be dead and she wouldn't have met Cameron Tremayne. So, it was a very good thing she'd sent that letter to London.

But now she was leaving her whole life behind to go to a strange new place. This cottage had been her home for many years and Jamie had been her family and protector. She hadn't felt so desperately upset and confused since her father had thrown her out of her childhood home. She shuddered at the memory of that morning's staring male eyes after she'd been stripped of her burning clothes. But if the workers who tore off her clothing hadn't acted so swiftly, she would have been badly burned or worse. As it was, her back felt barely scorched.

She allowed herself a few moments of remembering the terror she'd felt when her clothing was on fire. Then she drew a deep breath and reached inside to the stubbornness that had refused to surrender when she had been disowned. She had survived that, and would survive this.

After opening her eyes, she set Gentleman Jack on the floor, then set to making herself more respectable. She laid Cameron's coat over the back of a chair before going into her bedroom to wash the soot from her face, neck, and hands. Then, shivering with cold, she studied herself in the small mirror over her washing stand and tried to think of her appearance as female.

Her features were regular and unremarkable. Since she was beardless, she looked like a young boy but could equally be a young woman. She wondered what color her hair would be after the brown coloring had been washed out with vinegar. She guessed that her blond hair had darkened over the years, perhaps to a light brown.

Since she was nude above the waist, she studied her figure. She would never have the kind of voluptuousness many men admired, but her breasts were large enough to make her gender obvious when her clothing had been ripped away.

At least now that her masquerade had ended, she wouldn't have to bind them anymore. She wouldn't miss *that*!

After changing into a clean shirt and trousers, she studied her image again. In her usual clothing she still looked like a youthful male, but one with some subtle, unexpected curves. Though she didn't feel quite ready to end the charade yet, she knew that today had ended her life as a young man whether she was ready or not.

She blocked that thought and moved into the kitchen to start making a pot of tea. She was adding honey to a steaming cup when Cameron returned with a bulging carry bag. After unlocking the door and coming inside, he studied her intently. "You look very collected for someone whose life has just been shattered."

She gave him a wry smile. "I learned early that when disaster strikes, all one can do is get up, keep moving, and have a cup of tea. Would you like one?"

"Yes, thank you." His brow furrowed. "You look different now."

She gestured at her torso. "I'm no longer binding my breasts."

"True, but it's more than that," he said thoughtfully. "Before,

"It is to me." He glanced at Cameron. "You're one of the Tribe of Tremayne? If so, Miss Harris will be in good hands."

Cameron nodded. "We'll help her find a new path."

The burly man stepped forward. "I'm Tom Burton and I work in the smithy, Miss Harris." He swallowed hard. "You pulled my boy Tommy to safety. He would have died today. I can't offer anything but the thanks of me and my wife."

Casey smiled at him. "I'm very glad that I saw him despite the smoke, and that I was able to bring him to safety. I hope he wasn't seriously injured?"

"He's more than a bit bruised." Burton gave a sudden smile. "He says an angel rescued him, and I reckon he was right."

Casey blushed. "Give him my best wishes. Were there any other casualties of the explosion and fire?"

Mr. Burton shook his head. "Nay, the men that set the explosion were aiming to just kill Sir Samuel. Bad luck that my Tommy was there, too."

"Do you know who set the explosion?"

Mr. Norman nodded. "Once the police chief was notified, he brought in two men he'd been suspicious about. They've confessed. They were from the procurement department, Mr. Farrell and Mr. Broughton."

The names stirred a vague memory of the voices she'd overheard. She frowned, sensing that there was more to the conspiracy.

Cameron's hand came to rest lightly on her left shoulder. Her perceptions immediately sharpened. "They are not the only conspirators. Someone in London paid them to kill Sir Samuel."

There was a gasp of shock from her visitors. "You're sure of this?" Sir Samuel asked grimly.

Cam's hand tightened a little on her shoulder. She was very aware of how his power strengthened her own abilities. "As sure as I was that you would be attacked today," she replied. "I'm coming to terms with being gifted and knowing things I wouldn't normally know."

Sir Samuel swore under his breath. "I knew I had enemies, but there are more of them than I suspected."

"I'll report this to my superior and the Home Office," Cameron said. "Perhaps we can find the man in London."

"Do your best, Mr. Tremayne," Sir Samuel said. "Again, I offer my thanks to you, Miss Harris."

The three visitors bade them farewell and left. As the door closed, she realized she was shaking with nerves and fatigue.

Cameron also noticed and he drew her into his arms for a long, warm hug. "I'm glad they called on you. You deserved acknowledgment for what you did today. It was remarkable."

She sighed into Cameron's shoulder, appreciating the warmth and strength of his arms. She realized that she had been starved for human touch. There had been no one since Jamie had died. "It was a proper ending to my life here. But I can't imagine what my new path might be."

"You can take all the time you need," he said in a soft voice. "You'll meet other gifted people. You'll learn more about your abilities. You'll make friends who will accept you as you are." He gave a low chuckle. "You'll be able to attend the upcoming Tremayne Christmas ball if you wish."

"It all sounds exciting, and more than a little alarming." She realized that she didn't want to leave his embrace, which was not only warm and comforting, but something more. A stirring of her blood that she was unfamiliar with.

With a silent shock, she realized that it must be desire, a craving for male closeness. She almost jerked out of his arms at the recognition. She didn't feel ready for this! But she still didn't want to move away from his embrace.

"Are you hungry?" he asked. "We should eat while the food from the cook shop is still warm."

"That's a good idea." Reminding herself that Cameron was just being kind, not romantically pursuing her, made it possible for her to step away from him. "Then I . . . I'd like to rest for a while." Her gaze swept over her familiar surroundings. "It won't take long to pack. I don't have many clothes, besides the ones that were ruined this morning. I'm wondering what to do about my cottage."

"You can always return here if you want to," Cameron said. "No life-changing decisions need to be made right away. For now, do you have a neighbor you can ask to keep an eye on this place?"

"I'll ask the Smiths, two doors down. Mrs. Smith would look in on Jamie during his final illness when I had to be at work. They're good people."

She opened the bag Cameron had brought from the cook shop. It was easier to think of simple things than it was for her to try to imagine what her new life might be.

As they settled at the table to eat, her cat appeared, showing a clear interest in the food. She scratched his head and fed him another piece of cheese. "Can you find something that will be suitable as a carrier for Gentleman Jack? I don't want him to run away."

Cameron grinned. "I am experienced at transporting cats. We'll all arrive safely in London tomorrow."

And her new life would begin. She'd think about it tomorrow.

She covered a yawn, suddenly so tired that she could barely finish her meal. "I'm going to lie down for a bit."

"That's a good idea. You've had an exhausting day. I'll clean up here." He stood and began clearing the table. "Tomorrow should be an easier day."

"I have my doubts," she said as she got to her feet. Yawning, she made it to her small bedroom. She'd lie down for just a minute . . .

CHAPTER 8

The next morning the weather was cold but fair. While Cameron walked to the livery stable to collect his horse and the small carriage he'd hired for the trip to London, Casey took her perishable food supplies to the Smiths. The promise of food made it easy to catch Gentleman Jack, though he protested loudly when he was boxed.

When they were ready to leave, Casey stood in the street for long moments regarding the cottage after she'd locked it.

"It's hard to leave a place where you've lived so long and well," Cameron said quietly. "You can return if you wish to."

"I won't live here again," she said in a low voice. "It was Jamie who made this cottage my sanctuary."

"You'll always have him in your heart wherever you go."

She nodded, then turned to the carriage. She didn't need his help to climb in. He climbed in on the other side and they were off. Two humans, one cat, and one horse hitched behind. Casey looked very self-possessed, but he sensed the tension inside her.

He was tempted to pull over to the side of the road and draw her into his arms and tell her everything would be all right, but he knew that she must handle her situation in her own way. She wasn't ready to face the possibility of romance, no matter how much his inner voice kept whispering *This one!*

As he turned the carriage onto the London road, he asked, "Do you have any idea what you might like in your future?"

"I actually liked working with numbers and doing accounts," she said slowly. "Might it be possible to find a position with a business that doesn't mind hiring a female if she can do the job?"

"Definitely. It would have to be a smaller business, though, one more interested in skills than in government regulations."

"That would suit me."

"You'll have time to find a position that you like and where people appreciate you." As the road opened ahead and he increased their speed, he asked, "Have you ever been to London?"

"No, I grew up just outside of Faversham. My father sometimes went to London, but he never took me," she said dryly. "He generally ignored me, until he realized that he'd been nurturing a poisonous asp in his bosom and threw me out."

"It doesn't sound as if much nurturing was going on," Cameron said with equal dryness. "It's been years since you left. Do you know if he's alive or dead? Do you care?"

She considered. "I don't really care. If he's dead, he's probably in a much warmer place than Britain."

Cam laughed. "My father, Rhys, has a theory that the reason Britain has numerous overseas colonies is so that Britons can work in warmer places."

"That's not a bad reason!"

Seeing that Casey looked chilled, he reached behind his seat and pulled out a folded travel rug. "Speaking of warming up, this wrap should help."

"Thank you." She tugged the wool travel rug around herself and looked much warmer.

"Though you haven't visited London, you've surely heard much about it. Are there any particular attractions you'd like to visit?"

"Astley's Amphitheatre?" she replied. "I'd love to see all the riding tricks!"

"Astley's is always great fun, but when we go, there will certainly be other Tremaynes coming with us. We all enjoy it." He gave her a sidelong glance. "Though for the first visit, it can just be you and me."

"I'd appreciate that." She gave him a rueful smile. "Your family sounds lovely, but . . . I'm not used to being around so many people."

"Not surprising when you've had to hide so much of yourself from others. You'll get to decide which changes you like and which you don't."

"I'd like to see Westminster Abbey," she said tentatively. "And go to a theater."

"Those are both easy," he replied. "I try to visit the abbey when the choir is practicing. The music is stunning. And there are a number of theaters."

"They sound wonderful." After a lengthy silence, she said, "Can you tell me more about the kind of work you do in the Home Office?"

He considered before answering. "The Home Office is vast and deals with many aspects of British life. My foster father, Rhys, is in charge of the gifted department. In particular, we investigate potential French threats. Sometimes we find them, other times we find British criminals."

"Is your work always as dangerous as this mission was?" she asked. "You were knifed and had to go into a fiery inferno to rescue Sir Samuel."

"Usually my work isn't particularly dangerous, but one never knows," he said as he slowed the carriage when they encountered a half dozen chickens in the road. "This mission isn't over yet, though. We need to find the man in London who was behind the attempt to kill Sir Samuel. And we'll need your help since you are connected to what happened."

"I'll be happy to help in any way I can," she said wryly. "I'll probably be better at that than learning to be a lady."

He smiled to himself. It was going to be very interesting to watch how she would bloom, now that she was no longer required to be as invisible as possible.

CHAPTER 9

They traveled at a good speed, but the winter days were short and it was dusk by the time they arrived at Tremayne House. Casey studied the house, which was prosperous and imposing. A cheerful wreath made of greens and scarlet ribbons decorated the door. "Do you live here or have separate rooms?"

"I've thought of getting my own place but I travel a fair amount so it hardly seems worth the effort of moving. Besides, I like living here. The food and the company are first-rate." He handed her the reins and swung out of the carriage. "I'll get someone to bring in our luggage and Gentleman Jack. I'm sure he'll be glad to get out of his prison."

A loud *MROWP!* from behind their seats confirmed that. Cameron climbed the steps and gave several hard raps with the knocker. The door swung open almost immediately and he exchanged a few words with the person who opened it.

The man who followed Cameron back to the carriage was tall and dark and not wearing a servant's livery. Cameron offered his hand to help Casey out, saying, "This is the oldest of my brothers, Caden Tremayne. Cade, this is Casey Harris, who was vital in saving the life of Sir Samuel Bentham."

His brother's brows arched. "I want to hear more about that!"

Gentleman Jack yowled again as Casey lifted his box from behind the seats. "A new gifted person and a cat!" Caden said with a friendly smile. "I definitely want to hear more about what you've been up to, Cam."

"Later," Cameron promised as he removed their bags from the carriage. "Are Rhys and Gwyn having tea now?"

Cade nodded. "Yes, in their private parlor." He swung into the carriage and took the reins. "I'll see you after I return the carriage to a livery."

Casey and Cameron climbed the stairs and entered Tremayne House, he with their few bags and she with her cat. He closed the door behind them. A cheerful garland of greenery and scarlet berries twisted up the banister of the stairway on the left of the foyer. "I'll leave the bags here so we can go right to my parents. You might want to leave Gentleman Jack in his box till we get there."

Since a large gray tabby had entered the front hall and Casey could hear feline growls, she said, "Lead on, Cameron!"

He took the cat box from her. "I'll carry Gentleman Jack. He's heavy."

"He does like his food." Casey was trying to keep her voice light, but she was knotted with nerves.

Cameron led her through a long passage toward the back of the house. He stopped at a closed door and gave a couple of quick knocks, then entered. The pleasant study overlooked a quiet winter garden behind the house. "Rhys, Gwyn, let me introduce you to Casey Harris, who saved Sir Samuel Bentham's life."

Lord and Lady Tremayne were attractive people of middle years and dressed with quiet aristocratic elegance, but what struck Casey most was her sense of how connected they were by love and shared purpose. There was a kind of invisible glow between them. From what Cameron had said, they'd dedicated their lives to helping gifted children and young people who had been shunned and abandoned by the families that should have loved them.

People like Cameron, his brother Cade, and now her. Casey felt their penetrating gazes on her and wanted to retreat, but she wouldn't allow herself to turn coward.

"Well done, Cam!" Rhys said as he rose and shook his son's hand.

Gwyn also stood and moved toward the newcomers. She had a warmth that filled the room. "And this is surely Miss Casey Harris, not Mr. Harris. Is Casey your preferred name?"

Casey hesitated. "Once I was Cassandra and called Cassie, but I prefer Casey."

Gwyn extended her hand. "Welcome to Tremayne House, my dear Casey."

Casey took the older woman's hand and felt warmth spreading through her. "You remind me of my mother," she managed to say.

"Gwyn is mother to us all," Cam said quietly.

Casey dissolved into shocking tears. Gwyn's arms came around her, and she began crying even harder.

Gwyn said softly, "You've had a long, hard road, my dear girl. But you're safe now." She drew Casey down to the sofa, still holding her.

Casey wasn't sure how long she cried but it seemed like a very long time. When she straightened up, Cameron tucked a handkerchief into her hand. After blotting her eyes and blowing her nose, she said unsteadily, "I'm sorry. Cam has been telling me that I'd be welcome in Tremayne House, but . . . I didn't expect to dissolve into a watering pot."

"We're glad you're here," Rhys said as he reached for the cord that hung by the fireplace. "I'll ring for more tea and something to eat."

"Thank you," she said, glad her voice was steadier.

Cam had released Gentleman Jack from his box, and he now landed on her lap with a solid thump. She began petting him. "Cam also said that cats were welcome. This is Gentleman Jack."

"And a very fine fellow he is. When you move through Tremayne House, you'll notice that most of the rooms have little cat doors. They also have latches so they can be closed against feline invaders," Cameron said as he settled on Casey's other side. He handed a folded paper to Rhys. "Here's the official report of my mission."

"I'll read it later," his father said. "First tell us what happened."

Casey let Cam do the talking. She was content to be sitting between him and his mother. If she were a cat, she'd roll on her back and wave her paws in the air just as Gentleman Jack was doing.

Cam's verbal report was concise and covered everything that had happened, but Rhys frowned when Cam ended by saying, "Though the two men who tried to kill Sir Samuel were identified and captured, Casey said that someone here in London was behind the attack. I'm hoping she'll be able to help us find whoever it is."

Rhys's thoughtful gaze moved to her. "That will be very helpful."

"That's a discussion for tomorrow," Gwyn said firmly. "You both need to eat and rest first."

The door to the study opened and two servants brought in trays of food and more tea. Though they'd stopped for a quick meal at a tavern on the trip from Chatham, Casey realized she was famished. The meat pies and sliced cheese and ham and pickled onions were delicious, and she ate an unladylike amount. Cameron did justice to the food as well. A small plate of cut-up meat and cheese had been prepared for Gentleman Jack.

When the meal had been polished off, Gwyn said, "I think you both need to rest since you've had several challenging days."

Cam finished his tea, then asked, "Is Tamsyn here? Cade was just leaving as we arrived and I wondered if they'd come together."

"No, he just came by to drop off a report," Rhys said. "So no Tamsyn, alas. She'll want to meet Casey."

"Tamsyn is the oldest Tremayne daughter and wonderful at helping newcomers settle in," Cam explained. "I assume that Naomi, who is the next oldest daughter, will take charge of getting Casey outfitted and settled."

Gwyn rose. "I'll take you up and introduce you to Naomi, Casey."

"I'll come as well," Cameron said. "So you'll have a familiar face with you."

Gwyn's interested gaze moved from Casey to Cameron, but she said only, "I'll be back soon, Rhys."

"Gentleman Jack will keep me company," he said as he scratched the cat's neck. "I'll see if I can persuade him and Lord Stripes to become friends."

As the three of them headed up the broad staircase, Gwyn said, "Luckily this house is large enough so that anyone who wants a private room can have one."

"Not everyone does," Cam added. "I understand that when Cade and Bran arrived here as very small boys, you couldn't have separated them with a crowbar."

"Very true," Gwyn said with a laugh. "We're a flexible household. I'm guessing that having lived a quiet life for so long, you would prefer a single room?"

"Yes, I would," Casey admitted. "As I told Cameron earlier, I'm not used to living with a lot of people." She suppressed the brief thought that living with a pleasant, attractive male like Cameron might be rather nice.

They climbed to the third floor and turned left into the corridor. Gwyn tapped on the first door on the right and a female voice called, "Come in!"

Cameron opened the door to a sizable, well-filled, and well-warmed room, revealing a slender, dark-haired young woman who was sewing by the light of several lamps. A fire in the fireplace warmed the room. The young woman looked up with a smile. "Is this a new Tremayne I see?"

Gwyn laughed. "Perhaps. Casey has only just arrived. Cameron worked with Casey on a vital mission down at the Chatham Royal Dockyard. A new wardrobe will be needed." Gwyn turned to Casey. "Naomi is our master seamstress and fashion expert. She'll help you figure out what you want and need."

Naomi rose and studied Casey. "A pleasure to meet you, Casey. Which kind of wardrobe do you prefer?"

Casey blinked. Obviously gifted people were much quicker to identify gender than non-gifted ones were. "I've worn male clothing for years in order to have a job where a female would not be hired. Now . . . I'm not sure? I like the freedom of trousers, but I think I should try wearing skirts again to see what it feels like. I haven't worn a dress since I was ten years old."

"Interesting times ahead," Naomi said cheerfully.

Casey glanced at Cameron. "I'd like to be able to ride again, but wearing breeches would be best since I'd rather not ride sidesaddle if I can avoid it."

"We have plenty of horses," Naomi replied. "Most of the female Tremaynes, including me, are tomboys who prefer riding astride.

It's much safer and gives better control of your mount. I've designed a split skirt that looks like a gown when one is walking around, but it's perfect for riding astride."

"I like that idea," Casey said with interest.

"We'll start with that kind of outfit then," Naomi said as she made a shooing motion with her hand. "Go away, Cameron. I need to take Casey's measurements and discuss colors and fabrics and other such things that drive men mad."

He laughed. "As you wish, Naomi. I'll see you in the morning, Casey." He put a brief, warming hand on her left shoulder. "Rest well tonight."

Gwyn said, "I'll go to make sure your room is ready. Naomi, Casey will be in the last room on the right on this corridor." With a final warm smile for Casey, she left Naomi's room, Cameron at her side.

"I feel like I've fallen into a dream," Casey said to Naomi after the door closed.

"I felt that when I first came here," the other young woman said. "I still do. Now as to what garments you'll need . . ." Her eyes narrowed. "We'll start with a split-skirt riding outfit with a shirt and a jacket for warmth since it's winter. Then a simple morning gown so you can try to become accustomed to wearing a skirt. Of course you'll need a ball gown since the annual Christmas ball is just a few days away."

"I've never had so many garments made at once," Casey said, alarmed. "It's too much! I can't imagine needing a ball gown when I've never been to a ball."

"You'll need an evening gown even if you only stand against the wall of the ballroom looking lovely and mysterious like a shy Cinderella," Naomi reassured her.

"I'll feel foolish attending when I have no idea how to dance," Casey argued.

"Then it's time you learned," Naomi said imperturbably. "Dancing is great fun."

Casey hesitated. "I just recalled that I had dancing lessons when I was quite small, before I was ten. I enjoyed it then, but I remember nothing now."

"You may find yourself remembering some of the steps. If not, it's easy for even a novice to manage a simple reel." Naomi hesitated, then said, "You won't like the next thing. You'll need stays."

Revolted, Casey said, "Stays? Why do I need to torture myself?"

"Stays are needed to make the gowns fit properly, but well-made stays won't torture you," Naomi assured her. "I have an excellent corsetiere. Her stays will feel different from wearing unstructured garments, but they won't hurt, I promise."

Casey gave the other woman a miserable look. "Is all this necessary? Corsets, evening gowns, and who knows what else?"

Naomi met her gaze. "No, you don't have to do anything you don't want to do. But in order to decide if you wish to be female, you must give it a fair try. Which means wearing female garments long enough to be comfortable with them.

"If you then decide they're not for you, the clothes will make splendid castoffs for some other woman and you can return to male garments. You wouldn't be the first woman to dress like a man to have more freedom. But I do think you should try being a woman, or you'll always wonder who you really are."

Casey drew a deep breath as she considered Naomi's words, remembering when Cameron asked if she'd ever dreamed of dancing at a ball in silken skirts and flirting with young men. Now she imagined dancing with Cam, being held in his strong arms as her skirts whirled around her ankles.

The thought made her blush and look away from Naomi. "Your words are wise. As a child I was quite fine with being a girl. I really do need to learn if that is still who I am."

"Good!" Naomi said, pleased. "Some other things to consider. Might you like to have your ears pierced? Earrings are pretty and feminine."

Casey gasped sharply and her hands immediately flew to her ear lobes.

"You needn't have your ears pierced," Naomi said immediately. "Now or ever!"

Casey exhaled and her hands dropped to her sides. "My mother pierced my ears not long before she died. She put in a pair of her own gold studs. I was so proud of them. Then . . ." Her voice stumbled. "When my father threw me from the house, he jerked the gold studs out because gold is valuable. When I left, my ears were bleeding."

"Dear God!" Naomi gave her a swift hug. "What a monster! Is he dead? If he isn't, can I send one of my brothers to make sure that he is?"

Casey gave a choke of laughter as she hugged Naomi back. "I don't know if he's dead or alive, and I really don't care. But remembering that makes me *want* to have my ears pierced!"

"Very well, that can be done tomorrow to give your ears time to adjust to them. But I do think that earrings will look lovely with your delicate features."

"Delicate features?" Casey looked into the tall pier glass mirror. "Me?"

"Yes, you," Naomi said firmly. "You've spent years trying to look like an unmemorable young man. How you see yourself now will be changing."

Casey moved closer to the mirror to study her face. Naomi was right. Her features now seemed more delicate and feminine. "Have you ever done this before? Helped a person change from one gender to the other?"

"Not a situation exactly like yours, where someone has lived for years as the opposite sex, but I've worked with others who want to change how they look. I quite enjoy helping people do that." Naomi circled around Casey, studying her head. "Your hair is a bit short, but with a little trimming it will look girlish." She ran her fingers through Casey's hair. "Is your hair colored? It doesn't feel quite natural."

Casey brushed a curl from her cheek. "Yes, as a child I was very blond and it was rather distinctive. When I was taken in by my foster father, we both thought it would be safer to have nondescript hair, so I've been using a brown rinse ever since. Jamie said the color could be washed out with vinegar. I imagine my natural hair has darkened over the years."

Naomi looked closer at Casey's scalp. "The roots of your hair are light. Perhaps not as light as when you were a child, but definitely blonder than the brown shade you've been using. Rinsing the color out will also leave your hair softer and shinier. This is going to be *very* interesting! Cameron won't even recognize you."

"I'm doing this for me, not him," Casey said firmly. Which was . . . mostly true.

"That's wise. Now let's look at some fabric samples to see what suits you," Naomi said as she produced a box containing a number of differently colored squares of cloth.

Casey said, "Surely you can't do all the sewing for a household this large?"

"No, we use seamstresses and tailors," Naomi said. "But I do love helping people decide what they like and how they choose to be seen."

"That is so reasonable!" Casey exclaimed. In a softer voice, she said, "Everyone I've met here has been so kind."

Naomi smiled. "Since the world often isn't, we need to be kind to each other. Every member of the Tribe of Tremayne has a story about how we arrived here."

"I'm sure that some of those stories don't bear repeating." Casey sensed that was true for Naomi.

"Indeed." Naomi pulled out pieces of fabric in different shades of blue. "Hold these up to your face one at a time and look in the mirror. The color will enhance your pretty silvery blue eyes."

Casey followed the instructions, starting with a soft, sky-blue fabric that felt as lovely as it looked. She brushed it against her cheek. "If this is female fun, I like it!"

"This is only the beginning!" Naomi said with a laugh. "Next we'll talk about shoes and boots."

Chapter 10

After leaving Casey with Naomi, Cameron returned to his parents' private parlor. Rhys was there petting Gentleman Jack with one hand and Lord Stripes with the other. "Your lady friend has a fine cat," he commented. "Would you like another cup of tea, perhaps with something extra added?"

"I certainly would. It's been a demanding several days." Cameron took a bottle of brandy from the cabinet. "Shall I enliven your tea as well?"

"Please."

After their cups of tea had been enhanced, Cameron sank wearily into one of the chairs opposite the sofa. Gentleman Jack promptly left Rhys and came to sprawl on Cam's lap. "Saving Sir Samuel was a very near thing. If we'd been a couple of minutes slower, he and a young apprentice would have died."

"But they didn't. Enjoy your success." Rhys sipped at his tea. "Do you have any idea what Casey wants to do now?"

"She's delighted to meet more gifted people. She's been very alone since her foster father, Jamie Harris, died." Cameron took a deep swallow of his tea. "In her position at the dockyard, she worked with numbers and accounting and apparently is very good with them."

"I could use help with that kind of work," Rhys said with interest. "Do you know what her gifts are?"

"She has an ability rather like Bran's, to put bits of information together to find an underlying pattern. She's also good at sensing people's emotions. She's very strong and might have other abilities I haven't seen yet."

"Would she benefit from more training?"

"Yes, though her foster father gave her a good foundation. I think she's hungry to learn more. To discover everything that she has been denied for so many years. To ride a horse as she did when she was a child and to visit Astley's Amphitheatre and go to theaters and to see the famous sights of London."

"And so she shall." Rhys's brows arched. "Am I wrong in thinking that you have a more than brotherly interest in her?"

Cameron made a face. "It's impossible to conceal anything from you or Gwyn. But it's much too soon to act on that interest."

"True, but you'll be working together to find the man behind the plot against Sir Samuel." Rhys's eyes twinkled. "Not to mention showing her the sights of the city."

"Why do I bother to have thoughts of my own?" Cameron said with amusement. "I can just wait for you or Gwyn to tell me what I'm thinking."

Rhys laughed. "It's not very difficult to read your mind at the moment. Did you observe anything else we should know about the dockyard?"

"As you probably know, Chatham dockyard has expanded since my last visit, which is good for the Royal Navy. With Napoleon conquering most of the Continent, we must rule the seas or start learning to speak French."

"You already speak French, but you're right that the Royal Navy is critical to our future. We need engineers like Sir Samuel, as well as sailors and soldiers." Rhys covered a yawn. "It's getting late. Sleep well."

Cameron glanced down at the purring cat on his lap. "I'll take Gentleman Jack up to Casey's room. He might have trouble finding his way to her."

"It's a good excuse to say good night to Casey," Rhys said, his voice sober but his eyes amused.

"Indeed it is." Cameron hoisted Gentleman Jack over his shoulder. "See you in the morning."

He climbed to the third floor and turned along the left corridor. At the end, a crack of light showed under the door to Casey's room, so he knocked lightly.

She opened the door wearing a long blue robe, her expression relaxed and happy. "Oh, you've brought Jack!" She lifted the cat and cuddled him before he jumped down to sprawl in front of the small fireplace.

"Are you overwhelmed by all the newness?" Cameron asked.

"Not yet. Naomi is *amazing*!" She opened the door wider and gestured for him to come in. "I loved the way she kept saying that I didn't have to do anything I didn't want to do, after so many years of doing only what I needed to survive. After talking with Naomi, I'm thinking seriously about what it will mean to live a female life."

"Female Tremaynes are an independent lot, as you'll learn as you meet more of them. You'll see there are many possibilities." He laughed. "And they'll give you a wide variety of opinions."

"I like the idea of having female friends after living so many years in a masculine world." She gave him a slanting glance. "One female experience I've not had . . ." She fell silent, and her cheeks colored.

"As I said, the females of the family will help you in any way you want," he said encouragingly.

Casey hesitated, then blurted out, "I've never been kissed!"

He felt as if he'd been kicked in the solar plexus. He drew a deep breath. "That can be taken care of, if you really wish it."

"I do." Her gaze was half shy and half hopeful.

He placed his hands on her shoulders and drew her toward him. "You're sure?"

"Quite."

He bent his head and pressed his lips gently to hers. He liked that she was tall. Easy to kiss.

She gave a soft sigh and pressed closer. Sparks cascaded through him and he encircled her with his arms. She leaned into him, her warm lips opening under his, her hands starting to knead his back.

Though she was slim, she had feminine curves in all the right places. After long, dizzying moments, he pulled back and said raggedly, "You're doing very well at embracing your feminine side."

"Thank you. I'm liking it!" she said, eyes shining as they separated. "I'm reminding myself to take one step at a time."

"That's wise." He reminded himself that he also needed wisdom. "There is a very real attraction between us, but it's best we act on it slowly."

She made a face. "I know you're right. Unfortunately."

He caught her right hand and brushed a kiss across her knuckles. "Sleep well, my lady. I'll see you at breakfast."

He left her room while he still had the sense to do so, but the sweet smile she'd given him lingered in his mind.

CHAPTER 11

Casey slept well with Gentleman Jack purring on her pillow. She woke when a distant clock struck six times. She stretched her limbs under the blankets. She felt so *safe*! It was similar to the way she felt when Jamie took her in as a hungry, frightened waif. He had given her love and survival. Now she was being given a whole new life in a houseful of gifted people. She didn't have to hide anymore.

Dreamily she allowed herself to think about Cameron, and her thoughts thrilled her to the tips of her toes. Was it because he was the first man who had ever kissed her, or was it Cameron himself? Some of both, she thought, but mostly it was Cameron. His warmth, his intelligence, his kindness . . . and his beautiful strong male body.

Her imagination created a vivid image of him in her bed, both of them naked so that they were pressed skin to skin. He was kissing her again and heat burned through every fiber of her body. She pulsed against him, wanting more and with a fairly good idea of what *more* meant.

She reached to draw him closer—and fell out of the bed onto the carpeted floor. The impact and the cold air jarred her to full wakefulness. Good lord, she was going mad! She scrambled to her feet and crossed the room to freshen the coal fire, then dived under the warm bed covers again. From his place on the top of the pillow, Gentleman Jack patted her head with one paw, then returned to his rest.

She buried her face in her pillow, feeling an absurd desire to giggle. She hadn't giggled since she'd been thrown from her home as a child, but she was feeling deliciously mischievous. Clearing her mind, she systematically relaxed all her muscles, starting with her feet and working her way up her body.

She was halfway asleep when Cam returned to her mind. She was dozing on her side when she imagined him lying down behind her, his arm around her waist, his breath against her hair. Before, she'd dreamed of passion. This time she dreamed of tenderness, which was perhaps even better.

Was he thinking about her as much as she was thinking about him? Surely not. Cameron was a man of the world, one who was very relaxed around females. But she was allowed to keep thinking of him. And she did as she drifted back into sleep.

She dozed until sounds of the household stirring made her decide it was time to get up. As she stood and stretched, Gentleman Jack did the same, then jumped from the bed and padded over to the shallow box of sand that had been tucked discreetly into a corner. Tremayne House was as hospitable to cats as to people. How had she gotten lucky enough to be here?

Since she still had only her male clothing, she dressed in that, but when she looked in the mirror, she realized that she looked different. More feminine. She was changing, and it reflected in her expression.

She made her way down to the ground floor and followed the delicious scent of food toward the back of the house. She reached the breakfast room to find Gwyn, Rhys, and Cameron serving themselves from heated food dishes laid out on a sideboard. Cam looked up with a smile. "Shall I pour you a mug of tea?"

A hearty mug instead of a dainty cup. Perfect for a cold winter morning. "I'd love that."

"Did you sleep well?" Gwyn asked.

"Yes, Gentleman Jack and I had a wonderful, restful night." After a moment of hesitation, Casey said, "I feel so safe here. Thank you for your welcome."

"All gifted people are welcome here," Rhys said seriously. Then he smiled. "And after you've had a good breakfast, we'll get to work on finding the man behind the attacks on Sir Samuel Bentham."

"But breakfast first!" Gwyn said firmly. "Help yourself."

Casey did, filling a plate with shirred eggs, fried potatoes, and a slice of ham. Then she sat down with the tea Cameron had poured, and feasted.

After all four of them had finished eating, Rhys said, "It's time to take our tea to the study and hunt for a villain."

Cameron topped up everyone's tea, and they adjourned to the study. After they were seated, Casey asked, "How does this work?"

"The four of us join hands," Gwyn said. "Casey, think of the men that you sensed plotting against Sir Samuel. Cam, you were also there, so add what you sensed. Rhys and I will amplify the energy. That might help lead us to the man behind the plot."

Casey obeyed, startled how the addition of each new person sharpened her sense of the villain they were seeking. "I think he's a Frenchman, though I believe he can pass as English. And . . . he's gifted!" she added with surprise.

An instant later the man sensed her mind touch and shoved angrily back. It *hurt*! Like a swiftly passing headache. She yanked back into herself, breaking the link and muttered a rude word under her breath before saying, "That was . . . interesting. Are there many gifted people who can use their abilities as a weapon?"

"It's rare, I think," Rhys said, "but there is much we don't know about gifts."

"So true," Gwyn agreed. "Do you have any idea where we might find him?"

Casey focused, drawing on the power of the other three but not directly touching the Frenchman. "He likes going to a particular coffee house. They can be almost like clubs, can't they?"

"Yes, for a penny any man can enter and have a cup of coffee and join the conversations," Rhys replied. "Men of humble backgrounds can discuss affairs of state with members of Parliament.

Customers visit their favorite houses regularly and become friends with other regulars. Can you identify a particular coffee shop?"

"I think it's not far from here," Cam said slowly. "Around Bond Street. The Frenchman goes there regularly. Usually in the afternoon, I think."

Gwyn glanced out the window. "The day is going to be sunny and rather mild for December. Rhys and I can wander a bit around Bond Street and look in shop windows, and perhaps sense the correct coffee house."

Cameron also gazed outside. "Casey, I have a good idea for how to spend the next few hours since it's relatively warm. Let's go riding. That's one of the things you wanted to do and we have a couple of very gentle mounts in the stables."

She caught her breath. "I can go riding with you? Astride?"

"You certainly can." He grinned at her. "Did Naomi find you an acceptable pair of riding boots?"

"Yes, she did."

"Then run upstairs and put them on along with your warmest coat and hat!"

As Casey swallowed the last of her tea and headed for the door, Gwyn said indulgently, "Enjoy yourselves!"

Chapter 12

Going for a ride in the sunshine on a fine horse with a handsome male companion was bliss. Casey laughed out loud with pure happiness when they entered the nearby park.

Cameron chuckled. "You may have sore muscles later, but clearly you haven't forgotten how to ride."

"Never." She patted the neck of Cinnamon, her handsome chestnut mount. "I used to dream of riding again but couldn't imagine how that might happen."

"Proof that dreams can come true," Cam said with a smile.

Together they explored several of the riding paths, chatting amiably as they did. When the sky began to cloud over, Cameron said, "It will be dark soon, so it's time to head back. But we'll ride again another day."

"I look forward to that."

They were getting close to Tremayne House when Cameron halted and said sharply, "Rhys and Gwyn are in trouble!"

Casey pulled up beside him and caught his hand. She felt power surge between them. "What kind of trouble?"

His brows drew together as he used her energy to clarify his concern. "When they went out walking, they found the Frenchman's coffee house. Rhys went inside to talk to him, but the devil was with several friends and some were armed. I think the coffee house is run as a meeting place for the Frenchman and his associates. Several of them surrounded Rhys and they went outside and caught Gwyn as well. Rhys sent out a mental call for help. We have to go to them!"

"Lead the way!" As Cam kicked his horse into a swift canter, Casey followed. They rode for several blocks, then turned down a narrow alley. Ahead of them she saw Rhys and Gwyn surrounded by several dangerous-looking men who were roughly moving them along. Though Rhys and Gwyn seemed calm, Casey saw the glint of at least two pistols held by the men around them.

Casey slowed Cinnamon so they were walking single file along the alley. To her surprise, at the farther end of the alley she saw Cade, the man she'd met the night before as he was coming out of Tremayne House. Beside him was a petite blonde, and the two of them were moving at a pace just short of a run.

Cam exchanged a swift glance with Cade, then gave a shrill whistle as he came alongside the Frenchman's group. Arthur reared up, his smashing hooves knocking down two of the captors. In the next instant, Cameron dived from his saddle with a furious shout and took down the man whose hand was clamped onto Rhys's arm.

At the same time, Cade Tremayne attacked from the other side. There was a flurry of movements too fast for Casey to sort out, but acting on instinct, she jerked her left foot from its stirrup and kicked the throat of the man holding Gwyn. As he fell back, she leaned over and caught Gwyn's arm and hauled her up onto Cinnamon's rump, using more strength than she thought she had.

Gwyn caught Casey around the waist and added a kick of her own into the face of another of their captors. The Tremaynes fought together as if they'd practiced this in advance. Even the petite blonde slammed a pistol over the head of a man who was trying to grab Rhys. He went down immediately.

In a matter of moments, all the captors were sprawled on the ground and targeted with pistols. Casey said weakly, "Is this the way Tremaynes live their lives all the time?"

The petite blonde laughed. "Not usually." She shot her pistol into the air to draw attention to the fracas. "You must be Casey. I'm Tamsyn. My husband, Cade, met you last night when he was leaving Tremayne House. He said you'd fit in very well with our gang of ruffians, and he was right."

Tamsyn looked so much like Gwyn that she must be one of the natural Tremayne children. Gwyn slid from the back of Cinnamon, her cloak ruffled but her expression serene as she hugged Tamsyn. "This has been an unexpected afternoon's entertainment!"

Rhys joined them and wrapped an arm around Gwyn. "I'm so glad you were all nearby!"

Cameron opened Arthur's saddlebags and pulled out a coil of rope. Cade kicked the ribs of one of the Frenchmen who was struggling to get up, then handed Cam his pocket knife so the rope could be cut into lengths suitable for tying up the Frenchman and his fellow thugs.

The noise had drawn a crowd of onlookers. An official-looking man exclaimed, "Lord Tremayne, are you and your lady all right?"

Rhys nodded. "That man there is a French agent and the others are his associates. They attempted to abduct Lady Tremayne and me, but luckily several of our children were within call."

Cameron said, "I'll escort the ladies back to Tremayne House. If the authorities need testimony from us, you know where we'll be."

"That's a good idea." Rhys glanced at Casey. "Come to my office later today. I'd like to get your legal name and place of birth and other data for my records."

"Very well." Casey wasn't enthralled by the idea of revealing that ancient history, but she could understand why Rhys wanted it. Taking care of his Tribe of Tremayne was clearly a large job. She dismounted from her horse. "If anyone would prefer to ride, Cinnamon would be happy to oblige."

"We're not far from home and walking will steady my nerves," Gwyn said, taking Tamsyn's arm. "I'm glad you were all close enough to come to our aid!"

Casey and Cameron were both leading their mounts, but they each had a hand free, so he quietly took hers in his. As always, his presence gave her warmth and strength.

She squeezed his hand back. "I'm grateful that you and Lord Tremayne are all right. My life has become rather too exciting lately!"

Gwyn laughed. "Usually, our lives are pleasantly calm. The biggest excitement coming up is our annual Christmas ball, and that's rather civilized. Would you like to have a few dance lessons before the ball? You'll enjoy the celebration more that way."

"I'd like that." Casey swallowed hard. "Everyone is being so kind!"

"It's our pleasure," Gwyn said. "You've already proved you're an asset to the Tribe of Tremayne."

"Am I really a member of the Tribe when I've only just arrived?" Casey asked shyly.

"You most certainly are!" Tamsyn said with a smile. "And a very welcome addition."

After dinner, Rhys called Cameron into his private study. "The authorities at Chatham Naval Dockyard want you to return for a couple of days to study some issues they're concerned about. And there's another matter for you to look into as well."

Cam winced slightly. "As long as I'm home before the Christmas ball."

"You will be," Rhys assured him. "And you'll be spared much female frenzy as the ballroom is decorated!"

Cam laughed. "I won't miss that."

More seriously, Rhys added, "Casey will be well looked after."

"I know." It was just that Cameron wanted to be the one looking after her.

Soon.

CHAPTER 13

Casey slept well again that night, and again woke with Gentleman Jack on her pillow. She suspected he'd gone out the cat door during the night to explore his new home. Scratching his head, she said, "You've already discovered the kitty breakfast room, I imagine. We've found ourselves a fine nest here."

She rose to add a few coals to the fire, then saw that a note had been slipped under the door. She picked it up and saw that it was from Cameron.

> *Casey—I must go down to Chatham for a couple of days. But I'll be home in time for the Christmas Ball. Please save a dance or two for me. Cameron.*

She hadn't realized how much she looked forward to seeing him later until she learned that she wouldn't. With a sigh, she splashed cold water on her face, then dressed and descended to the breakfast room.

She found Gwyn and Rhys enjoying breakfast. She smiled and said, "Cameron left me a note saying he was going to Chatham for a couple of days, so I hope the two of you won't have to deal with any villains today."

They both laughed. Gwyn said, "Today we'll be decorating the ballroom and similar innocent activities. Though there might be some disagreements about the decorations!"

After Casey helped herself to breakfast and settled at the table, Rhys said, "I do have a task in mind if you're interested. Cameron told me that you're very good with accounts and numbers and rather enjoy working with them. I'm currently without a secretary and rather overcome with paperwork. Would you be willing to help me out?"

"I'd love to," she said. "I'm not used to being idle."

Naomi entered the breakfast room then. "You won't be idle! I'll need some of your time for fittings later today."

Casey made a face. "I would prefer doing accounts, but I shall cooperate with your struggles to improve my appearance."

Rhys said, "Naomi, I have her in the morning so you can do your fittings in the afternoon, if Casey agrees."

"I love that everyone always asks what I want to do," Casey said quietly. "It's a luxury I haven't had."

"You do now," Gwyn said with a smile. "Though you'll find it difficult to avoid Naomi and her alterations!"

"I'll invite Tamsyn over so she can join in the fun," Naomi said.

Casey frowned. "With two of you, I'll be outnumbered!"

"Tamsyn will be there for balance," Naomi explained. "Sometimes I get overenthusiastic. She's more practical."

Gwyn nodded. "Very true."

After finishing breakfast, Casey followed Rhys to his office. As they entered, he said, "I'm sure you can imagine the complexities of overseeing a large family and a number of properties, but it's certainly less than managing accounts for the Royal Navy!"

Casey laughed. "Numbers are numbers and I enjoy working with them, but I only did a few of the dockyard accounts. Granted they were large accounts, but I expect yours will be more interesting. Where do you want me to start?"

Rhys explained what needed doing first, and she fell happily into the familiar work. With all she was being given, she needed to be giving back.

By the end of her morning session, she'd learned that Rhys and Gwyn were excellent managers and that the earldom of Tremayne was vastly wealthy. Which was fortunate, given their large family and how well they paid their servants. They were good and generous employers.

As promised, Naomi carried Casey off to her lair in the afternoon. She started with ear piercing. The process made Casey wince, but it reminded her of her mother, who had pierced her ears the first time when she was a child. Thoughts of her mother were good, but the needle still hurt.

After Naomi finished the piercing, she produced a pair of simple gold posts. "These are a gift from Gwyn," she said as she showed the posts on her open palm. "Since she is mother to us all, she wanted you to have them."

Casey bit her lip, then nodded. After the posts were gently inserted, Naomi handed her a bottle containing a clear liquid. "Clean your ears with this twice a day."

"Is it water?"

"No, gin. Very good for keeping wounds clean," Naomi explained.

Casey chuckled. "So I'll have drunken ears?"

"Only if you let them overindulge," Naomi said with a straight face.

A knock sounded on the door, and Tamsyn entered followed by a maid carrying a tea tray and a plate of biscuits. "It's always time for tea," she explained. "How are matters proceeding? I don't see any blood or bandages."

Naomi chuckled. "I've been very well-behaved so far."

After they'd had their tea, Naomi said, "Now it's time for dressing you from the skin out. You can stand behind that screen to remove what you're wearing now, and I'll pass over the proper female undergarments."

Casey sighed, but she'd promised to give female clothing a fair try, so she moved behind the screen and stripped to her skin. Naomi passed over her new underclothing. "Here are a shift and drawers. When you have those on, I'll help you with the short stays."

As Naomi said, the stays were reasonably comfortable when

properly adjusted, but wearing them was . . . odd. They shaped her torso in a distinctly female way. She supposed that was the point.

"Now it's time for the morning gown Naomi had made up," Tamsyn said as she lifted the garment and handed it over the screen. "I think this will look lovely on you."

Curious, Casey asked, "How do you get things made so quickly, Naomi?"

"The seamstresses I use are the sole supports of their families, so they're always happy to have more work." Her eyes twinkled. "Especially since I paid twice as much for a rush job this close to Christmas."

That explained the quickness. Now it was time to evaluate the results. Casey dropped the gown over her head. The fabric was a light but rich blue shot through with darker threads, and the skirt fell in pleats from the high waist to her ankles.

She stepped out from behind the screen so Naomi could do the fastenings on the back. The bodice was fitted closely and made it clear why the stays were needed. It felt *very* odd that after years of concealing her breasts, she was now emphasizing them! She wanted to grab a shawl and cover herself, but the goal was to look like a proper female, breasts and all.

After fastening the ties, Naomi brushed down the pleats. "Now take a look at yourself in the pier glass."

Casey swallowed hard when she regarded her image in the long mirror. She made a partial turn and the skirts flowed around her ankles. It was a lovely gown, but . . .

"It's beautiful. But . . ." She hesitated before continuing. "I don't recognize myself! I don't *feel* like this woman. Does that make sense?"

"It does," said Tamsyn said soothingly. "You've spent many years pretending to be a different person. That's not going to change overnight. Walk around a bit and see how the gown feels."

Casey obeyed. The slippers that Naomi had given her were much more lightweight than any other footwear she owned. "These slippers feel very flimsy."

"Indoor female footwear is usually very light. This pair of slippers is leather and heavier than dance slippers, which are often made of silk," Naomi explained. "Those are very elegant and very easy to wear out!"

Casey sighed. "Are half boots allowed?"

"Yes, though they're usually worn outdoors. I'll find you a pair that are for indoor use. You'll like them better than the slippers." Naomi circled around Casey, studying the gown and how the fabric fell. "No alterations are needed. This isn't a very fitted gown, except for the bodice, which makes it easy to wear."

"But I'm *cold*!" Casey said with a shiver.

Naomi turned and dug a folded square of multicolored fabric from a shelf. "This Kashmiri shawl will help."

Casey unfolded the fabric and found that it was a marvelously soft mixture of rich colors and patterns. She draped it around her shoulders and found that it immediately warmed her, as well as covered most of her torso. "This is beautiful!" she said as she stroked the fabric. "With so many colors, it will go with everything. I may never take it off."

"That's quite acceptable, especially in winter," Tamsyn said. "Now you can practice walking around in that gown to get used to the feel of it. You can wear the shawl in this afternoon's dancing lesson if you need it, though dancing is warming."

Casey made a face. "I'm really going to be taught how to dance? Everything has been happening so quickly!"

"You have years to make up for." Tamsyn tilted her head thoughtfully. "What would you like your new life to look like?"

Casey frowned as she considered. "I love being surrounded by other gifted people so I don't have to worry about saying things I shouldn't know. I like being busy, I enjoyed working on the accounts with Rhys, and I loved riding with Cameron. Beyond that, I really have no idea what kind of future I want."

"It will probably take you time to figure this out." Tamsyn grinned. "Or realization might strike in an instant. We all have our own paths."

Tamsyn was a good example of Tremayne understanding and kindness. Casey turned to look in the mirror again. Was that really her? The image felt a little more like her than it had earlier. Step by step . . .

Turning to Naomi and Tamsyn, she said, "Cameron told me that the Tribe of Tremayne is large. I would have expected to see more people here."

"The youngest children spend much of their time in the nursery and the bedrooms on the top floor, where they make a great deal of noise and are occasionally forced by their patient tutors to learn things like reading, writing, and history," Naomi said with a grin.

"Several of the older Tremaynes are pursuing their interests elsewhere," Tamsyn added. "For example, Giles is studying medicine in Edinburgh and Alan is an ensign in the navy. It's very rare for all of us to be home at the same time, but we try to have a family gathering in the summer when travel is easier."

Naomi said shyly, "I want to become a modiste with my own shop. Next month I'll start working as an assistant to a very successful modiste so I can learn the business."

"You certainly have the fashion sense," Tamsyn said. "Putting up with the customers will be the difficult part!"

Naomi rolled her eyes. "I've had plenty of experience putting up with Tremaynes, so I should be very successful."

They all laughed.

Later, it was time for Casey's dancing lesson. She enjoyed it more than she expected. There was an amiable dance instructor, and for partners she had Cade, Rhys, and also Bran Tremayne, who had just arrived from Cornwall with his wife, Merryn. Tamsyn, Merryn, and Gwyn joined in, and they all had a fine time.

Casey could sense the bond between Cade and Bran, who were clearly brothers of the heart. Tamsyn had told her how as very small children, the two boys had escaped together from a horrible childhood. At the end of a dangerous journey from Cornwall, they'd found Rhys and Gwyn. The senior Tremaynes had done so much good with their warmth and generosity!

By the end of the lesson, Casey was stepping on fewer toes and she wasn't tripping on her skirts. And as Tamsyn had said, dancing was *fun*!

That night Cameron stayed at an inn close to the Chatham dockyard. He could have stayed at Casey's cottage, but it would have felt strange to be there without her. Yet even at the comfortable inn, she was in his mind.

He recognized how deeply she was rooted in his heart. He'd always been very fond of people of the female persuasion, but something about Casey touched his soul. He'd liked having her under the same roof. Even more, he wanted her in his bed.

But what was it about her that was so special? Her combination of strength and vulnerability? That was part of his attraction, but even more was her essence, which was unique and enchanting. With sudden shock, he realized that this was love: the essence of Casey that resonated with his own essence. He'd seen this with others, but now felt it himself. So strange. So wonderful.

He knew he mustn't rush her when she was experiencing so many dramatic changes. He'd never even seen her in female clothing, yet he knew beyond doubt now that she was the woman for him, now and forever more.

As he rolled into his bed, he reached out to her mentally, trying to touch her essence. To his delight, he succeeded, feeling first her surprise, then her pleasure. The feeling was extraordinary. There were no words between them. Only warmth, and that carried him into sleep. Together . . .

CHAPTER 14

After breakfast the next morning, Casey headed to Rhys's office to work on the Tremayne accounts. She was smiling since she still felt the warmth that had flowed between her and Cameron in the night. Was this a common thing between gifted people who were close? She'd have to ask Cameron when he returned.

As she and Rhys finished the morning accounts, he said, "If you're looking for a permanent job at Tremayne House, I'd be happy to take you on for this kind of work."

Startled and pleased, she raised her gaze to his. "I'd like that. I'm receiving so much from the Tremaynes that I'd like to give something back."

"The benefit is mutual." He gazed out the window at a leaden gray sky. "A winter storm is coming. A severe one, I think."

Casey frowned. "Will it prevent Cameron from making it home before the ball?"

"It could," Rhys said seriously. "We'll have to wait and see. But I know he'll do his best to be here. Luckily most of the Tremaynes and other friends who planned to attend the ball have already arrived in London."

Casey had really been looking forward to dancing with Cameron at the ball, but if the roads were too treacherous, better he be delayed than risk himself. Sending him good travel wishes, she headed downstairs and lunched on a hot bowl of potato leek soup, fresh bread and cheese.

Then she warily presented herself to Naomi. "What will you be inflicting on me today?"

"We'll start by going down to the kitchens to wash the brown color out of your hair," Naomi said. "Once you've returned to your true color, we can choose the ball gown fabrics that best suit it."

"Your seamstresses will have to work very fast to have the gown ready for the ball. Perhaps I can skip the ball and spend the evening reading in my room instead," Casey said as she followed Naomi down to the basement kitchen. She was wearing the shawl and morning gown Naomi had had made for her and was becoming more used to the skirts. But wearing men's clothing was easier and warmer.

Naomi made her remove the shawl and morning gown and swathed her in a vast piece of oilskin to protect her shift. "I'm going to smell like a pickled onion!" Casey muttered under her breath during the first vinegar rinse.

"Luckily most men love pickled onions!" Naomi said cheerfully. "It's going to take several rinses to get your hair to its original color."

Since Casey was curious what her hair would look like after all of these years of drab false coloring, she endured Naomi's ministrations patiently through several rinses. After two final rinses with warm clear water and thorough towel drying, Naomi held up a hand mirror so Casey could see the results. "Your hair is a really lovely color," she said admiringly.

Casey looked into the mirror, and gasped. Her hair had darkened a bit over the years, but now it was an even richer golden blond. It was not the hair of an unmemorable clerk. "Now I *really* don't recognize myself!"

"There are wealthy women who would pay a fortune to have hair like yours," Naomi said. "But no matter how much they spend, it won't look as good as your natural color."

Casey was still staring at the mirror. "This is . . . really upsetting," she said, her voice unsteady. "I don't know who I am anymore."

"You're still you," Naomi said with unexpected understanding. "Put your morning gown and shawl back on and I'll take you to Gwyn."

Casey numbly obeyed and they went up the stairs to Gwyn's private office, which adjoined Rhys's. On the way, Naomi flagged down a maid and ordered tea and cakes to be sent to Gwyn's office.

When they reached their destination, Naomi opened the door and ushered her inside. "I'll leave you and your wardrobe alone for a while," she promised.

Gwyn was sitting at a wide desk with neat stacks of paper in trays. She glanced up and was still for a long moment before she rose and offered a comforting hand. "Casey, you look like a butterfly emerging from your chrysalis with great reluctance."

"*Very* great reluctance!" Casey said, trying to conceal how upset she was. "I'm a stranger to myself."

"After so many years of disguising your true self, it's not surprising that you don't recognize who the mirror shows you." Gwyn moved to the sofa opposite the desk and tugged Casey down beside her. "But this is as much a part of who you are as the very skilled accountant and the brave young clerk who saved two lives. Would it have been easier if your transformation was being done more slowly?"

Casey thought a moment, then shook her head. "The sooner this is over, the better. But the changes are stirring up so many old memories." She stared down at her knotted hands. "When I was small, my hair was waist length and shining blond. My mother would brush it out and tell me how beautiful I was. I looked very much like her, actually."

"So that's a good memory?" Gwyn prompted.

"Yes, but before he threw me from the house, my father chopped my hair off to a boy's length," Casey said, shaking. She drew a deep breath and touched her hair with her right hand. This was her, the blond daughter of a blond mother. She had been so lucky to have a wonderful mother even if it wasn't for long enough.

"The more I hear about your father, the more I hope he died in a ditch," Gwyn said in her soft voice. Soft but implacable. "Preferably in agonizing pain."

The words were so startling coming from Gwyn that Casey gave a choke of laughter. "One can only hope! But he is the past. Now I'm concerned with the present and the future."

"You have so many possibilities ahead of you, and you can take as long as you need to make your choices."

I choose Cameron. The thought blazed through her. Luckily the tea and cakes arrived, which were a welcome diversion.

As the last of the tea disappeared, Gwyn said, "Have you seen the ballroom? The decorations are almost finished."

Casey swallowed her last bite of ginger cake. "I'm not even sure where the ballroom is. I'd love to see it."

"Then let's go down." Gwyn rose and led the way.

Intrigued, Casey followed Gwyn down and across the house. Gwyn opened a door to reveal a sweeping expanse of polished wooden flooring and high-ceilinged grandeur. "Here we are. Impressive, isn't it?"

"It's huge! I had no idea there was such a magnificent ballroom here."

"It's only a part-time ballroom. Three rooms on the west side of the house have been opened up into each other and the furniture was removed so there's plenty of space for dancing," Gwyn explained. "Most of the decorating is done, but as you can see, there is still plenty of activity."

Gwyn introduced Casey to several young Tremaynes who were creating bouquets of looped red ribbon to decorate the tartly scented garlands of greenery. Casey scanned the room, her gaze stopping when she reached the nearest corner. "Is that a decorated spruce tree? It's lovely!"

"Decorating trees at Christmas is a German tradition and the royal family brought the custom to England with them. Rhys and I saw one when we visited one of the royal princesses. We liked the idea so now we always have a Christmas tree here."

Casey moved closer across the room to inspect the tree. The top almost reached the ceiling and the tree was decorated with bright ribbons and ornaments. "What a fine custom," Casey said as she studied the ballroom, and imagined dancing here with Cameron. If he made it home in time.

CHAPTER 15

Late the next day, Naomi summoned Casey for the final fitting of her ball gown. Apparently, there had been much discussion in the house about the gown, and half a dozen other females were present to view the results. Casey wasn't comfortable with being the focus of so much attention, but everyone was so kind, and Naomi deserved the chance to demonstrate her skills.

By the time Casey arrived in Naomi's room, a full-fledged tea and cakes party was in progress. Gentleman Jack was curled up on a pillow, watching with what looked like amused approval. Even Gwyn was there with an interested smile.

Naomi shooed Casey behind the screen and helped her remove her morning gown. Then she produced the ball gown, which was covered with muslin to protect its grandeur until it was time for the grand unveiling.

"You enjoy putting on a show, don't you?" Casey asked as Naomi carefully removed the muslin, then gently lowered the ball gown over her head.

"I certainly do, a trait that will serve me well when I have my own shop," Naomi agreed as she did up the ties on the back. She brushed the skirts down, then combed and fluffed Casey's hair before gesturing for Casey to turn around for closer examination.

She gave a nod of satisfaction. "You look splendid! Now step around the screen to show the breathlessly waiting audience. And be sure to look in the mirror yourself!"

Casey obeyed and was greeted with gasps of delight. She turned slowly so that the onlookers could admire the whole gown. Finally, she looked into the tall mirror, and gasped herself.

The gown was made of lustrous gold satin that shimmered and dazzled and was trimmed with a silvery lace that enhanced the gold satin. Her hair was a golden crown that matched the gown. She still wasn't entirely sure that she felt like a lady, but she certainly looked like one.

She looked like her mother, who was the greatest lady she'd ever known. And looking like her mother warmed her heart.

After swallowing hard, she said, "Thank you, Naomi. This is magnificent! I will never look better."

"You will if you patronize Naomi's shop when she opens one," Tamsyn said with a smile. "She'll be able to support the shop with just Tremaynes as customers!"

There was general laughter, and then everyone dived into the tea and cakes. Casey removed the gown with Naomi's help and put on the morning gown again. She hoped that Cameron would return in time to see her in all her glory.

That night, she once more slept in the warmth of his emotional presence. But it would be even better when he arrived back in person.

CHAPTER 16

Once more Cameron slept in the peace of Casey's warmth, which didn't last once he'd dressed, eaten, and set off for Faversham. He felt the advancing storm, but it hadn't arrived yet. With luck, he'd be able to take care of his business and be home in time for the ball, but he figured the odds of making it in time were about even.

He and Arthur made good time to Faversham, where he planned to learn about Casey's vile father, if the man was alive or dead, and if there was an inheritance for Casey. She must understand her situation to help her plan for her future.

He was returning to the livery stable where he'd left Arthur when he passed a small but elegant jewelry shop. On impulse he went inside. The well-dressed man behind the counter asked, "Are you looking for something in particular, sir?"

"Yes. A ring." It wasn't something he'd thought about before, but now he was quite certain that he needed a ring, and he'd find exactly the right one here.

"For a lady, sir?"

"Yes."

The jeweler pulled out several flat display cases containing rings, but it took Cameron only a moment to find the right one. It was made of gold with delicate designs etched between the plain edges. "This one."

"An excellent choice, sir. Subtle but rich," the jeweler said. "If it doesn't fit the lady, you may bring it back for a size adjustment."

"This one will do," Cameron said, hoping he had enough money to pay for it.

He did, barely. After sliding the slim velvet box inside his coat for safety, he left and headed for the livery. Now it was time to *ride*!

He was able to make good progress toward London before it was time to stop for the night. Once more he slept with the feeling that Casey was near. Just not near enough.

The ball would be held the next night. He set out the next morning. As the first snowflakes began drifting from the sky, he wondered if he would make it home in time. His progress slowed as the snow deepened. Anxious though he was to get home, he had to take care to ensure that he and Arthur arrived home safely.

As the snow deepened and the part of his face not covered by a scarf numbed from the cold, he reminded himself that even if he didn't make it home this evening, he would be able to see Casey tomorrow.

That might have to do.

CHAPTER 17

Cameron still hadn't returned by the time Naomi came to dress Casey for the ball. "He might still arrive tonight," Naomi said comfortingly.

Casey moved to the window and looked at the deepening snow. It was falling so thickly that she could barely see the street. "It's much more important that he and Arthur arrive home safely."

"True," Naomi said as she finished with the ties on the back. "But it will be lovely if he can see you in all your splendor! Shall we go down now?"

Casey nodded. As they stepped into the hall, she heard music floating up from the ballroom. She was equal parts excited and nervous. When they entered the spacious ballroom it sparkled with lights and greens and bright ribbons.

"It's just starting," Naomi whispered. "Our balls always start with Gwyn and Rhys performing a minuet together."

Guests were gathered around the edges of the ballroom as Rhys and Gwyn stepped out together in the minuet. They danced with such exquisite grace that Casey had to choke back tears. They were not only excellent dancers, but love incarnate.

When the dance ended, they held hands and bowed to the other guests. Then the music struck up again and dancers flooded onto the floor of the ballroom. Rhys cut through the chattering guests and offered Casey his hand. "Dance with me, Casey?"

"Of course," she said with a smile. As she stepped into the music with Rhys, it was almost as good as dancing with Cameron would be. But not quite.

Cameron and Arthur were both exhausted by the time they reached Tremayne House, but the lights were on inside and he could hear the whisper of dance music as he headed back to the stables. He slid off Arthur and wearily started to remove the saddle.

"I'll take care of Arthur," a voice said at his elbow. It was Farrell, the head groom. "You go inside and claim your lady."

Cameron gave a twisted smile. "Does everyone know my business?"

Farrell grinned. "Yes. Now inside with you!"

Cameron turned and crossed the backyard to the kitchen. The sudden warmth made him want to sink down on a kitchen chair and fall asleep on the table, but not yet. He tossed his coat, scarf, and hat over the back of the chair, then followed the music.

He paused as he passed a mirror in the hall, grimacing at the sight of himself. His clothing was disheveled and his breeches were wet from the snow. Not to mention that his overlong hair was tangled and his prickly chin proved that he was overdue for a shave. He looked like a shiftless vagabond who would be banned from any decent household, but he couldn't bear to wait any longer to see Casey.

Passing through the refreshment room, he grabbed a lobster tart and wolfed it down in two bites while he walked. When he opened the door to the ballroom, a tidal wave of music and warmth flowed over him and he paused, dazzled by the bright colors and dancing couples.

At first he couldn't see Casey. He frowned, thinking that he was tall enough that he should be able to see her, but where. . . ?

Then he caught his breath, wondering if that was Casey waltzing with his older brother Bran. She was the right height and build for Casey, but Cam didn't recognize the shining gold hair, and her magnificent and equally shining gown looked like the garb of a royal princess, not a Tremayne, even a very fashionable one.

The woman must have felt the pressure of his interest, because she half turned and caught his gaze with hers. A bolt of pure energy flared between them. She abandoned Bran and raced through the dancers as a pathway opened before her. *"Cameron!"*

"Casey!" He moved toward her and she sailed right into his open arms. His golden lady was so warm, so sweet, so *Casey.*

He pulled her close, delighting in the warmth and feel of her slim body. "You look like Cinderella, and I look like a beggar from Seven Dials," he said ruefully.

"Really? I think you look quite wonderful. Very kissable." She raised her face and they kissed for an endless moment of delight.

When they separated to breathe, he asked huskily, "Dance with me, my lady?"

"Of course!" she said with a dazzling smile.

Ignoring his battered riding boots and his general dishevelment, he swept her into the waltz. He suspected that she'd had some recent dancing lessons because she glided across the floor very smoothly, perfectly in step with him.

An advantage of the waltz was that it gave a couple the opportunity to have a real conversation. He said succinctly, "I visited Faversham before returning and talked to your family solicitor. He explained that your father died about six months ago, and you're something of an heiress."

"Oh?" she asked quizzically.

"The title and estate will go to your father's heir—a second cousin, William—whom you probably don't know," he explained. "But your parents' marriage contract specified that your mother's rather sizable fortune would be divided equally among the younger children. Since you're the only one, it will all come to you."

She blinked. "You mean I'm well-off? What an odd thought after so many years of watching every sixpence! I'm not sure what I'll do with it apart from being able to afford having your sister Naomi make all my clothing once she opens her shop. She did an amazing job with this gown."

"Naomi created this?" He studied it more closely. "It's magnificent, even for her. You really do look like a princess."

"That's how I feel tonight." She blushed. "I've been having trouble feeling really female, but perhaps the final piece of the puzzle of feeling like a proper woman is to dance with a proper man."

He smiled back at her, intoxicated by her closeness. "You certainly feel like a real woman to me. In a tomboyish sort of way!"

She laughed. "That sounds right."

The waltz music ended. Knowing that the moment had come but feeling profoundly nervous, he reached into his inside pocket and retrieved the small velvet box. Should he go down on one knee? But he didn't want to draw that much attention to them so he simply offered her the box, feeling shy. "Please?"

She opened the box and caught her breath at the sight of the ring. Raising her gaze, she asked, "Does this mean what I think it means?" Her eyes were wide with wonder.

He said softly, "If you think it means that I love you and very much want to marry you, yes."

Tears glinting in her eyes, she mutely held out her left hand so he could slide the ring onto her third finger. It fit perfectly. "This is beautiful, Cam!"

He kissed the ring on her finger. "Always and forever, my matchless Cinderella tomboy, and light of my life."

"Always and forever," she whispered as she went into his arms again. "Because I love you, too, my most handsome, charming, and mischievous hero!"

They kissed again and the other guests began to applaud, the sound going from a soft patter to a torrent of joyous approval.

Always and forever, amen.

A Winter's Wish

Anna Bradley

Chapter 1

Chester, England
December 1801

"Harder! Come, Estella! Surely you can pull harder than that?"

Stella had been wrestling with Cornelia's corset for the better part of an hour already. She'd nearly broken a finger, her palms were red and raw, and sweat had gathered at her hairline, but she didn't dare argue with her stepmother.

"Yes, Phillippa." She propped one foot on the bedframe, braced the other on the floor of her stepsister's bedchamber and tugged on the laces until her arms ached and her head was swimming.

"For pity's sake, is that the best you can do?" Phillippa eyed Cornelia's corset with a frown. "It must be tighter! Put your back into it, girl!"

"Careful, Mother." Beatrice, who'd fallen into a graceless sprawl over the settee, glanced over the top edge of her book. "Another wrench like the last one and both Cornelia and Stella will tumble out the window."

"Quiet, Beatrice," Phillippa snapped. "No one asked you. Hold on to the bedpost, Cornelia, dear. That's it. Again, Estella."

Stella gripped the damp laces in her fists, sucked in a fortifying breath, and yanked with such force the bed jumped a foot across the floor.

"One would think you could manage a bit more effort for your sister's sake, Estella, especially given how good she is to you." Phillippa gave a disapproving sniff. "But I suppose your meager efforts will have to do, as we're out of time. Fetch Cornelia's gown and be quick about it. Our guests will be arriving soon."

"And with no earthly idea of the torment that's about to be inflicted upon them." Beatrice sat up, tossing her book aside. "She's not playing the 'Christmas Gambols,' I hope? Poor Charles Dibdin is likely turning in his grave."

Stella hurried to Cornelia's dressing closet. "Mr. Dibdin is still very much alive, Beatrice."

"He is *now*, yes, but wait until he hears Cornelia banging out his music on the pianoforte." Beatrice gave an exaggerated shudder. "Our poor guests have no idea what they've set loose upon themselves."

No, they hadn't, and there was no way to warn them Cornelia's attacks on the pianoforte would sound less like holiday cheer, and more as if a dozen feral cats had been released into the drawing room.

But there wasn't anything she could do about it, and even if she could, she'd long since learned to keep her opinions to herself. She wasn't Cornelia's music master and could not be blamed for her stepsister's tuneless shrieking.

She stepped into Cornelia's dressing closet and a fleeting moment of quiet joy rushed through her. *This* was her domain. Ballgowns, riding habits, walking dresses, pelisses—every article of clothing a lady could dream of was stuffed inside, in every color and fabric imaginable.

And she'd sewn every stitch of it herself.

Every bodice and skirt, every bit of lace and every perfectly straight hem was a product of her needle. She'd even made the hats and gloves herself.

But this wasn't the time to admire her handiwork, so she bypassed all this glorious finery and reached for a cream silk confection with a pale pink overskirt, the sleeves and neckline trimmed with the finest Belgian lace she'd ever touched.

It had taken her most of the week to sew the gown, long nights spent bent over the worktable in her cramped bedchamber, her fingertips sore and her eyes burning with exhaustion, but the gown was worth every pinprick and sleepless night.

It had turned out just as she'd envisioned it would. It was exquisite, the silk as delicate and soft as a cloud. It had taken her ages to get the draping right, but it moved like a dream.

"Estella!" Phillippa called, her voice ringing with irritation. "Whatever is taking you so long? Make haste, will you? We haven't got all day."

"Yes, Phillippa. I'm coming." She hurried back to the bedchamber with the gown cradled as tenderly in her arms as if it were a newborn infant. "Here we are."

"Well, don't just stand there!" Phillippa glanced at the watch dangling from a gold chain at her waist and let out an impatient huff. "I already told you we're in a hurry. Dress her!"

"Yes, Phillippa."

She unfastened the row of dainty gold buttons at the back of the gown and lowered it over Cornelia's head, taking care not to wrinkle the delicate fabric as she helped Cornelia find the sleeves, but instead of falling to the floor in a graceful arc of pink and cream silk the gown bunched at Cornelia waist and hips.

"The bodice is too tight!" Cornelia squirmed, jerking at the fabric with careless hands, then whirled to face Stella, her cheeks flushing an ominous shade of red.

Stella took a hasty step backward. She'd seen that same red flush a dozen times before, and it only ever meant one thing. Cornelia was mere seconds away from a—

"It doesn't fit!" Cornelia stamped her foot, her hands clenching into fists. "You stupid girl, you made it too small!"

—a screaming tantrum.

"I-I don't understand." Stella tried to smooth the folds of the gown over Cornelia's torso, but it was so tight, the seams at Cornelia's waist and back were threatening to tear. "How could this be? The gown fit you to perfection just last week!"

If there'd ever been a wrong thing to say, that was it.

Cornelia's face turned positively purple, and she took a menacing step toward Stella. "You horrible girl! Do you mean to imply—"

"That the snugness of the gown has something to do with the dozens of Cook's jam tarts you consumed this week?" Beatrice spoke in honeyed tones, but her wicked grin gave her away. "A ravenous sweet tooth is a dreadful thing, is it not, Cornelia?"

Cornelia turned on her sister with an outraged gasp. "Why, how *dare* you—"

"Quiet, both of you! I can't hear myself think with you two shrieking. Stand still, Cornelia." Phillippa circled Cornelia, examining the dress from every angle. "It's a bit tight, but it will do well enough."

"Certainly, it will, so long as you don't attempt to inhale." Beatrice eyed the waistline of the gown, one eyebrow aloft. "Or exhale, for that matter. You can manage a few hours without breathing, can't you, Cornelia?"

Cornelia sucked in another furious breath, but Phillippa cut her off before she could deliver what would undoubtedly have been an outburst for the ages. "This is the dress we intended for this occasion, and this is the dress you shall wear."

"Do you really think it's all right, Mamma?" Cornelia turned back toward the glass, her bottom lip quivering.

"Yes, dearest. You look a perfect vision." Phillippa snapped her fingers at Stella, who'd retreated to a corner and was doing her best to avoid notice. "Why are you just standing there, Estella? See to Cornelia's hair at once."

But the gown was far from perfect, despite Phillippa's insistence. The row of gold buttons marching down the back of it were positively bulging, Stella's tiny, careful stitches threatening to burst. One deep exhale and the whole lot of them would pop off, one after another. "Er, I beg your pardon, Phillippa, but I think perhaps the pale blue gown might be a safer—"

"Not another word." Phillippa turned on her, her dark eyes

ablaze. "Do you imagine anyone here cares what *you* think, Estella? You've done enough damage for one day. Indeed, it amazes me how you always manage to be such a great disappointment."

Beatrice rolled her eyes. "I don't see how it's Stella's fault Cornelia gorged herself on jam tarts."

Stella gave her a grateful smile. Beatrice had always been kinder to her than Cornelia and Phillippa. They weren't friends, exactly—Phillippa would never allow it—but they shared a silent camaraderie in the way of prisoners suffering under the same cruel jailor.

"Silence, Beatrice!" Phillippa turned on her youngest daughter with such violence that even Beatrice, who was far from a shrinking violet, took a step backward. "As for you, Stella, you will leave us this instant." Phillippa pointed a shaking finger at the bedchamber door. "Get out of my sight."

There was no use trying to defend herself. Her protests would only enrage Phillippa further. Yet somehow, her mouth was opening. Words rushed to her lips, but she never got the chance to say them.

"Get *out*!" Phillippa thundered. "I can't bear the sight of you."

Stella turned and fled the room as if the hounds of hell were nipping at her heels.

When she reached the safety of the corridor she paused, her back against the door and her palm pressed to her throat. One breath, then another, slow and calm, and . . . yes, that was better. Her heart was no longer threatening to beat its way out of her chest.

Why hadn't she included a bit of extra room in the bodice? This wasn't the first time Cornelia's ferocious sweet tooth had come back to haunt her. She might have known this would happen as soon as those tarts made their way to the breakfast table.

But there was nothing to be done about it now but pray her stitches would hold.

She eased away from the door and tiptoed down the corridor to the stairs, as silent as a mouse. When she reached the kitchens she paused in the doorway to take an appreciative sniff. "My, it smells lovely in here."

"Shortbread biscuits for Lady Featherstone's company."

Mrs. Neville gave a derisive snort as she set the tray of shortbread down beside a plate loaded with her famous raisin buns. "We must have shortbread *and* raisin buns. I swear, the whole lot of them are fussier than spoiled children."

Stella leaned over the buns and inhaled the yeasty steam rising from the pan, her stomach growling at the mouthwatering scent of cinnamon. "You've outdone yourself, Mrs. Neville."

Without a word Mrs. Neville wrapped a clean cloth around one of the buns, and a thick slice of shortbread. "Here you go."

"Oh, how kind. But that's not necessary, Mrs. Neville."

"Nonsense. Your cheeks are pale, and I can hear your empty belly protesting from here." Mrs. Neville held out the warm bundle. "I daresay you haven't been allowed any time for breakfast this morning."

Stella gazed at the treats, saliva pooling in her mouth. She had missed breakfast, as Cornelia had demanded she sew another row of silk rosettes onto the gown she intended to wear to Lady Townley's dinner party this evening.

She *was* a trifle hungry.

"Out to the garden with you while you have the chance." Mrs. Neville waved her away. "Shoo, before Her Ladyship gets after you to beat the dust from the carpets, or something equally unpleasant. You must seize your freedoms when they present themselves."

That was true enough. When she wasn't sewing until her fingertips were bloody, Phillippa invariably assigned her another task. She only ever got a moment to herself when her stepmother and stepsisters were away from the house or engaged with company.

If she didn't eat now, she may not have another opportunity until supper. Her stomach let out another demanding groan as she took the bundle. "You're too good to me, Mrs. Neville."

"Oh, aye. I'm a perfect saint, I am." Mrs. Neville brushed off the thanks, but her eyes were twinkling. "Go on, then."

Stella opened the kitchen door and stepped out into the courtyard, gasping as a blast of frigid winter air stole her breath. It had been a terribly cold December, but the sky above her was a pure, unbroken blue, the winter sun setting the frost on the stones at her feet sparkling like bright, tiny diamonds.

She made her way down the pathway that wound around the outside of the house toward the walled garden. As she passed the drawing room window, she could make out the faint plink of pianoforte keys. The first note of the "Christmas Gambols" rang in the drawing room, and she closed her eyes on a wince.

For better or worse, Phillippa's much anticipated musical afternoon had begun.

Worse, most likely, as Cornelia wasn't quite the musical prodigy Phillippa imagined her to be, but that was a worry for another time. For now, all that mattered was the pathway stretched out before her, dappled with sunlight.

She couldn't help but give an excited little skip at this perfect, fleeting slice of freedom.

Goodness knew it was rare enough. Phillippa had made certain of that. Her stepmother had done a thorough job of snatching away everything that had once brought her joy, and she'd delighted in doing so.

Oh, she'd taken pains to hide her distaste, at first. She'd simpered and cooed over Stella for the first two years of the marriage, and proclaimed herself the most affectionate of mothers, but her mask had fallen away after Stella's father had died from a tragic fall from his horse.

That was two years ago, and since then, Phillippa had made no secret of her dislike. Why she'd become such an object of disgust to her stepmother was a mystery, but she'd always imagined it was because she was the daughter of an earl, and her stepsisters . . . well, they weren't, and goodness knew there was no one in all of England more obsessed with rank than Phillippa. Indeed, she made herself so unpleasant about it Stella had taken to using her mother's maiden name, Harley, to avoid inflaming Phillippa's temper.

But she wouldn't waste the few precious moments she had ruminating on her stepmother's whims and cruelties. It was too lovely a day for that, with birdsong echoing in the cold air and the ice gilding the bare tree branches glittering in the winter sun.

When she did have a rare moment to herself, she always came here. One would never guess to look at it, but this had once been a thriving garden. The beds were dormant now, but in her mind's eye it was the same as it had been when her father was alive, a wild profusion of colorful flowers.

He'd loved this garden, and he'd taught her to love it just as he did. They'd used to wander here together for hours, and he'd tell her stories about her mother, Caroline. She didn't remember her mother—she'd died of a fever shortly after Stella was born—but her father had brought her mother to life for her during those long walks together.

She reached for the locket hidden inside her pocket, stroking her fingertips over the smooth case. Her father had given it to her on her sixteenth birthday, and since then she'd opened it hundreds—no, thousands—of times to gaze at the portraits inside.

One of her, and the other of her father.

She carried it with her always still, but she rarely looked inside it anymore. She couldn't bear to see his handsome, smiling face, the warm smile that had been extinguished far too early.

But she didn't need to see his portrait to remember him. He was gone, but she'd always have her memories of him. No one could take those away from her.

And such sweet memories they were!

She'd come here with him every day as a child, her hand tucked into his as they strolled from one flowering bed to another, and she'd steal the plump, dark-skinned blueberries from the bushes as they passed.

How could it feel as if it were only yesterday that she'd strolled through these grounds with him, yet at the same time feel like a lifetime ago?

Gravel crunched under her feet as she made her way down the winding path, her head full of memories. There'd been a lovely cluster of hydrangeas to the left, just there, their flowers a vibrant shade of bluish purple, and there, in the center of the garden, her father's prize peonies had once held pride of place, a dazzling array of bright pink.

It wasn't the same now. How could it be?

But he was gone, and nothing would ever be the same again. The garden blurred before her, but she pressed her lips together and dashed away the tear in her eye before it could drop.

She turned her back on the beds of snarled weeds and wandered farther down the pathway, but her chest was tight, and there was a telltale sting in her nose.

There wasn't anywhere on the estate where her father's absence was more apparent than it was here, but what good would tears do her? She wouldn't waste her few stolen moments of freedom entertaining such maudlin thoughts, especially on such a perfect day as this.

It was strange, the way grief could sneak up on you and steal every pleasure. She might go an entire day without dwelling on her father's absence, but there were also times when every sound, every step reminded her of him, and it all became too much to bear.

This, alas, was one of those times.

Perhaps it would be better if she didn't return to the walled garden for a few weeks. The rush of memories only made her melancholy, and there was no sense in dwelling on what couldn't be changed—

"No!"

She stilled, her feet frozen to the pathway, a shudder jolting down her spine. The unholy shriek was coming from the drawing room, and there was no mistaking that voice.

It was Cornelia, and she was in a towering, incoherent rage.

Again.

The childish part of her wanted to slap her hands over her ears, but she'd never been a coward, and anyway, forewarned was forearmed. She braced her palms on the windowsill, rose to her tiptoes and hefted herself up so she could peek through the glass.

Cornelia was seated at the pianoforte, her head thrown back, a scream that threatened to shatter the windows coming from her wide-open mouth.

Dear God, what was happening? Cornelia threw frequent tantrums, yes, but she'd never done so in front of company before, and every aristocrat within a ten-mile radius had been invited to today's performance. This was Cornelia's first formal appearance in society, and both she and Phillippa had high hopes it would lead to a successful London season.

What could have gone so dreadfully wrong?

Nothing seemed to be amiss. The drawing room had been scrubbed until it shone, the pianoforte had been tuned to perfection, and Cornelia looked lovely in her new gown—

Wait. Was that. . . ?

Oh, no. No!

It was Cornelia's gown. Instead of a row of pretty gold buttons marching down her back, there was a gaping opening where they'd once been, and Cornelia's shift and the top third of her stays with the straining laces were perfectly visible to the guests seated in gilt chairs behind her.

Every aristocrat in Chester had attended today's party, and now they were all getting a shocking glimpse of Cornelia's underthings! Already some of the young ladies were tittering behind their hands, and goodness knew it wouldn't end there.

Only a few dozen people were in attendance today, but each guest had been carefully selected by Phillippa. Only the loftiest aristocrats had been invited, and most of them were likely planning to go to London next month for the season.

And now they'd all seen Cornelia's stays! Soon enough Almack's would be abuzz over Cornelia's wayward buttons!

Oh, dear. This was very bad. Cornelia's first season was over before it could even begin. It was an utter disaster, and it didn't take a fortune teller to know who'd be blamed for it.

The one who'd wielded the needle, of course.

The last button was still clinging to the silk, but it was just barely hanging on, and Cornelia's shrieking was putting quite a lot of pressure on it.

Stella waited, her gaze locked on the last remaining button, her fists clenched and knuckles white as Cordelia inhaled, inhaled, inhaled, and then released the breath in a great gust, the silk pulling tight and the tiny stitches straining.

Her entire life was hanging by a thread.

Not figuratively, but literally.

Well, perhaps not her *life*, but her immediate future depended on one button and the resilience of a fragile length of silken thread.

There was nothing she could do to stop the impending tragedy. The thread would either snap or it wouldn't, and there wasn't a single, blessed thing she could do but mutter a quick prayer that fate would err on her side this time.

The odds weren't in her favor. Since her father's death two years ago, fate appeared to have abandoned her entirely.

Then, in the next instant, it happened.

The last remaining button gave up the ghost, but instead of dropping to the floor with quiet dignity and politely rolling under the pianoforte, it burst free with the force of a pistol shot, flew across the drawing room and landed with an audible plop next to Viscount Lawton's shiny black Hessians.

Viscount Lawton, the object of Cornelia's most ardent affections.

She released her hold on the windowsill, lowered her feet to the ground and pressed her back against the stone wall, closing her eyes.

Fate, gravity and a dozen jam tarts had been her undoing.

If only she could stay here forever with the sun-warmed stones at her back and the winter breeze on her face! Better still if she could scale the stone wall surrounding the garden and disappear. But it was hopeless. She had no money, no friends, and no place to go.

She was utterly at Phillippa's mercy.

By the time she roused herself the rattle of the departing carriages had faded to silence. The guests had made a hasty retreat, and there was nothing to be done now but to face the consequences.

Her feet dragged with every step back to the house. She slipped through the front door, bracing herself for a tumult, but there wasn't a sound to be heard.

The house was silent. Ominously so.

How strange. She was halfway down the corridor that led to the drawing room when the soft murmur of voices reached her. She crept closer, uneasiness tugging at her, and paused in the corridor, just out of sight.

". . . afraid we have no choice but to delay your season until next year, dearest."

"Delay it! But what of Viscount Lawton, Mamma? Miss Grimshaw says he intends to wed this season. I can't give him up! I simply can't. I shall never recover from the loss of him. Indeed, my heart will break."

Cornelia burst into a flood of noisy tears, and Phillippa was obliged to raise her voice to be heard over the din. "Never mind Viscount Lawton, dearest. Why should you settle for a Viscount when you could have a duke?"

The screeching stopped at once. "A duke? What duke, Mamma?"

"The Duke of Hawthorne, my love. I wasn't going to mention it, as I know you had your heart set on London." Phillippa held up a thick, cream-colored card. "He's having a house party, and just listen, dearest! The party will culminate in a Christmas Eve ball, where the duke will choose his future duchess. All the best people will attend. I daresay the London season will be quite dull this year."

"The Duke of Hawthorne?" Beatrice, who hadn't any use for either dukes or viscounts, gave a dismissive sniff. "Never heard of the man."

"He's only just returned to Scotland after six years in Brazil. Or was it some other godforsaken place? I can't recall, but he's a scientist of some sort and reputed to be quite brilliant."

"Six *years*?" Cornelia wrinkled her nose. "He must be quite savage by now."

"Perhaps," Phillippa allowed. "But he's a savage who also happens to be a duke. For pity's sake, Cornelia, don't you want to be a duchess? Hawthorne Castle, his country seat in Annan, is meant to be spectacular, indeed. Imagine being mistress of a castle, Cornelia!"

"If Cornelia is meant to land a duke, Mamma, you'd best keep her away from the pianoforte." Beatrice popped a bite of shortbread into her mouth. "The jam tarts, as well."

Stella didn't wait to hear any more. She tiptoed back down the corridor, ran up the three flights of stairs to her tiny room and closed the door with a quiet click behind her.

A house party, and a Christmas Eve ball? A beautiful Scottish castle, and a betrothal to a duke?

It sounded like a fairy tale waiting to unfold.

She'd believed in fairy tales, once upon a time. She'd believed in dazzling pink peonies and plump berries and a father who would live forever. She'd believed that life was sweet, and people were good at heart.

Of all the things she'd lost, she missed her faith the most. She wanted it back more than she wanted her next breath, but her eyes had been opened, and there was no closing them again.

Fairy tales weren't real. At best, they were pretty stories, nothing more.

At worst, they were lies.

And no good ever came of lies.

Chapter 2

Hawthorne Castle
Annan, Scotland

If Gabriel hadn't seen the tragedy currently unfolding with his own eyes, he wouldn't have believed it was happening.

"Will you wear the blue superfine this evening, Your Grace?"

What difference did it make which coat he wore, when his peace of mind was under direct threat? And was that *another* carriage coming up his front drive?

A Christmas Eve ball, of all wretched things. If that wasn't horrific enough, this ball came with a two-week house party attached to it and was meant to culminate with a betrothal.

His betrothal.

For the next fortnight, Hawthorne Castle would be overrun with ladies. A few gentlemen too, perhaps, but mostly ladies. Ladies, and their marriage-minded mammas.

Petite ladies, plump ladies, and tall, slender willowy ladies. Fair, dark, and redheaded ladies. Ladies who appeared to be scarcely out of pinafores, and ladies on the verge of toppling headlong into spinsterhood.

Every sort of lady one could imagine had appeared at his doorstep at some point today, and none of them were dreaming of sugarplums.

No, they'd come for only one reason.

To become the Duchess of Hawthorne.

"The blue, Your Grace?" Rowan held up two coats for his inspection. "Or do you prefer the bottle green?"

Gabriel turned from the window with a weary sigh. It hardly mattered what color coat he chose. It would still be *him* inside it, either way. "I shall defer to your superior fashion sense, Rowan."

"The blue, then. It only just arrived from London yesterday." Rowan set the green coat aside and selected a boar's head brush from his array of tools. "I do hope you don't catch a chill, lingering so long by the window, Your Grace. It's quite raw this morning."

A chill, indeed. "I can't help but feel, Rowan, that your concern has less to do with my health, and more to do with our guests catching me gawking at them from above."

"Not at all, Your Grace." Rowan attacked the right sleeve of the blue coat with his brush. "I have never known you to observe anything less than the strictest propriety."

Gabriel stifled a snort. Rowan was unfailingly loyal, but they both knew it was only a matter of time before he cocked this whole thing up.

Still, a retreat did seem like a wise course of action. He'd already wasted half the morning spying on his guests as their carriages stopped below his bedchamber window, and it had done nothing to quell the swarm of uneasy butterflies dancing a jig in the pit of his stomach.

"I'm not certain this house party was a good idea, Rowan."

It wasn't the first time he'd said so, but Rowan's head jerked up, as if his clothes brush had just delivered a nasty static shock. "But the ladies have already arrived, Your Grace."

They were still arriving, in fact. The first carriage had come just before nine this morning. It was nearly noon now, and the endless parade hadn't yet concluded. Even as he spoke, a smart gray coach trundled up the drive and came to a stop at the castle's front door, the bells fixed to the horses' bridles ringing merrily as they stamped their hooves and tossed their heads, frosty air streaming from their noses.

One of the carriage doors flew open and disgorged its passengers onto the drive.

"Look, Rowan. More ladies. How wonderful." There were three of them, their richly embroidered velvet cloaks fluttering in the wind. "I don't suppose we can send them away again."

"Of course we can, Your Grace." Rowan set his brush aside and joined Gabriel at the window, peering over his shoulder. "You can do whatever you wish to do. You are the Duke of Hawthorne, and this is your castle."

"Very reassuring, Rowan, but why do I feel as if there's an unspoken 'but' coming?"

Rowan twitched the heavy silk draperies to hide their faces from any curious gazes. "We will send them away at once, if Your Grace commands it, but—"

"Ah, there it is."

"But banishing the ladies will not solve your difficulties. Your castle will be your own again, but your problem will remain. If you don't wed, Your Grace, you'll be left at Hawthorne Castle alone."

"Would that be so terrible?" His work would keep him busy enough, wouldn't it?

But Rowan was shaking his head. "Annan is a tiny, remote place, as you know, Your Grace. You're not accustomed to a solitary existence. I'm afraid it will be a lonely life for you to live here by yourself."

Gabriel looked away. If he could persuade himself that wouldn't be the case, he'd do so in a heartbeat, but he'd returned to Annan nearly a year ago, and it had been the quietest year of his life.

The threat of him wandering about this castle until he expired from loneliness was all too real.

"All will be well, Your Grace." Rowan took up his brush again. "I promise it."

Promises were breakable things, and it was on the tip of his tongue to say so, but Walter Rowan had never, in all the years Gabriel had known him, broken a promise to him.

He was a man of his word, so Gabriel bit back his complaints and turned once again to the activity unfolding below his window. "Good Lord, that's a great many trunks. How long do they intend to stay?"

"Perhaps one of them will stay forever as the Duchess of Hawthorne."

Forever. "What a strange thought that is."

He pushed the draperies aside and resumed spying on the ladies below.

The tallest of the three was of a matronly age, and likely the mother of the two young ladies who'd emerged from the carriage after her. They were dark-haired, red-cheeked young ladies, and quite pretty, at least from this distance.

How odd, to think one of them might become his duchess. How odd that he should need a duchess at all! He stared hard at the two young ladies, trying his best to feel *something*. Surely, he should be able to tell if he was looking at his future betrothed? Shouldn't there be a shiver of awareness, or a delightful pang of some sort?

There was nothing. Well, unless one counted indigestion. There was plenty of that.

For as long as he could remember his father had told him he'd know at once when he found the lady meant to be his duchess. He'd described it as a lightning strike, the sudden clarity like a gift from fate herself, but Gabriel had turned thirty years old this year, and he remained unstruck.

He'd never felt a twinge of anything that might be love.

Had it all been romantic nonsense? Sentimental claptrap? He hadn't thought so at the time. At the time, he'd believed every word his father said. Since then, he'd dreamed of the day he'd find the lady his heart recognized as his own.

But it had never happened, and there was no one left to ask about it. His father was dead and tucked into the family mausoleum at the north end of the property, and with him Gabriel's beloved older brother James, who'd succumbed to a fever just over a year ago.

Now, against his every expectation, he found himself the Sixth Duke of Hawthorne, of all cumbersome things, and every duke must have a duchess.

So, here they were.

Someone must become the Duchess of Hawthorne. Why shouldn't it be one of the two young ladies standing in his drive, mere steps away from the front door of his castle?

Even as he watched, a fourth figure emerged from the carriage, a threadbare cloak wrapped around her, the deep hood pulled low over her face, as if she were hiding.

No richly embroidered velvet for her, then. She must be a servant.

"I believe that's Lady Featherstone," Rowan murmured. "I recognize the crest on the carriage. Her two daughters, Cornelia and Beatrice, have accompanied her here. The eldest, Cornelia, is reputed to be a beauty."

"What of the other lady, the one who's just stepped onto the drive. Who is she?"

Rowan observed the ladies through the window, his brow creased. "I couldn't say. I'm certain Lady Featherstone accepted the invitation on behalf of herself and her two daughters. I daresay the other must be their lady's maid."

Yes, that made sense, given that shapeless cloak she was wearing.

She didn't have the bearing of a servant, though. There was something regal about her, an innate grace that marked her as a gently born lady, but she was dressed in what looked like a bundle of rags.

How odd.

He watched from his perch at the window as she wandered to the far side of the drive. The eastern edge of the formal gardens could be seen from there, and she stood for some time gazing at the grounds before a sharp word from Lady Featherstone recalled her.

She turned to rejoin her party, but she paused for an instant first, and then, almost as if something had compelled her, she tilted her head back, her gaze moving up the castle's façade—up, up, up—until she appeared to be gazing right at him.

He stumbled backward, away from the window, shock rushing through him.

That face. He'd seen it somewhere before, hadn't he? Fine, pale skin, wide eyes, and an adorably stubborn, pointed chin . . .

Just then the castle's front door flew open. A half dozen servants streamed onto the drive to attend to the new arrivals, and the young lady looked away.

The moment was gone, but . . . dear God, his hands were shaking! He peered down into the drive again, but it was too late. She'd returned to her party, and even through the thick panes of glass he could hear Lady Featherstone's voice, sharp with command, one long finger pointed imperiously at the mountain of luggage piled on his front drive.

She was a bit of a harridan, by the sound of her, and likely not the only one currently under his roof. God above. What was he meant to do with a dozen or more preening young ladies and their exacting mammas?

They'd all be expecting an elegant, gallant duke, a gentleman of the world, and instead they were going to find . . .

Well, *him*.

Awkward, bumbling, tongue-tied, wild-haired, and nothing at all like a proper duke. This whole ill-conceived scheme was far more likely to end in disaster than a wedding.

"Shall we see to your ensemble for the evening, Your Grace?" Rowan retrieved the blue coat from the back of the settee where he'd left it neatly folded. "This will look very well with your gold and blue silk waistcoat. Quite ducal, indeed."

That was the problem. If he donned the navy superfine and the figured silk waistcoat he'd look like a duke, and then people would expect him to act like a duke.

And if *that* happened, then this would all be real, wouldn't it?

He rose, strode across his bedchamber and dropped into a chair in front of the fire, stretching his legs out and studying the glossy tips of his Hessians. The words were right there on the edge of his tongue, burning to be free, but how could he say them when Rowan and his other servants had gone to so much trouble to arrange this party?

But alas, the words must be spoken. "I'm going to make a bloody mess of this."

"Your Grace—"

"Come, Rowan. You know it as well as I do."

Rowan set the coat aside. "May I, Your Grace?" He nodded at the chair opposite Gabriel's.

"Of course."

"Thank you, Your Grace." Rowan seated himself, his face giving nothing away. If he was perturbed, or angry, one couldn't tell it from his expression.

Rowan was always calm, always the perfect gentleman. He'd

known Rowan since they'd both been in short pants, and he'd never heard an ugly word pass the man's lips.

"If you'd be so good as to explain your concerns to me, Your Grace, perhaps I can help."

Gabriel huffed out a breath. "It's obvious, isn't it?"

Rowan smiled. "Not to me, Your Grace."

Dear God, how to put such a thing into words? "I'm not a proper duke."

"No? How peculiar. I was under the impression that you're the Sixth Duke of Hawthorne and have been ever since your elder brother's unfortunate passing." Rowan leaned closer, as if imparting a great secret. "Hence my referring to you as 'Your Grace,' Your Grace."

"Was that a joke, Rowan?"

"I'm afraid so, Your Grace." Rowan's eyes twinkled. "I do beg your pardon."

"Nonsense." Gabriel waved the apology off. He and Rowan had attended Eton together, and later Oxford, and Rowan had spent the last six years with him while he'd pursued his studies in Brazil. Strictly speaking, Rowan was his valet, but they were friends too, and there was a frankness between them unusual for a duke and his valet.

"I don't deny that legally speaking, I am the Duke of Hawthorne. What I mean is . . ."

What the devil *did* he mean? It was difficult to put into words, but it was there like a sharp stone in his boot digging into his flesh with every step.

The trouble was that none of the young ladies Rowan had brought to Hawthorne Castle would want him. He knew it in the same way he knew the beat of his own heart.

He was tall, yes. Dukes should be tall.

But his ducal qualifications began and ended there.

He was outfitted to perfection, thanks to Rowan's efforts, but the fashionable clothing made him feel as if he were masquerading as someone else, like a boy dressed in his father's finery.

He was clever, yes, but not in the way a duke was meant to be clever. He wasn't charming or charismatic like James had been, and he didn't have James's gift for putting people at ease, because he was so rarely at ease himself. He'd suffered from a stammer when he was younger, and it still occasionally reared its ugly head when he was nervous.

Which was often, particularly with the ladies.

When it came to flirtation, he was an utter disaster. He'd never really understood how to do it. On occasion, he even had difficulties conversing properly, and his awkwardness had only grown worse during the years he'd been in Brazil.

The few airs and graces he'd once possessed had utterly worn away.

The last time he'd attempted polite conversation with a lady, he'd somehow gone off on a tangent about the nuptial flight of the virgin queen bee, and it had been too, er . . . descriptive for the young lady in question, who'd burst into a flood of tears.

Then there was the blushing. He was prone to the most humiliating blushes. Gentlemen weren't supposed to blush, especially dukes.

"Your Grace? You were saying?"

He met Rowan's gaze. "They won't want me. The young ladies."

"They want the Duke of Hawthorne, Your Grace. It's why they've come."

They'd come, yes, and from every corner of the kingdom, too, but they'd all soon discover it was a wasted trip. "They're expecting someone else entirely."

"They're expecting a gentleman, and that is what you are. I beg your pardon, Your Grace, but I think you give yourself far too little credit."

And Rowan gave him far too much, but what was the point in arguing over it? The ladies were here now, and he couldn't simply toss them out of his castle, no matter how much he might want to.

There was nothing for it but to make the best of it, and that's what he would do.

Soon. Very soon, indeed.

But not right now. Not when he could put off his imminent doom just a bit longer.

"Never mind the coat right now, Rowan. I'm going to pop down to the conservatory and check on my bees. The work will settle my nerves."

"Oh, but Your Grace, Cook has arranged a special tea for your guests—"

"Yes, but that's hours away yet. Not to worry, Rowan. I'll return in an hour, and you may fuss over me and primp to your heart's content then. I'll even sit there meekly while you go at my hair with those infernal curling tongs."

Rowan studied him, tapping his lip with one finger. "The Brutus would look very well on you. Curls for gentlemen are the fashion, Your Grace."

Gabriel paused at the door. "You do recall what happened to Brutus, do you not, Rowan?"

Rowan's lips twitched. "I do indeed, Your Grace. A nasty business, indeed, but not to worry. I'll have the footmen check the young ladies for swords before they're permitted to enter the drawing room."

"Good man, Rowan. Good man."

CHAPTER 3

Hawthorne Castle was just as Stella expected it to be, yet at the same time nothing at all like she'd imagined.

On the one hand, it was undeniably ducal. His Grace the Sixth Duke of Hawthorne's country seat was as ducal an estate as she'd ever seen. To be fair, it was also the *only* ducal estate she'd ever seen, and goodness knew it was just the sort of place one might expect a duke to live.

But there was nothing cold about it, nothing stiff. Somehow, despite its grandeur, Hawthorne Castle was warm and welcoming. Stepping over the threshold and into the entryway had been like stepping into an embrace.

It was rather a paradox, really, but no matter how one chose to look at it, it was a sprawling, massive affair, a monolith of pale gold stone with dozens upon dozens of windows with diamond-shaped glass panes gleaming in the early afternoon sun.

Then there were the turrets. Why in the world did the Duke of Hawthorne need so many turrets? Not that it was any business of hers, of course.

He might do as he pleased with them.

Dukes might do as they pleased, but the same thing wasn't true for lady's maids. She had no excuse for peeking behind doors and nosing into corners as if this were her home, yet here she was, creeping about like a pickpocket eyeing a gold watch.

Phillippa had ordered her to remain in her bedchamber in the servants' quarters while she, Cornelia and Beatrice rested from the long journey. If she had any sense at all she'd have done as her stepmother bade her, but good sense never led to anything amusing.

When would she ever have another opportunity to explore such a grand estate?

Never, so as soon as she'd dropped her tattered valise on the narrow bed she was out the door and tiptoeing down the staircase.

Goodness knew she needed a bit of an adventure after four endless days trapped in a carriage with Cornelia, who took all the space for herself and never ceased fretting for the entire journey, despite everything being arranged specifically for her convenience.

Dear God, what a drive that had been! She'd begun to despair of ever escaping that carriage. After such a penance as that, she deserved this brief wander around the castle. Soon enough she'd return to her quarters, and Phillippa would never be the wiser.

Fortunately, none of the other guests were wandering about. The grand entryway was deserted aside from one housemaid, who paused her dusting to give Stella a curious glance when she reached the bottom of the staircase. The girl didn't speak to her, but it didn't seem wise to linger, so she marched down an adjacent corridor as if she knew precisely where she was going.

That was her first mistake. Four corridors and a half dozen turns later and she was lost. She'd passed a breakfast parlor a few turns back, across from the main staircase, hadn't she? If she could find her way back there, it would be simple enough to retrace her steps to her bedchamber.

As it turned out, it wasn't simple at all. The breakfast parlor and the main staircase appeared to have vanished into thin air, and after another dozen fruitless turns she was no closer to her tiny attic room than she was half an hour earlier.

She wandered blindly from one corridor to the next, the beamed ceilings seemingly miles above her and the paneled walls closing in on her with every step. Once or twice, she heard the faint echo of voices, but it was impossible to tell which direction they came from. When she tried to follow them, she only became more confused.

No one appeared, not even a servant.

Eventually she found herself at one end of a long corridor with a checkerboard of black and white marble on the floor and handsome arched doorways that led to extensive formal gardens outdoors.

The corridor seemed to go on forever, but gradually it widened until at last she came to an ornate stained-glass doorway. The air was thicker here, damper, and through the door she could just make out an ornate structure of wrought iron and what looked like thousands of pounds worth of glazing.

A conservatory? She'd never seen a proper conservatory before. She'd only ever been inside Lady Bastable's conservatory in Chester, but to her disappointment it wasn't truly a conservatory so much as a breakfast room with a great many windows.

It stood to reason that the Duke of Hawthorne's conservatory would be terribly grand, as befitted a duke. There was no harm in taking a little peek inside, surely. No one ever had to know, and she'd come this far, hadn't she? She'd never forgive herself if she didn't get just a tiny glimpse of it.

She grasped the handle and pushed, and the heavy door swung slowly open.

She stumbled to a halt, her mouth falling open on a gasp.

She'd never seen anything like *this* before! It was another world entirely, one scented with roses and citrus and bathed in rainbows of light.

"Oh, my." She turned in a circle, her breath catching.

Floor-to-ceiling arched windows dominated one entire wall, but ordinary glazing wouldn't do for the Duke of Hawthorne. No, the top third of his windows were fitted with intricate pieces of colored glass in a pattern of flowering trees, the tiny white blooms scattered among the leaves glowing in the late afternoon sun.

Was there any place in the world as lovely as this? She'd never seen so many growing things in one place in her life!

She hardly knew where to look first.

Bright pink bougainvillea bloomed next to vibrant orange and blue birds of paradise, and alongside the profusion of colorful flowers there were figs and passionfruit, and olive trees with their shiny silver leaves. There were even a few new citrus trees with lemons no bigger than the tip of her thumb.

She hardly dared to breathe as she crept down the checkerboard pathway past a collection of blooming orchids. She rounded a deep bend, and on the other side of it was a . . . dear God, was that a *pond*?

It was. A circular pond, a fountain at its center spurting a sparkling stream of water. The pond's surface was covered with a profusion of water lilies, their pointed petals a delicate shade of pale purple.

Settees and small, wrought-iron tables were tucked snugly among all the growing things, and she gave in to the temptation to lounge on one of the apricot-colored velvet chairs and inhale the fragrant air.

She couldn't linger, of course. Phillippa would go mad if she knew her orders had been disobeyed, but it was so lovely here, and so utterly outside of anything Stella had ever experienced before.

A few moments more wouldn't do any—

"Such industriousness this afternoon! I'm pleased to find you all so contented with your new home."

She jumped to her feet, her heart vaulting into her throat. Not five paces away from her, leaning over a collection of woven straw baskets, was a man, half hidden behind a spray of palm fronds.

Goodness, where had *he* come from?

He was quite a tall man, and he was dressed in a loose-fitting, er . . . dressing gown? No, it was more akin to a painter's smock except it covered him entirely, from his feet to the voluminous hood pulled over his head.

She hovered beside her abandoned settee, frozen with indecision. If she moved, he'd almost certainly see her, but if she didn't . . . well, he'd almost certainly see her then, too.

Dash it, how had she managed to get herself into such a scrape?

They'd only just arrived at Hawthorne Castle, and she'd already made a grievous error. She'd sneaked into the duke's conservatory without a word of invitation, even knowing it wasn't meant to be enjoyed by a servant.

Why couldn't she learn to accept her place?

There was nothing for it but to make a hasty retreat and pray he didn't notice her. He did seem to be rather preoccupied with his baskets, or . . . were they baskets? They were woven from straw as one might expect, but they didn't look like any basket she'd ever seen. These were cone-shaped, rather like an upside-down flowerpot. There was no opening at the top, only a small notch carved out of the bottom.

They were arranged in a neat row atop a series of wooden tables, and there was some sort of insect buzzing around them.

Insects that looked very much like—

No, surely not.

But there was no mistaking those tiny, furry black-and-yellow bodies. "My goodness, are those *bees*?"

She slapped her hand over her mouth, but it was too late. The man whirled around, and the deep voice that had been speaking so soothingly only moments before barked, "Keep back!"

She took a hasty step backward, speechless.

He was wearing a mask. Or no, not a mask, exactly, but a thin piece of woven straw was fixed to the inside of his hood, entirely covering his face.

How strange! He looked quite frightening.

If an encounter with this faceless stranger wasn't enough to convince her she'd much better have remained in the servants' quarters as she'd been told to do, then nothing ever would.

"Who are you?" His deep voice echoed in the enormous space. "Where did you come from?"

Oh, dear. He sounded angry. "I . . . I beg your pardon! I shouldn't have—"

"I asked you a question, miss. Who are you?"

Oh, no. She'd have to tell him her name now, and one way or another Phillippa would get wind of her little foray, and she'd be forced to spend her Christmas locked alone in a freezing attic.

Much as she'd done last Christmas, and the Christmas before that.

One would think she'd have grown accustomed to it by now, but still, she'd just as soon avoid giving this man her name if she could possibly manage it.

"My name is Stella Harley, but I'm no one of any consequence, I assure you." She edged closer and peered over the man's absurdly broad shoulder to the baskets behind him. "I've never seen so many bees in one place before. What are you doing with them?"

For a long, tense moment he didn't say a word, just stood there staring at her, a cloud of suspicion as thick as London fog hanging about him.

At last, he spoke. "What do you know about bees?"

Not much, unfortunately. Her father had taken a passing interest in entomology at one point, and she'd picked up a few bits of knowledge here and there, but she'd gladly pretend to be an expert if it kept him from questioning her further. "They're, er . . . black and yellow and rather adorably plump and furry."

"Adorably furry?" He crossed his arms over his chest. "Is that your official entomological assessment?"

He was raising his eyebrow at her, wasn't he? She couldn't see his face through the straw covering, but the heavy skepticism in his tone gave him away. No one could speak with such condescension without raising their eyebrows. It wasn't physically possible.

"No, that's my official Apian assessment." Yes, that was very good, indeed! Her father's vast collection of scientific tomes was proving useful at last.

"Your Apian assessment," he repeated flatly.

"Yes." She crossed her arms, mirroring his pose, and nodded at the baskets. "Those are honeybees, aren't they? I believe the study of honeybees is referred to as apiology."

Ah. He hadn't expected *that*. She could sense his eyebrows rising another notch, but she rushed into speech before he could say a word. If he asked her another question, she'd have to answer him, and that simply wouldn't do.

"They, ah . . . they're . . ." Why couldn't she recall a single fact about honeybees, for pity's sake? "They have a queen," she blurted. "There's a honeybee queen, then the worker bees who, er . . . do all the work, and then the drones, who . . . who . . ."

Oh, no. What did the drones do? "They, ah . . . they . . ."

"The drones mate with the queen. That is their sole purpose."

"Er, yes, of course. I remember now," she mumbled, her cheeks heating. The less said about bee mating rituals while she was alone in a conservatory with a strange, masked man, the better. "I confess I didn't know they lived in baskets."

"It's not a basket. It's a skep."

A skep? She'd never heard of such a thing. "I see. The bees live inside of it, I presume?"

"Yes. Each skep holds a single colony of bees. They attach their honeycombs to the walls and ceiling of the skep, and the queen lays her eggs inside."

"Does she, indeed?" She edged closer, taking care to keep a wide berth between herself and the man. It wouldn't do to get too close, particularly while his face was shrouded with that menacing face covering, but she rose to her tiptoes to get a better look at the skeps over his shoulder. "It seems a bit of an awkward place to do it. How does she manage it?"

Silence, and for far longer than was comfortable.

At last, he spoke. "Do you really wish to know?"

"I wouldn't have asked if I didn't, sir." Really, she was starting to lose patience with him.

"The queen squeezes her body into the honeycomb cells, lays a single egg, and then repeats the process a single cell at a time."

"I see. How many eggs can a queen lay before she expires of exhaustion?" Honestly, why was it always the females who had to do all the work?

"A healthy queen can lay up to two thousand eggs a day."

"Two thousand! Why, how marvelous she is! I had no idea bees were so fascinating."

He let out a derisive snort. "I don't know many young ladies who find them so."

Goodness, he was rude. No wonder the duke hid him in the conservatory. "I'm not a young lady."

"No? How strange. Because you look very much like a young lady to me."

Her distinctly shabby clothing indicated otherwise, but this man, whoever he was, didn't seem to know the difference. For pity's sake, what sort of man couldn't tell a servant from a lady?

"You're mistaken, sir." She had been a young lady, once upon a time, but she was a servant now, and if the past two years had taught her anything, it was that those two things were *not* the same. "In any case, I don't see how you can tell what I look like with that covering over your face. Why, I might be a kangaroo, for all you know."

"I doubt that. Kangaroos are native to Australia. This is Scotland, madam."

"Still, you can't possibly know for certain unless you—"

"Very well." Without warning he swept the hood from his head, stepping away from the skep as he did until he was only a few paces away from her. "There. Is that better?"

Better? Hardly. It was a great deal worse, because she wasn't prepared for the face that emerged from behind the mask. If he intended to startle her, he'd done a good job of it. It was terribly disconcerting to find such a face as that hiding behind that dreadful mask.

He had smooth olive skin, an angular jaw with a hint of dark stubble that matched the untidy mop of dark hair on his head, and a pair of bright green eyes peering curiously at her from behind an elegant pair of silver spectacles.

There was no use denying it. He was handsome.

Quite the handsomest man she'd ever seen. His eyes alone were enough to tongue-tie the most collected of young ladies, or they would have been if he hadn't been glaring at her with such narrow-eyed suspicion. Why, he looked as if he imagined she was about to snatch up his baskets and run away with them.

"Ah, just as I expected." He offered her a slightly awkward bow, but there was a hint of amusement lurking at the corners of his lips now. "You're not a kangaroo at all, but a young lady, just as I suspected."

"You've caught me out, sir. I am, in fact, not a kangaroo."

"A vast relief, indeed. I presume you're here for the Christmas ball?"

This time it was her turn to give a derisive snort. *Her*, attend a ball? Phillippa would sooner see her hanged at the gibbet than attend the Duke of Hawthorne's ball alongside Cornelia and Beatrice.

But she wasn't about to explain herself to this man, no matter how handsome he was. The less he knew about her, the better. So, she said only, "Something like that, yes."

His eyebrows rose. Really, he had the most expressive face.

"I see. Are you well acquainted with the duke?"

"No. I'm not at all acquainted with him." She wasn't inclined to think well of him, however. Perhaps that was unfair, but after two years as a servant she was persuaded that noblemen were, for the most part, as petulant and mean-spirited as spoiled children.

And dukes were likely the worst of the lot.

But one didn't disparage a gentleman while at the same time enjoying his hospitality. Or enduring it, more accurately. Yes, that was closer to the truth.

"You're not acquainted with the Duke of Hawthorne." His gaze swept over her, lingering on her lips. "Yet you've already decided you don't like him."

Her mouth fell open. How had he known that she didn't—

"The curl of your lip. It was subtle, I'll give you that, but I'm rather an expert at reading disgust on a lady's face."

What in the world did that mean? Better not to ask.

She rushed into speech before another inconvenient truth could emerge from his absurdly perfect lips. "What nonsense. Why should I feel disgust for a gentleman I've never met?"

He shrugged, as if it mattered not a whit to him how she felt, but that telltale quirk was still at the corners of his lips. "I haven't the vaguest idea. Why don't you tell me, madam?"

For pity's sake, how had she gotten herself into such a ridiculous conversation? She cast a longing glance at the door, but it was on the other side of the enormous conservatory, and he was standing between her, and it.

There would be no quick escape.

She huffed out a breath. "Very well, if you insist upon knowing, I find this house party and Christmas Eve ball to be in bad taste."

The eyebrow jumped, threatening to leap off his face entirely. "Oh? How so?"

"Do you not think it's in bad taste for a gentleman to summon dozens of young, aristocratic ladies to his remote country estate so he may choose a bride from amongst them, much as he would a prime bit of horseflesh?"

His head jerked back. "I never thought of it that way."

"No, I expect not." Gentlemen rarely saw anything as it truly was. "But I've wasted too much of your time already, mister . . . er, mister . . ."

Silence, once again. A beat passed, then another, and then, "Ambrose," he said at last, offering her a shallow bow. "Christopher Ambrose. I'm the Duke of Hawthorne's gardener."

CHAPTER 4

The lie slid from Gabriel's lips as if his tongue were coated in ice.

He hadn't meant to say it. Even now he could hardly believe he'd spoken the words aloud, but the lie was there, still echoing between them.

Christopher Ambrose, the Duke of Hawthorne's gardener. His *gardener*!

What in the world was he thinking, telling this young lady such an egregious falsehood?

The answer was plain enough. He wasn't thinking at all. He'd been lost in a pair of eyes of such a deep, startling blue, one glance at them was like diving into the ocean.

Except this wasn't the ocean. This was his conservatory, and the young lady—the same young lady he'd seen from his bedchamber window only an hour earlier—was shifting uneasily from one foot to the other and worrying her lower lip.

And what a lip it was! Plump, pink, and as smooth as silk—

"I shouldn't have said that." She glanced at him, and then away again. "I beg your pardon. It was wrong of me to speak so ungraciously about the duke, particularly when I've never even seen His Grace."

"I wouldn't let that worry you. The duke appreciates honesty."

Good God, the irony was so thick he could taste rust in his mouth. "He might even agree with you. When you're introduced to him at the dinner tonight—"

He broke off, panic swelling in his throat. How in the world was he going to explain himself when he encountered her at the dinner tonight? He'd been away from England for some time, but unless things had changed a great deal, the gardening staff did not dine at the duke's table.

Damn it, this was what came of telling lies. The moment he took his seat at the head of the table his identity would be revealed, and she would think he was an utter madman. What sort of duke pretended to be a gardener?

"Oh, I won't be attending the dinner tonight, Mr. Ambrose."

"Of course you'll attend. All the young ladies will attend the welcome dinner this evening."

"Ah, but as I already told you, I'm not a young lady."

She held up the skirt of her cloak, as if that explained everything, but what did her cloak have to do with dinner? Unless . . . ah, that was it. She was pointing out how shabby it was, how threadbare. She meant for him to see it was not the garment of a genteel young lady.

"I'm Lady Featherstone's servant, Mr. Ambrose," she added, removing all doubt. "Her lady's maid."

"I see. I beg your pardon." Still, servant or not, this made no sense. Her cloak was a breath away from falling to bits. Lady Featherstone should be ashamed of herself for permitting her servant to go about dressed in such rags.

"Lady Featherstone will not be pleased if I'm seated at the duke's dinner table this evening alongside her daughters." She smiled, but there was a hint of bitterness in it. "It's just as well, as I have no wish to attend. I haven't much use for dinner parties."

Or dukes, by the sound of it.

"I'm not fond of them myself." Balls, routs, musical evenings, dinners—he invariably made a cake of himself at such grand events. Just a week before he'd returned to England from Brazil he'd attended a formal dinner at the Viceroy's estate. He'd been seated next to the Vicereine, which was a mark of great honor, and he'd proceeded to spill wine all over her gown.

Red wine, and the gown was a pale yellow silk. The poor lady looked like she'd been stabbed.

"Then I suppose we should both be grateful that we're not welcome at the duke's dinner table. There must be a great many other pleasant things to do on such an estate as this." Her gaze wandered to the row of arched windows behind him. "I daresay the grounds are lovely."

"They are, especially the formal gardens. We're famous for our . . ." He trailed off, an idea chasing every other thought from his head.

A foolish, ill-advised and perfectly delightful idea.

There *were* a great many pleasant things to do at Hawthorne Castle. What if, instead of the endless stilted dinners and dull musical evenings, he spent the duration of the house party squiring Lady Featherstone's lady's maid around his estate?

No, no. It was impossible. A dangerous thought, indeed.

Dangerous, and oh, so very tempting.

But it was out of the question, of course. He'd never be able to manage it. As Rowan had reminded him earlier today, the young ladies crowding his drive had come here to meet the Duke of Hawthorne.

But what if he *wasn't* the Duke of Hawthorne? What if he was simply Mr. Ambrose, the Duke of Hawthorne's humble gardener?

Pure madness, that. Insanity. Who would entertain the young ladies and their mammas if there was no Duke of Hawthorne?

If only there were two of him . . .

"Mr. Ambrose? You were about to tell me what Hawthorne Castle is famous for."

"I beg your pardon, Miss . . ." Good God, what was the matter with him? She'd utterly charmed him, and he couldn't even recall her name!

"Miss Harley."

"Hawthorn, Miss Harley. Hawthorne Castle is famous for hawthorn."

"Indeed? How shocking." Her lips were twitching. "Whoever would have guessed?"

"Yes, I daresay the first Duke of Hawthorne thought himself very clever. A particular type of hawthorn known as Glastonbury thorn grows on the estate. You must make time to see the one on the western side of the castle. It's been there for six centuries, at least."

"Six centuries! My goodness, how impressive."

"It is, indeed. It's over forty feet, which is unusually tall for a Glastonbury thorn. It reaches past the roof, and the trunk is as big around as my thigh."

A dainty eyebrow lifted. "Your *thigh*, Mr. Ambrose?"

Oh, no. He shouldn't have said that, should he? Gentlemen didn't discuss their thighs with young ladies. Or lady's maids either, for that matter. They didn't discuss thighs at all, with anyone.

Another apology hovered on his lips, but if Miss Harley was offended, she didn't show it. Delicate pink color flooded her cheeks, but she was smiling again, and this time there was no bitterness in it. It was the pure, unselfconscious smile of a lady who was enjoying herself.

He wanted more of it. More of *her*.

There was something forthright about her that put him at ease.

Her lovely blue eyes hadn't hurt matters, either.

All told, once he'd gotten over the initial shock of a strange young lady wandering around his conservatory, he'd spent a most delightful half hour with her.

She'd made him forget himself, in the best possible way.

A miraculous feat, indeed. No one had ever managed it before.

That was what made up his mind. "Would you care to take a stroll with me this evening while Lady Featherstone and her daughters are occupied with dinner? I'd be happy to show you the rest of the conservatory and the formal gardens."

He held his breath, waiting for her answer.

"How kind of you to offer. Yes, I would like that very much, Mr. Ambrose."

"Wonderful! I believe dinner will be served at eight. Shall we meet here at eight fifteen?" They'd be safe from prying eyes here. No one ever came to this wing of the house since he'd moved his bees into the conservatory. They were afraid of getting stung.

"Yes. I'll see you here at eight fifteen, but I'd best be off now. Lady Featherstone does not like to be kept waiting."

She gave him a brief curtsy, and then she was gone, and the thing was done.

Mr. Ambrose, the Duke of Hawthorne's fictional gardener, would be taking Miss Harley on a stroll amongst the flowers this evening.

There was only one small matter left to see to.

Poor Rowan was going to be beside himself.

He took the stairs two at a time and burst into his bedchamber with such force the door hit the wall behind it with a thud, startling Rowan, who was still fussing with the blue coat he'd selected for Gabriel for tonight's dinner.

"Good afternoon, Your Grace. I was just—"

"Never mind the blue tailcoat, Rowan. I won't be needing it after all."

There. That was as good a place to start as any.

"Very well, Your Grace. I daresay the bottle-green superfine will do just as well."

"I won't be needing the bottle green either, Rowan." Gabriel closed the bedchamber door behind him and dropped onto a settee. "I won't be needing a coat tonight at all."

"No coat?" Rowan's brow creased. "But it's a formal dinner to welcome your guests to Hawthorne Castle."

"Yes, I'm aware of that, but I, ah . . . well, you see, Rowan, the thing is that I've decided I won't be attending the dinner this evening."

"Not attending! I don't understand, Your Grace. The young ladies are here at your invitation. They've come here to meet *you*."

He'd wager every cent in his ducal coffers that none of the young ladies who'd crossed his threshold this morning had come all the way to Annan to meet Gabriel Scott, the man. They'd come for His Grace, and His Grace alone.

Therein lay the problem. "They haven't come for *me*, Rowan. They've come for the Duke of Hawthorne."

Rowan frowned. "You and the Duke of Hawthorne are one and the same person, Your Grace."

An inconvenient truth, to be sure. "Yes, but no one needs to know that, Rowan."

Rowan stared at him for a moment before carefully setting his clothes brush aside. "Forgive me, Your Grace, but I still don't understand."

How to explain? "I only mean to point out that none of our guests know anything about me. Not even one of them could pinpoint me as the duke if their life depended on it. We might present George, the first footman, as the Duke of Hawthorne, and none of them would know the difference, so . . . are you quite well, Rowan? You look a trifle green."

"Quite well, yes," Rowan replied faintly. "You're not suggesting we *do* present George as the Duke of Hawthorne, surely?"

"No, no. I haven't utterly lost my wits, Rowan."

"That's a great relief, Your Grace."

"George is a good fellow, but a footman won't do at all in this instance."

They needed someone with gracious manners and brilliant conversation. Someone elegant and gentlemanly. Someone who was confident, clever and amusing.

Someone impeccable. Someone like . . . well, like Rowan.

Yes, Rowan would do very well, indeed. He was the appropriate age, and he was intelligent, handsome, gracious and kind. He was everything a duke should be. Rowan was more ducal than *he* was, for pity's sake.

Once they outfitted him in properly ducal clothing, no one would ever guess he wasn't the Duke of Hawthorne. "I, ah . . . I have someone else in mind for it."

Gabriel didn't say any more, but Rowan must have guessed what he had in mind, because the color drained from his face.

"Ah, I see you understand me, Rowan. Shall we get on with it, then? Here, try on the blue coat."

Gabriel leapt from the settee, seized the coat and held it out for Rowan, who looked as horrified as if he were attempting to drape a venomous snake around his neck. "I-I . . . but Your Grace, I . . ." Rowan trailed off, his mouth opening and closing like a gasping fish.

They'd never come to an agreement at this rate. "Go on then, man. Just say what you wish to say, so we can get on with it. We're wasting time."

"I . . . you . . . we . . ." Rowan sucked in a deep breath and managed to collect himself. "Is there some reason we need a counterfeit duke?"

"Of course there is, Rowan. There's a reason for everything. But perhaps I should clarify that we only need a counterfeit duke for a fortnight, just for the duration of the house party."

"But I don't want to be a duke!" Rowan blurted, his eyes wide.

"Neither do I. Not just now, anyway. That's rather the problem, you see."

"Forgive me, Your Grace. I didn't mean to suggest there's something wrong with being a duke—"

"Never mind, Rowan." Gabriel waved the apology away. "I daresay you're in shock. I realize this is a bit sudden. Perhaps you'd better sit down. You don't look at all well."

Rowan collapsed onto the settee as if his knees had just given way beneath him. "I'm quite well, Your Grace, just, er . . . a bit shocked."

But Rowan wasn't well. He looked as if he were on the verge of casting up his accounts. Damn it. He was making a mess of this. "Forgive me, Rowan. Perhaps I'd better explain myself."

Rowan dabbed his forehead with the perfectly pressed handkerchief he'd pulled from his pocket. "Yes, that would be most welcome, Your Grace."

"I confess it's a trifle unorthodox." Some might even call it madness, but once one got over the unconventionality of the thing, it made perfect sense. Really, he didn't know why he hadn't thought of it sooner.

"I've reconciled myself to the need for a wife. Not only because I am now the duke, but also because I believe it's necessary for my future happiness."

"I agree wholeheartedly, Your Grace."

"If I can find the right lady, that is." It was rather a big *if*, matrimonially speaking. Aristocrats did not, for the most part, marry for love, especially dukes. They married for titles, money and power.

Was it any wonder so few of them were happy?

He didn't want that for himself. "I don't wish to marry for convenience, Rowan, or for money, or noble lineage. I understand it's expected of me to do so, but in my opinion there is only one reason a gentleman—or a lady, for that matter—should consider marriage."

"What reason, Your Grace?"

"Love, Rowan. *Love*, of course."

His parents had married for love. Since the day they'd met, they'd been utterly enamored of each other. His father had been heartbroken when his mother had died unexpectedly from an outbreak of scarlet fever. He'd rallied for Gabriel's and James's sakes, but he'd never been the same again.

A man couldn't grow up surrounded by such a love as that, and not long for the same love for himself. His brother had never said so, but he suspected James had never wed because he hadn't yet fallen in love.

Now he'd never have the chance.

James was gone. Gabriel was the last of his family, and the long, distinguished history of the Hawthorne dukedom rested on his shoulders.

He *must* marry. It was his duty to produce an heir.

It was a heavy responsibility, and one that had been weighing on him since he'd returned to Scotland, but it had taken on a new urgency since Miss Harley wandered into his conservatory and started quizzing him about honeybees.

He hardly knew her, yet somehow, that didn't matter.

He knew enough. After all, he'd spent a full half hour with her this afternoon, and he hadn't stuttered, or spilled anything, or maimed her in any way.

That must mean *something*, surely?

But he wouldn't confide in Rowan yet. Not about this. For all his gentlemanliness, Rowan was a practical sort. He'd panic if Gabriel declared he'd already chosen his bride after only a single day.

"And has Your Grace fallen in love over the course of the afternoon?"

"I see that sly grin, Rowan. You're not nearly as subtle as you imagine you are. I have not fallen in love this afternoon, no."

At least, he didn't think so, but then what did he know about love?

Not a blessed thing.

He knew only that he was intrigued by Miss Harley, more intrigued than he could ever recall being with any lady.

To be fair, he hadn't yet met any of the young ladies who'd come for the house party. No doubt some of them were perfectly lovely, but they'd all come to Hawthorne Castle for one reason.

To marry a duke.

But not Miss Harley. She didn't care for the Duke of Hawthorne. She'd said so herself.

"Forgive me, Your Grace, but if I may be so bold, what has prompted this sudden disinclination to appear as the Duke of Hawthorne?"

Gabriel dropped onto the settee with a sigh. How to make Rowan understand? A pretend duke sounded daft, even to him. But he couldn't ask such a great favor from Rowan while refusing to explain himself.

Rowan deserved to know the truth.

"I want a love match, Rowan, like my parents had. I daresay that makes me rather foolish. There are, I think, very few dukes who marry for love."

Good Lord, what a depressing thought. He let out another sigh.

"It's not foolish at all, Your Grace. Everyone wishes for true love."

"I suppose they do, yes, but only a lucky few ever seem to find it." He plucked up a pillow, avoiding Rowan's gaze as he toyed with the fringe. "If I meet our guests as the duke, how will I ever know for certain if I'm loved for myself, or only tolerated by a lady who merely wishes to become a duchess?"

Rowan was quiet for some time, but at last he said slowly, "I suppose you won't. I confess I hadn't considered that."

"Well, no. There's no reason you should have done." Fretting about such things was the province of dukes. Marquesses too, and perhaps the occasional earl or viscount.

"I can't say I'm comfortable perpetuating such an elaborate falsehood, Your Grace. These young ladies have come here in good faith. To lie to them feels quite wrong."

"There is that, yes." There was no denying his scheme was dishonest, and unfair to the young ladies who'd come to Hawthorne Castle in good faith. Well, no doubt some of them had come for selfish reasons, but none of them deserved to have such a trick played on them.

"Let me see if I understand you, Your Grace." Rowan cleared his throat. "You wish for me to pretend to be the Duke of Hawthorne in your place, so you might pursue true love with a lady who doesn't know your true identity?"

Gabriel tossed the pillow aside. "It sounds mad indeed when you put it that way, Rowan."

"I'm just making certain I understand you, Your Grace. What of the other servants? We must consider them, too. Won't they all be required to pretend, as well?"

Dear God, he hadn't even thought of that. They'd all have to lie for him, too. He hadn't considered the complications of pulling off such an elaborate scheme.

He'd only been thinking of himself.

"Forgive me, Rowan. I fear I've spoken too hastily. You're right, of course. I suppose I'm a bit of a romantic, just as my father was. I always hoped for a true love match, as my parents had."

"Your Grace—"

"If it were anything less than the rest of my life I'd never even consider such an underhanded scheme."

"Your Grace, I—"

"I just . . . I wish to wed a lady who wants *me*, and not just my title. I want to be loved for myself, Rowan."

Rowan was staring down at his hands folded in his lap, but at that, his head jerked up. "Very well, Your Grace. I'll do it."

Gabriel's mouth fell open. "You *will*?"

"I will. I don't entirely approve of it—you'll forgive me for speaking plainly, Your Grace—but I do understand your quandary. Everyone deserves to know they're loved for themselves," Rowan finished quietly.

Gabriel's throat tightened. "Y-you're sure?"

"I am. I don't wish for you to be condemned to a loveless marriage, Your Grace. But are you certain you want me to play at being the Duke of Hawthorne? A valet is not a duke."

"Not every valet, no, but you, Rowan, are a consummate gentleman. I haven't any doubt at all about your ability to see the thing through."

"Thank you, Your Grace. I only hope I prove worthy of your confidence in me."

"I have no doubt you will." Gabriel gave Rowan's back a hearty slap and rose to his feet. "You're a great deal more charming than I am."

"I'll inform the necessary servants, Your Grace."

"Good man, Rowan."

Chapter 5

Stella found her way out of the conservatory and back to the main staircase with little fuss, which was miraculous enough, considering how thoroughly she'd got lost on her way into it.

Perhaps Hawthorne Castle had a touch of Christmas magic about it. Perhaps it was a place where what was lost would be found once again.

It was a fanciful thought, and alas, a short-lived one.

Fanciful thoughts and Christmas magic were no match for Phillippa, who wasted little time snatching away every pleasing fancy the instant she opened her bedchamber door to Stella's knock.

"Where have you been, Estella? Lazy, wicked girl! I've been ringing for you for ages!"

Just like that, everything pleasant about the last half hour—the pink bougainvillea and the tiny lemons, the pond with the water lilies and green eyes the color of spring leaves—withered and died in the face of Phillippa's wrath.

"I beg your pardon, Phillippa. I got lost on my way to your rooms. Hawthorne Castle is an enormous and rather confusing place."

"Silence! I haven't the least interest in your pathetic excuses, Estella. If it happens again you will not enjoy the consequences.

Now, fetch Cornelia's blue walking dress and be quick about it. Lady Lassiter and her daughter have invited us to walk in the gardens with them this afternoon, and I don't wish to keep them waiting."

"Yes, Phillippa." What extraordinary luck! They'd be off again in a trice, and she'd be left at liberty to amuse herself. These were unexpected riches, indeed. Hawthorne Castle was magical, after all!

If she could have hugged Lady Lassiter and her daughter, she would have.

But her heart sank again as soon as she stepped into the bedchamber. "My goodness! What happened?"

Walking dresses, hats, gloves and dinner gowns had been tossed carelessly over the bed, dozens of shoes, walking boots and slippers were scattered in every direction, and one of Cornelia's fine linen shifts had been flung over a lampshade.

"Another of Cornelia's tantrums." Beatrice was seated in the window seat, a book open in her lap, but she looked up at Stella with a wince. "She's made a bit of a mess, I'm afraid."

A bit of a mess? For pity's sake, it looked as if Cornelia's trunk had exploded and spewed its contents over every available surface.

Amidst all this chaos stood Cornelia, her hands clenched into fists and her face stained with tears. The blue walking dress was lying in a crumpled heap at her feet. "I don't *want* the blue walking dress! No one is wearing that shade of peacock this season!"

"Nonsense." Phillippa gave a brisk clap of her hands. "You will wear the blue, and I don't want to hear another word about it. Well, Stella? What are you waiting for? Help Cornelia dress!"

It was no easy task, dressing Cornelia. She'd sooner try and dress a feral animal.

But after a great deal of shrieking, another torrent of hysterical tears and a rather nasty scratch on Stella's arm, Cornelia was properly outfitted.

"You will not stir from this room until we return." Phillippa turned at the bedchamber door to give Stella a menacing look. "Not a single step, Estella. If I discover you have disobeyed me, the repercussions will be dire, indeed. Do you understand me?"

"Yes, Phillippa." The lie slid easily off Stella's tongue.

Phillippa sniffed. "For your sake, I certainly hope so. Come, girls." With that final threat, Phillippa sailed out the door, Cornelia at her heels.

But Beatrice paused on her way out to whisper, "I overheard one of the footmen say dinner will be eight courses tonight. It's certain to drag on for hours. If you did pop out for a bit then, no one would ever know."

She didn't have the least intention of obeying Phillippa's order, but she wouldn't confess it to Beatrice, who'd be punished as surely as Stella would if Phillippa found out. "No, I daresay they wouldn't, but your mother said to remain here."

"My mother says a lot of things. Obeying her every command hasn't gotten you very far, has it? It's something to think about, Stella." Beatrice didn't wait for an answer but marched out the door with a rustle of pink silk.

That was strange. Beatrice had always been kinder to her than Phillippa or Cornelia, but she'd never advised outright defiance before.

But there was no time to think on it now. They'd be back soon enough and demanding she begin the laborious process of dressing them for dinner, and Phillippa would have her head if she wasn't right here waiting for them.

She didn't have much time. No more than an hour or so.

There wasn't a moment to waste.

She hurried up the staircase to her bedchamber and unearthed the bundle she'd hidden under her bed. It wasn't anything fancy, just an old flour sack that Mrs. Neville had given her, but there was treasure inside.

At least, to her it was treasure.

She upended the sack, and bits of fabric spilled across the coverlet. There were a few short lengths of plain muslin, a scrap of sprigged cotton, and some other bits and pieces that were too small to be of much use.

Phillippa had ordered her to discard the scraps in the rag bag, but she'd kept them instead. It was a small rebellion, to be sure, but if Phillippa ever discovered she'd taken them . . . an icy shudder went through her.

It was best not to dwell on such unpleasantness.

She sifted through the meager pile, searching for the length of netting left over from the fichu she'd made for Beatrice last spring.

Ah yes, here it was.

Would it work? She tested the sheer, finely woven fabric against her palm, then held it up to the late afternoon sunlight coming through the window.

Yes, this would do nicely. There wasn't much left, but it was enough.

A snip here and there, a few passes with her sewing needle, and she was finished. She stuffed the netting into her pocket and flew back down the stairs. By the time she'd finished tidying Phillippa's bedchamber her stepmother and sisters had returned from their walk.

She only had to get them dressed for dinner, that was all, and then her time would be her own.

It didn't go smoothly, of course. It never did, not with Phillippa complaining and nitpicking every detail, and Cornelia disintegrating into angry tears at every turn.

But the weight of the folded length of netting in her pocket was like a talisman against the despair that usually plagued her at such times.

Which was silly of her, really.

It was a small enough thing, that length of net, and hardly worth all the importance she was attaching to it, but it was a rare moment when she had the chance to offer anything to anyone.

When was the last time she'd given a gift to someone? It was so long ago, she couldn't recall it, but it felt as if she were the one being given a precious gift, instead of giving one to someone else.

It was this castle. There was something special about it. She couldn't put into words what it was, but she'd felt it the instant her foot touched the drive, as if the castle had gathered her close against it and wrapped its arms around her.

The warmth of it, the comfort was like magic flowing through her veins.

At last, Phillippa, Cornelia and Beatrice were outfitted in their finery, and there was no denying they looked very well, especially Cornelia. She was dressed in a very pale pink silk that fit her to perfection, and the walk earlier had put lovely color in her cheeks.

Perhaps the duke would marry her. It would be an easy way to be rid of her.

The ladies sallied forth, and just as the door closed behind them, the mantel clock struck the eight o' clock hour.

Dinner had begun.

She eased the bedchamber door open a crack and peeked outside, just in case Phillippa was lying in wait, but the corridor was deserted.

The ground floor was less peaceful, with servants scurrying about with silver platters and chafing dishes in their hands, but they were far too busy to pay any attention to her as she descended the staircase. She ducked into the corridor that led to the conservatory without anyone sparing her so much as a glance.

My, how thrilling this was! She'd never had a clandestine meeting with a handsome gentleman before.

By the time she reached the conservatory she was a bit late, but Mr. Ambrose was there, waiting for her, pacing from one end of the conservatory to the other, his brow furrowed. He looked almost grim, but when he saw her hovering uncertainly in the doorway the furrow vanished, and his face lit up with pleasure.

"There you are, Miss Harley! I was afraid you'd changed your mind."

"Good evening, Mr. Ambrose. I beg your pardon for my tardiness. Miss Cornelia's curls weren't cooperating."

"Far be it for me to naysay Miss Cornelia's curls. You're here now, and I am content."

He smiled at her, his green eyes twinkling, and goodness, what a smile he had! Surely there wasn't a lady alive who failed to blush when he turned the warmth of that smile on them.

She hurried toward him, the beekeeping veil she'd made for him in her pocket, her heart strangely aflutter. Which was ridiculous, of course. There was no reason she should be nervous. It was just a bit of netting, not a pocketful of gold coins.

Mr. Ambrose likely wouldn't spare it a second glance.

Yet she wanted him to have it, all the same. It had been ages since anyone outside of Phillippa's household had spoken to her, but he had, and he'd been kind to her. It only seemed right to return his goodwill.

She fingered the folded net in her pocket, her cheeks heating.

Oh, dear. It had seemed a harmless enough gesture this afternoon, but perhaps she shouldn't give him a gift, after all. Why, she hardly knew this man! A proper young lady didn't offer a gift to a man she'd met only once.

She may not be a proper young lady any longer, but she had been one, once upon a time. Had she already forgotten the manners her father had taken such pains to teach her?

The gift aside, it was highly improper for her to be here alone with him. Surely, he must know it, too?

But if Mr. Ambrose was scandalized by her brazenness, she couldn't tell it by looking at him. He didn't appear scandalized or even displeased. Far from it. He was beaming at her, those full, handsome lips curved in a grin that made her belly do somersaults.

Somersaults, for pity's sake, when it had never once somersaulted before.

What was happening to her? Had her wits finally deserted her?

"Shall we begin here in the conservatory, Miss Harley? I know I promised to take you to the formal gardens, but it's rather cold this evening. Perhaps we can see them tomorrow morning, instead?"

It wasn't likely she'd be able to escape Phillippa again so soon, but it hardly mattered to her where they went. When you'd been nowhere, everywhere was an adventure. "Oh, yes. I've never seen anything like it before, and I should like to see the rest of it."

"Wonderful." He held out his arm. "Shall we, then?"

"Yes, indeed, only I, ah . . . well, you see, I brought something for you," she blurted, and then instantly wanted to sink into the floor. It was bad enough she'd brought a man she hardly knew a gift, but for pity's sake, did she have to appear so eager about it?

"Did you, indeed? I'm intrigued, Miss Harley. What is it?"

"Nothing terribly exciting, I'm afraid, but I hope you might get some use out of it." She tugged the beekeeping veil from her pocket and unceremoniously pushed it into his hands. "There you are. Shall we go?"

She whirled around, turning her back on him before her face

had a chance to erupt in actual flames, but he caught her elbow and turned her gently around to face him again. "Wait, Miss Harley. You can't go until you've told me about this gift." He unfolded the piece of netting and stared down at it. "What is it, exactly?"

"It's a face covering, for when you're working with your bees. A beekeeping veil, of sorts." She nodded at the bit of netting. "It looked as if that woven face covering was difficult to see through. I thought this might be better."

He didn't reply at once but stood there staring at the netting spread over his hand.

She shifted from one foot to the other as the silence went on.

And on, and on, stretching into seeming infinity.

This had been a mistake, a most grievous mistake. "I daresay it was silly of me. I know nothing about beekeeping, after all."

Had anything ever been as mortifying as this? She began to edge toward the door, all thoughts of touring the conservatory vanishing.

"Wait, Miss Harley. A moment, if you would." Finally, he looked up, his gaze meeting hers. "You made this . . . for me?"

"It's nothing at all, I assure you. I already had the netting. I'm quite handy with a needle. It didn't take any time at all."

He weighed the netting in his palm. "But this is wonderful!"

"Do you really think so?" Her heart skipped a beat at the warmth in his expression. "Will it make a proper face covering, then?"

"I don't see why not. It's sheer enough to be transparent, but thick enough to protect my face from a sting. How does it work? Do I wear it over my head?"

"No, I designed it to be sewn into the hood, so as not to encumber the beekeeper with so much fabric." She took the netting from him and ran her finger over the thick band of cotton she'd sewed along one edge. "A few stitches here, and it should be sturdy enough."

"Remarkable," he murmured, then added quietly, "How kind you are, Miss Harley."

They stood there for a silent moment, each awkwardly avoiding the other's eyes, but then he drew in a deep breath. "Shall we try it, then? I mean, if you have time tomorrow morning, of course. I don't wish to disturb the bees now."

She *didn't* have time. There was no one in the world more vicious than Phillippa when she was obliged to wait for anything at all, yet somehow she couldn't make a refusal leave her lips.

Surely, a short meeting would be all right. Phillippa and her stepsisters never rose before the fashionable hour. She awoke far earlier than they did. She could meet Mr. Ambrose then.

Her eagerness had nothing to do with him, of course. Not at all. She simply wanted to see if her idea would work.

She gave him a shy glance. "I daresay I can spare a moment or two tomorrow morning."

"Wonderful!" Without another word he plopped the face net over his head and peered at her through it, his thick, full eyelashes catching on the rough fabric. "Perfect visibility! Well done, Miss Harley."

She bit her lip, trying her best not to swell with pride, but she wasn't accustomed to such effusive praise—or any praise, since her father had died—and it was more difficult than it should be. "I'm glad of it, Mr. Ambrose, but perhaps we should wait and see if you get stung before we celebrate."

"I daresay this will surprise you, but I rarely get stung. Stinging is a defensive maneuver, and I take care to make certain my bees never feel threatened."

"I see. The happiest bees make the tastiest honey, then?"

He laughed, the merry sound echoing around them. "Scientifically speaking, there is no evidence of that, but between you and me, Miss Harley?" He lowered his voice and beckoned her closer.

She went without a second thought, the sweet, earthy scent of him stealing her breath. "Yes, Mr. Ambrose?"

"Between you and me, Hawthorne Castle does the best figgy pudding in Dumfriesshire. There's only one thing that separates it from every other figgy pudding in Scotland."

"Let me guess. The honey?"

"The honey." He took her arm and drew it through his elbow. "Come, Miss Harley. The conservatory awaits."

CHAPTER 6

"Christmas Eve is upon us, Your Grace."

"So it is, Rowan." The past weeks had flown by in the blink of an eye. It seemed like only yesterday he and Rowan were debating whether the blue superfine coat was preferable to the bottle green.

If anyone had told him then what the next two weeks would hold, he'd have said they were mad. Shouldn't it take more than two weeks for a life to irrevocably change?

Before the house party, he would have said yes, but if the last fortnight had proved anything, it was that he was a perfect fool.

He gazed down at the drive below his bedchamber window. There were no carriages there today, no young ladies with mountains of baggage, and no horses stamping their hooves, the bells on their bridles ringing merrily in the crisp winter air.

The drive was empty, silent, deserted.

Why wasn't he pleased? It wasn't as if he'd *wanted* to have a house party. Yet he *wasn't* pleased. He was most decidedly displeased, and he didn't know why.

He was merely out of sorts, that was all. He'd woken to a gloomy, overcast day, the sky threatening snow, and he'd only grown more morose as the morning gave way to the afternoon.

It was too quiet. The castle was throbbing with silence.

How was a man meant to escape his own thoughts when he was surrounded by such confounded silence? They chased each other around in circles inside his head, like a buzzard circling a lifeless carcass.

Ah, such pleasing reflections! Was it any wonder he was morose?

But one thing was certain. This ridiculous melancholy had nothing at all to do with his house party coming to an end. Why would that upset him? God knew he'd been dreading the cursed thing, and now it was over, at last.

By this time tomorrow, his guests would be gone.

That was reason enough to celebrate, surely?

To be fair, the house party hadn't been *quite* the fortnight of torment he'd imagined it would be. There may have been a few moments here and there when he'd even enjoyed himself.

Perhaps even more than a few.

"In case you had any doubts, Your Grace, your guests had a wonderful time these past two weeks. I believe we can say your house party was a great success."

"If it was a success, we have you to thank for it, Rowan. You make an admirable duke." He hadn't seen much of Rowan these past weeks, but when they did happen to cross paths, Rowan seemed to be enjoying himself. "It's not as tedious as you imagined, being a duke."

Rowan had been buffing Gabriel's evening pumps to a blinding gloss, but his hand stilled, the buffing cloth still clutched in his fingers. "A counterfeit duke, Your Grace."

There was an uncharacteristic flatness in Rowan's tone that made Gabriel turn from the window. "Are you all right, Rowan?" The man looked a little peaked, and his cravat was a touch askew, which was unheard of for his fastidious valet.

"Of course, Your Grace." Rowan renewed his attack on the pumps, avoiding Gabriel's eyes. "Why wouldn't I be?"

"I couldn't say." That wasn't entirely true. He had his suspicions, but Rowan had been as tight-lipped as Gabriel had ever seen him. "I saw you walking the grounds with a young lady yesterday afternoon."

Rowan froze, then resumed buffing with enough vigor to strip the leather right off Gabriel's pumps.

"Nothing to say about this young lady, Rowan?" Perhaps a little nudge was in order. "You haven't been yourself this past week. I thought she might have something to do with it."

Rowan hesitated, then set his brush aside with a sigh. "Beatrice Featherstone."

"Lady Featherstone's daughter?" Now that *was* a surprise.

He'd overheard two of his servants whispering about the Featherstones the other day, and they hadn't had anything complimentary to say about Phillippa Featherstone. The word 'harridan' had come up more than once.

"Her younger daughter, yes. But Beatrice is nothing at all like her mother and elder sister." Rowan was too much of a gentleman to elaborate on that point, but his shudder gave him away. "She's clever, and funny and . . . well, a bit odd, really, but charming in her own way."

Was Rowan . . . glowing? By God, he was. As soon as he said the lady's name, his face lit up like a sky filled with stars. "My God, man. You're in love with Beatrice Featherstone, aren't you?"

"It doesn't matter if I am or not, Your Grace."

"For God's sake, Rowan, of course it does! Love matters more than anything."

"I don't disagree, Your Grace, but there is no possible chance of a future between myself and Miss Beatrice." Rowan shrugged, but his voice wasn't quite steady when he said, "She thinks I'm the Duke of Hawthorne."

There was no accusation in Rowan's voice, no blame, but his words cut through Gabriel as surely as if Rowan had plunged a dagger into his heart.

Why had it never occurred to him that Rowan might fall in love?

Because he'd only been thinking of himself, of course. He'd behaved abominably. "I've made liars of us both, haven't I, Rowan?"

"You never intended to hurt anyone, Your Grace. You couldn't have known how it would turn out."

"Always unfailingly loyal, Rowan."

He hadn't known, no, but that didn't change the facts.

This entire debacle was *his* fault. The lies, the schemes, the counterfeit duke. All of it. Now Rowan's heart was broken, and likely Beatrice Featherstone's, too, all because of his selfishness and cowardice.

And what of Stella's heart? Her lovely, warm, open, trusting heart?

He'd known who she was the first day she came to Hawthorne Castle. The beekeeping veil she'd made for him had been a gesture of pure kindness, and she'd made it for Mr. Ambrose, the duke's lowly gardener, and not for the Duke of Hawthorne.

Everyone was kind to a duke, after all.

He couldn't give her up. He *wouldn't*. She was holding his heart right in the center of her dainty pink palm.

He had to fix this. For Stella, and Rowan, and yes, even for Beatrice Featherstone.

For himself, too. He was the Duke of Hawthorne, and it was time he started behaving like it. Nothing would ever be good or happy or true again until he did.

"Don't despair yet, Rowan." He leapt to his feet. "I've made a terrible mess of this, but I'm going to put it right again. I promise it."

Rowan blanched. "*How*, Your Grace?"

"I will pretend I didn't notice that wince, Rowan. Never mind the details. All I ask is that you appear at the ball tonight as the Duke of Hawthorne, and I will take care of the rest. Do you have one final performance in you?"

"I daresay I can manage it, Your Grace."

"Good man. I have a few things to do this afternoon, but I'll be back here in time to prepare for the ball."

"You plan to attend the ball tonight as well, Your Grace?"

"Of course, Rowan. Have you forgotten I'm meant to announce my duchess's name tonight? I wouldn't miss it for the world."

The days had passed in a happy haze of honeybees and flowering hawthorn, leisurely strolls among blooming beds of white Christmas roses, and before Stella knew it, Christmas Eve had arrived.

The duke would select his bride at tonight's ball, and her time here would come to an end. They would leave for Chester tomorrow morning, and life would go on much as it had before she knew a place as magical as Hawthorne Castle existed.

Her father was still gone. She was still trapped under Phillippa's thumb. On the surface, nothing had changed. She was still a servant, her fingertips rough from repeated pinpricks.

But the heart that beat underneath her shabby clothing had awoken at last.

She was not the person she'd been two weeks earlier. How could she be? Her heart was irrevocably changed, transformed. She would never be the same lady she'd once been.

It was this place. Somehow, in just a few short weeks, Hawthorne Castle had become a home to her. She couldn't say when it had happened, or why.

Was it the scent of the evergreens in the entryway, or the cinnamon wafting from the kitchens? Was it the low, comforting buzz of Mr. Ambrose's honeybees, busy with their morning's work? Perhaps it was something as simple as the afternoon sun streaming through the stained-glass windows, throwing rainbows of colorful light around the conservatory.

Or was it easy laughter, and twinkling green eyes?

It was none of those things, and all of them, at once.

It was a fairy tale, come true at last.

But like all fairy tales it was ending, and the time had come to bid Mr. Ambrose goodbye.

It had taken her ages to escape Phillippa's clutches this afternoon. She didn't make it to the conservatory until after two o' clock, and there was no sign of Mr. Ambrose. Aside from the honeybees buzzing happily in their skeps, the conservatory was deserted.

Perhaps he was taken up with preparations for the evening's festivities, as she had been. Phillippa and Cornelia had certainly kept her busy. First it was a dozen rows of additional lace for Cornelia's ball gown. Then Phillippa had demanded she add more beading to her green velvet ball gown, and then Cornelia's white ribbons had gone missing . . .

It was one task after the next, almost as if they were trying to keep her occupied, but at last, she'd managed to slip downstairs while

Phillippa and her stepsisters were engaged in a game of charades with the other guests in the drawing room.

She perched on the edge of a settee, but her heart was sinking with every minute that passed. Oh, why hadn't she made time to come early this morning? She could have come down to the conservatory early in the morning, before Phillippa woke, and bidden goodbye to Mr. Ambrose.

How could she leave Hawthorne Castle without seeing him one more time? It was unfair, unbearable—

"Miss Harley! Good afternoon. I was hoping I'd find you here."

She jumped to her feet, and there, as if she'd conjured him from thin air, was Mr. Ambrose, coming toward her from the other end of the conservatory. "Were you really? I mean, good afternoon, Mr. Ambrose."

"Good afternoon." He ducked his head, his cheeks reddening. "I already said that, didn't I?"

"I don't mind hearing it twice." Oh dear, now *she* was blushing, too. They were like a pair of besotted schoolchildren.

Not that she was *besotted* with Mr. Ambrose. Of course she wasn't. She'd never do something so silly as to become besotted with the Duke of Hawthorne's gardener, for pity's sake.

"Besotted" was entirely too strong a word, but she was . . . fond of him.

Fond, yes. That was much better.

Quite fond, in fact. Very fond, even.

Very well, she was inordinately and irrevocably fond of Mr. Ambrose. What of it? It wasn't as if she had any other friends. It was only natural that she should feel an overwhelming, er . . . fondness for him.

"It occurred to me last night, Miss Harley, that I haven't yet taken you to see the ancient Glastonbury thorn on the western side of the property, and I did say I would. It's a bit blustery outside, but if you still wish to see it, we could—"

"I do wish to see it, Mr. Ambrose." Goodness, why was she so breathless?

He smiled, his green eyes crinkling at the corners. "Shall we go, then?"

He draped his coat over her shoulders and held out his arm to her in a gesture that had become so familiar over the past weeks that she took it without a second thought. He led her out of the conservatory and through the dormant formal gardens to a pathway that wound toward the back of the castle.

She closed her eyes and inhaled the cold, fresh air. It smelled like the snow that had just begun to fall, the wintry scent of it tickling her nose. They didn't speak, but his arm was warm and sturdy beneath her fingers, the rhythmic crunch of their footsteps on the gravel pathway like a clock ticking away the last of her time at Hawthorne Castle.

How odd, that walking beside him should feel so natural, as if they'd walked this path together hundreds of times, and would do so again, another hundred times hereafter.

It was a foolish fancy of hers, but it felt as if she'd known him forever.

"Here we are, Miss Harley. The famous Hawthorne Castle Glastonbury thorn."

She kept her eyes closed for an instant after he spoke. If she could only linger in this moment for a little longer, stop time while the winter sun was warm on her face and his deep, rich voice was in her ears, she'd have this memory right at her fingertips whenever she needed it.

"Miss Harley?"

"Yes?"

He leaned close, his warm breath stirring the hair at her temple. "If you want to see it, you'll have to open your eyes."

"Yes, of course. How clever you are, Mr. Ambrose."

She opened her eyes, and not ten feet in front of her was an enormous tree with a constellation of tiny white flowers in such riotous bloom it looked as if the branches were dusted with a layer of snow. "Oh, how pretty! I didn't expect it would be in bloom."

"This type of hawthorn blooms at Christmastime. It's a magnificent old tree, isn't it?"

"It is, indeed." The trunk was a bit gnarled, and the entire tree leaned toward the castle as if seeking protection from the thick stone walls, but it was a grand old tree with its stately trunk and spreading branches and the dainty little flowers like a spinster's white lace cap atop its head.

"I've yet to find another Glastonbury thorn as tall as this one." He nodded at the tree. "It reaches past the windows on the uppermost floor."

"It's quite . . ." She paused, her gaze catching on one of the windows as the first light snowflakes fell from the sky, wetting her cheeks. The branches rested directly against the glass, as if the tree were attempting to reach whoever was on the other side. "I believe you said this is the western wing of the castle?"

"Yes. This tree loves the light, and it gets as much uninterrupted sun here as a tree can reasonably expect in Scotland. I daresay that's one of the reasons it grew so tall."

"That's my bedchamber! The last window on the left, just there. How marvelous!" There was no reason she should be so delighted, but it was a barren, lonely room, and somehow the tree being just beneath her window cheered her.

"That can't be your bedchamber." Mr. Ambrose was staring up at the window, a dark frown marring his brow. "I think you must be mistaken. Those are the attic windows."

"Yes, I know. My bedchamber is in the attic."

There was a long silence, then, "Lady Featherstone requires you to sleep in the attic?"

Oh, no. He looked utterly thunderstruck. She'd said too much.

"Well, yes. It's not as if I expect silken sheets and thick Aubusson carpets. I'm a servant, Mr. Ambrose. I'm not anyone special."

"Yes, you are. You *are* special, Miss Harley."

He gazed down at her with fierce green eyes, but the large hands that closed over her shoulders were heartbreakingly gentle. "You're clever and amusing and one of the kindest ladies I've ever known."

She unfurled like a flower starved for sunlight at his praise, but after suffering Phillippa's endless barbs and merciless castigations she couldn't quite make herself believe his words. "I-I am?"

Could it be that after two years of aching loneliness and deprivations, some part of the girl she'd once been still lingered? Under the shabby clothing and raw hands, was a tiny part of her heart still beating?

"You are." He closed this distance between them, cupping her chin in his palm. "You're beautiful, Stella."

A thousand words rushed to her lips, but she never got the chance to say them.

He brushed his thumb over her lower lip, his touch lingering, and gazed down at her as if transfixed by the sight of his darker skin against her pale pink lips.

Then slowly, slowly, he lowered his mouth to hers.

Chapter 7

The kiss was shy at first, a tentative caress as light as the brush of a feather, but the spark of desire between them instantly caught alight, and he couldn't stop himself from taking her lips in a deep, hungry kiss.

"Let me taste you, Stella," he murmured against her mouth. "Will you open for me?"

She met him eagerly when he slipped his tongue into the heaven of her mouth, the soft whimper that left her throat sending a delicious shiver through him. There was nothing in the world he wanted more than to kiss her forever.

So he did. He kissed her again, then again, his lips clinging to hers. She let out another quiet, maddening sigh when she opened her mouth to him, welcoming him into that devastating heat. Their tongues tangled in a slick dance, one kiss blurring into the next until his head was swimming with dizzying pleasure.

When she twined her arms around his neck and pressed closer, her breasts against his chest, he ceased to think at all and gave in to the soft pressure of her lips against his and the maddening sensation of having her in his arms at last.

It should have ended with a kiss, but her inexperience and his restraint were no match for the heat that erupted between them the moment their lips met. The passion between them had been simmering and building for days, and now she was all he knew, all he could see.

There was nothing in the world like the give of her plump bottom lip against his, her fingers in his hair, the delicious languor in his limbs and the explosion of heat in his belly. He shouldn't be holding her like this, shouldn't be kissing her. He had dozens of guests roaming his castle, and any one of them might come upon them at any moment and catch him with Stella in his arms.

But rationality was no match for the passion between them. Nothing mattered except Stella and the brush of her lips against his, the subtle arch of her body as she tried to get closer, the restless tug of her fingers in his hair and their mingled panting breaths.

How many times had he dreamed of this moment? How many times since their first meeting in the conservatory had he imagined kissing her, holding her? He'd dreamt of her every night since she'd come to Hawthorne Castle and awoken every morning thinking of her.

She was the one he'd been waiting for. He'd known it since the moment he'd seen her face turned up to his as she stood on the drive below his bedchamber, and with every day that passed he'd only grown more certain.

She was *his*. Kissing her felt like coming home at last.

He might have missed this. He might have gone his whole life without finding her. He might never have met her, never have held her in his arms, and there would forever have been an empty place in his heart where Estella Harley should have been.

She sighed against his mouth, and his heart jumped in his chest at the soft puff of her warm breath against his damp lips. He broke the kiss, her protesting whimper going straight to his cock, and trailed his lips down the smooth, pale skin of her throat.

Dear God, she was sweet. The sweetest thing he'd ever tasted.

He needed her closer, as close as she could be.

He couldn't get enough of the softness of her skin, the silky tangle of her hair in his hands, the delicate citrus scent of her that put him in mind of blooming magnolias. It was more concentrated in that maddening space behind her ear and in the tempting hollow of her throat.

Was every part of her as sweet as her lips? Was the long, graceful line of her neck as silky as it appeared, as delicious? That place at her waist just as it gave way to the swell of her hips, her slender wrists and dainty fingers enthralled him.

It would take a lifetime of exploring her to do her justice, and there was nothing he wanted more than to lay her on his bed and take his time learning every inch of her.

Would she cry out for him when he touched her?

"I've dreamed of you, Stella." Day after day, he'd lost himself in his fevered imaginings of her standing before him, breathless and with the flush of arousal on her fair skin.

He brushed his lips over hers again, a rumble of satisfaction rising in his chest as she rose onto her tiptoes to get closer, meeting him halfway and sliding her hands down to his forearms to steady herself.

Her kiss-swollen mouth had darkened from pale pink to cherry red, and he couldn't resist sucking her generous lower lip into his mouth, so sweet and red and plump. He couldn't resist sucking and nibbling on it, coaxing sighs and gasps from her.

It was a miracle that he'd found her, a miracle that they were here together, and he wouldn't squander it. "May I . . . let me . . . wrap your arms around my neck, Stella."

She did as he bade her and he took her mouth in deep, drugging kisses, his desire ratcheting higher as she tangled her tongue with his. His hands flew to her waist, and he held her tightly against him as he plundered her mouth, his tongue tracing the delicate bow of her upper lip.

"Is this all right, love?"

"Yes." Her fingers sifted through his hair. "More, please."

How could he ever deny such a breathless plea?

He couldn't. He could do nothing but press closer, his lips skimming over her neck before settling in the warm hollow of her throat, her pulse beating frantically against his tongue as he tasted her.

God, he wanted to touch her everywhere, bare every inch of her skin so he might worship her as she deserved, but they were out in the open on the castle grounds. If someone should happen to glance out a window . . .

She was an innocent and a guest in his home.

Good Lord, what was he doing? He was no rogue, no debaucher of innocent young ladies.

He must release her at once.

And he would, in another moment, but first he'd taste the skin of her throat and neck once more, and . . . dear God, he'd never seen collarbones as perfect as hers. He brushed a fingertip over one, his gaze darting to her face when she gave an involuntary shiver.

He traced her other collarbone then dipped lower, his fingertips drifting over the satiny skin between her breasts, his eyes closing at the warmth of her, the softness. He'd been with other ladies, but nothing compared to her.

It was as if she had been created for him alone.

But she wasn't his. Not yet, and so with a restraint that should have qualified him for sainthood, he set her gently away from him.

"Mr. Ambrose?" She swayed toward him, her lovely blue eyes hazy with desire, and he was obliged to clench his hands into fists to stop himself from snatching her right back into his arms.

But if he did, he'd never let her go.

"Gabriel." He brushed golden strands of hair from her cheek, smiling down at her as he tucked it behind her ear. "Gabriel Christopher Ambrose."

Soon, he'd tell her his full name. He'd tell her *everything*.

Soon, but not quite yet.

"Gabriel." She rolled the name on her tongue, tasting it. "It suits you."

"Hmmm." He rested his forehead against hers. "Will you dance with me tonight, Stella?"

"At the ball?" Her face dimmed. "There's nothing I would love more than to dance with you, but I can't possibly attend the ball. Lady Featherstone—"

"Shh." He pressed a finger to her lips. "Not at the ball. In the conservatory, this evening. Will you come to me here as soon as you're at liberty? Please, Stella?"

He was meant to dance the first dance with the lady he'd chosen as his duchess. He'd chosen her. She would be his duchess, and no other lady would take her place tonight.

"Yes." She smiled at him. "I'll dance with you."

"Tonight, then." He didn't trust himself anywhere near her lips, so he pressed a chaste kiss to her forehead. "Until then."

He'd confess the truth to her tonight. All of it. His name, his title, everything.

If all went well . . .

His first dance, and every dance from this moment on, would be hers.

Stella skipped up the stairs as if she were walking on air.

Tonight, she would dance with Mr. Ambrose, and—

No, not Mr. Ambrose, but Gabriel, like the angel. It was an extravagantly romantic thought, but if a lady couldn't be extravagantly romantic when she was in love, when could she?

She could deny it no longer. She was in love with Gabriel Christopher Ambrose.

The guests were still playing charades when she passed the drawing room, and there was no sign of Phillippa or Stella's stepsisters in their bedchamber, so she drifted up to her attic room, dozens of delightful thoughts unfolding in her head as she made her way down the corridor.

If only she had a proper gown to wear tonight! One that would billow around her in a graceful arc as Gabriel led her through a dance—

"Well, Estella, here you are at last. I've been waiting for you for an age."

"Phillippa." Stella stumbled to a stop, her heart leaping into her throat. What in the world was Phillippa doing, lying in wait outside her bedchamber door?

"You're a clever girl, Estella." Phillippa eyed her calmly, as if her sudden appearance in the servants' quarters was the most natural thing in the world. "I don't deny it. But you're not as clever as you think you are."

Stella lifted her chin. She knew better than to challenge Phillippa. She'd learned that lesson mere days after her father's death. He hadn't yet been cold in his grave before she was ordered from her bedchamber in the family wing to a bare, chilly room set deep among the rafters, far away from the rest of the family. All her pretty gowns and shoes had been taken from her and replaced with a coarse linen pinafore.

Overnight, she'd gone from being her father's beloved daughter to a servant in her own home. Since then, she'd become a master at holding her tongue.

But no longer. Words burned in her throat, and then they were tumbling from her lips. "I haven't the vaguest idea what you're talking about, Phillippa."

"No? How curious." Phillippa smiled, her teeth gleaming in the meager light coming from the window at the end of the hallway. "Why, it's just this, my dear. Do you know the name of that gentleman you were so shamelessly kissing in the garden just now?"

Phillippa had been spying on her? The blood rushed from Stella's head with a violence that left her chilled and shaking.

This was bad. It was very, very bad.

"I'd be happy to enlighten you, Estella."

A shiver darted down Stella's back at her stepmother's amused tone. She'd heard that note of suppressed glee enough times to be wary of it. She pressed closer to the wall, instinctively protecting her back. "Of course I know his name. He's Mr. Ambrose, the Duke of Hawthorne's gardener."

"Is that what he told you?" Phillippa threw her head back in a laugh. "You poor child. How foolishly naïve you are. That gentleman is no more a gardener than I'm a coachman."

Stella stood silently, waiting. Phillippa had always taken great pleasure in toying with her, just as a cat did with a mouse before it strikes the killing blow.

"That gentleman, Estella," Phillippa announced with a triumphant sneer, "is none other than the Duke of Hawthorne himself."

Stella froze, her mind going blank aside from the one word echoing in her head.

No. It couldn't be true.

Mr. Ambrose—Gabriel—the Duke of Hawthorne? No. It was impossible.

Wasn't it?

Yes, of course it was. If Mr. Ambrose were really the duke, every young lady attending this house party wouldn't have given him a moment's peace.

Unless they didn't know, but that would mean Gabriel had lied to them all.

No. He would never do something so devious, so underhanded. Phillippa was just being cruel. "If Mr. Ambrose is the duke, who is the gentleman with the auburn hair who claims to be the Duke of Hawthorne?"

"He's the duke's valet, a man by the name of Walter Rowan. Rather gentlemanly, isn't he? For a servant, that is. I suppose the duke must have asked him to engage in a bit of charades, and naturally this Rowan wouldn't dare refuse the duke."

"How?" Stella whispered. "How did you find out?"

"Oh, I have my ways, Estella. Servants are never as discreet as one might wish. A quick visit to the portrait gallery confirmed my suspicions. The previous dukes' portraits are hanging in there, and none of them looks at all like Mr. Rowan." Phillippa leaned closer, her eyes gleaming with malice. "But they all bear a striking resemblance to your Mr. Ambrose. If you don't believe me, go and see for yourself."

She didn't need to see it for herself. Phillippa was far too satisfied for it to be otherwise.

Gabriel had lied to her. Not a small, harmless lie either, but an egregious, hurtful one, the sort of lie that broke a lady's heart.

He must have been playing with her all along, from their first meeting in the conservatory the day she'd arrived at Hawthorne Castle. He'd taken one look at her, and he'd chosen to lie to her.

Dear God, she was going to be sick. She pressed a hand to her stomach as bile flooded her throat.

"I see I've shocked you. A pity, but you've no one to blame for this but yourself, Estella." Phillippa tutted. "Such ridiculous credulity! It's quite tragic, really."

Stella hardly heard her. The dozens of questions tearing through her head drowned out everything else. Why would he play such a cruel trick on her? What could he hope to gain from it? She had nothing to give him, nothing to offer.

It didn't make any sense.

"Tell me, Estella. Why do you suppose a duke would go to all the trouble to lie to an insignificant personage such as yourself? A lady's maid, and a shabby one at that." Phillippa's gaze swept over her, an ugly sneer twisting her lips. "I can only think of one reason a duke would chase a servant."

One reason. Stella pressed her fingers to lips still tender from Gabriel's kisses.

There could be no mistaking Phillippa's meaning.

"Alas, it's a tale as old as time, and from what I saw in the garden just now, you've been happily obliging him since we arrived."

"I didn't . . . I never—"

"Silence!"

Stella's lips closed. What was there to say? Not a thing.

Phillippa closed in on her, pinning her against the wall. "Make no mistake, my dear. Two days from now, Cornelia, Beatrice and I will embark on our return journey to Chester. As for you, I'm afraid you're destined for Bridewell Prison. I believe that's where they take female thieves."

"Thief! I'm no thief!" For pity's sake, had Phillippa gone mad?

"But you are, Estella. You've been stealing muslin and thread, among other things. There's no point in denying it. I found the flour sack stuffed with your ill-gotten prizes under your bed."

"Bits and pieces destined for the rag bag only!" Dear God, this was a nightmare.

"I don't see what difference that makes. Stealing is stealing, and thieves go to prison."

Without warning, Phillippa wrenched the bedchamber door open and with one hard push she shoved Stella over the threshold. She lost her balance and fell to her knees, Phillippa looming over her.

"Why?" Stella whispered, the word scraping her throat. "Why do you hate me so much?"

"Because you're nothing special, Estella, and it sickens me that such a fuss has always been made over you. It was the same with your mother, you know. Lovely, kind and perfect Caroline Harley! She was the light of every eye, and the belle of every ball. She stole your father from me. Did you know that? I should have been the first Countess Featherstone, not *her*." Phillippa spat the words, her eyes glittering coldly. "But you see the tables are now turned, and it's given me great pleasure to see you brought so low."

Stella stared up at her stepmother, into eyes as cold as ice and a face twisted with fury. This was never going to end, was it? Such hatred as this was a sort of madness, and it would only grow more ruthless, more barbaric as time passed.

"You will therefore remain in this room until the magistrate comes to fetch you, Estella. I don't like to interrupt the man's holidays, however, so it will have to wait until the day after Boxing Day."

"But that's days from now!" Stella cast a stricken glance around the barren room, the thin mattress with the threadbare blanket, the bare, cold floors, and panic swelled in her chest. "You can't keep me locked in this room for three days!"

"On the contrary. I can, and I will. We can't have a thief running about the duke's castle, after all. But not to worry, my dear. I'll see to it you're provided with food and water. When I remember, that is." Phillippa gave her a smile that froze Stella's blood in her veins, then turned to the door.

"Wait!" Stella snatched at a fold of her stepmother's skirts and held on, her knuckles turning white even as she knew it was hopeless. There wasn't a shred of empathy or understanding in Phillippa's face. "You can't just leave me here."

"Of course I can." Phillippa gave her skirt a sharp tug, snatching it from Stella's grip.

Then she was out the door, slamming it closed behind her, the metallic click of the key turning in the lock like a death knell.

Soon enough the faint thud of Phillippa's retreating footsteps gave way to silence, and Stella was left alone.

She stumbled to her feet, her knees shaking, and collapsed on the bed.

Outside the window the sky was darkening, the shadows in the tiny room lengthening. It must be nearly time for the ball to start.

The snow that had begun this morning was still falling, the howling wind blowing against the window and setting the glass rattling. The moon was shrouded by clouds, and not a single star was visible.

It would be pitch black soon enough, and she had no lamp, and no fire.

She'd been alone a great deal over the past two years. Alone in her bedchamber, alone in the garden, and alone in the kitchens, taking her meals by herself.

But never, since her father's passing, had she been as alone as she was right now. What was she to do? She couldn't wait here for days on end only to be hauled off to Bridewell.

Perhaps Phillippa hadn't locked the door properly? It was a slim hope, given that she'd heard the click of the lock engaging, but this was an old castle, with old doors and old locks. If a bit of manhandling could lead to her freedom, wasn't it was worth an attempt?

The door was a massive slab of solid oak. There'd be no battering through it, but the lock . . . yes, if there was a weak spot, that would be it.

She pulled a hairpin from her hair and sank to her knees in front of the door. She'd never picked a lock before, but how difficult could it be?

Quite difficult, as it turned out. Fifteen minutes of poking at the lock got her precisely nothing, aside from a sadly mangled hairpin.

There wasn't any chance she could escape through the door.

There was no other way out. She was trapped, and there wasn't anything to do about it but wait until Phillippa relented or three days passed, and then she'd be dragged off to prison.

She dropped onto the battered stool in front of a rickety, three-legged table. A small looking glass sat atop it, leaning against the wall. It was a poor, cracked thing, no more than a shard. No doubt it had been purloined from another part of the castle by a previous occupant of this room.

The crack bisected the entire surface of the glass like a lightning bolt, dividing her face into two halves and distorting her reflection, but she sat there staring at herself for some time.

She might have kept it up all night if the sound of a carriage arriving in the drive below hadn't roused her. The duke's Christmas ball was about to begin, and here she was, once again watching life unfold from a distance like a forlorn child with her nose pressed against the glass.

It was always thus now, but there'd been a time when she'd been a part of things, a time when she would have spent the evening dancing until she was breathless and her feet ached.

Only two years had passed since then, but it felt like a lifetime ago. She scarcely remembered the carefree girl she'd once been who'd delighted in roaming the grounds with her father at Christmastime, the rhythmic crunch of the snow under their boots. That girl had spent long, cozy hours warbling Christmas carols to her father, and had delighted in making gingerbread at Mrs. Neville's knee.

She'd been happy, once upon a time.

It all seemed like a dream now, one that was fading with every moment she spent under Phillippa's roof. There was no gingerbread now. There was no singing now. No music, no kindness, and no warmth.

Soon enough there'd be nothing left of those memories but hazy fragments, and what would become of her then? Her heart was freezing, one degree at a time. How long would it be before it froze through, and splintered into a thousand tiny, icy shards?

She rose to her feet and went to the bed, leaving her broken reflection behind, and reached under her mattress. Her locket was still there. Phillippa hadn't found it, thank goodness.

She snapped open the lid, and a sigh fell from her lips.

Her father gazed out at her from the left side of the locket, and goodness, how handsome he'd been! He was sitting at his desk, a book spread out in front of him, the afternoon sunlight streaming in from the window behind him lighting up the threads of gold in his hair. His eyes were as blue as the summer sky and twinkling with warmth.

Gabriel's eyes were like her father's. She'd thought so the first time she'd gazed into them, and every time since then. Of course, Gabriel's eyes were green, and nothing like her father's blue, but she'd seen that same twinkling warmth in them.

Perhaps that was why she'd been taken in so completely by him.

Phillippa was right. She *was* a naïve fool.

Except . . . well, weren't the eyes meant to be the windows to the soul? Surely even a duke, as grand and mighty as he was, couldn't feign that sort of warmth in his eyes.

Could there be some other explanation for the lies Gabriel had told her? Perhaps he hadn't set out to trick her at all. It could be that it was all a misunderstanding, but even if it was, what of it?

He was a duke, and she was . . . well, nobody who mattered.

She gazed down at the portrait, her chest tightening at the sight of her own face gazing back at her from the right side of the locket. Her smile had been as bright as her father's, back then. It was the smile of a girl who'd never known a moment of sadness.

Had that really been her, once upon a time? It seemed impossible that she'd ever been that happy, smiling lady.

It wasn't her any longer. There was no carefree smile on the face of the lady staring back at her from the cracked looking glass. No, that lady was pale, her eyes blank and her cheeks too thin.

Two years. In two years Phillippa and Cornelia had reduced her to a shadow of herself. They'd bled her dry until she was nothing more than a husk of the lady she'd once been. What would become of her a year from now? Two? Would there be anything left of her then?

It was still snowing outside. Downy snowflakes gathered in the corners of the window behind her, reflected in the looking glass. It would be a slippery endeavor, climbing out that window. Slippery, and cold.

She wanted to be free of this room, yes, but not if it meant breaking her neck. Hawthorne Castle was a massive old pile, and she was on the uppermost floor. The ground was miles away, so far below that she couldn't even see it from here.

Madness, in other words. Yet was it any less treacherous to stay and endure a slow, inevitable fading away until there was nothing left of her?

She had to get out of this room, this castle, this life she'd fallen into.

She rose to her feet, tucking the locket safely into the neckline of her dress, and as if in a dream she fetched her cloak and donned the thin gloves tucked into the pocket. They wouldn't do her much good, as the wool was nearly worn through, but they were better than nothing.

There, that was the easy part done. Now for the more challenging part.

She gulped in a breath and turned to face the window. Had it always been that small and narrow? Alas, it didn't get any larger as she crept closer until she was standing right in front of it, the cold already making her shiver.

It didn't open easily, but after a good deal of heaving and some rather unladylike cursing she managed to wrench it open an inch or so. Snowflakes swirled around her, dampening the front of her cloak, but this was no time to turn coward. She braced her feet against the floor, closed her eyes and pushed at the window with a strength born of desperation.

Ah, some luck at last! By some miracle, the window lurched open the rest of the way. She braced her hands on the sill, heaved herself up, then somehow she managed to twist about until her belly was resting on the sill and her feet were braced on a branch of the Glastonbury thorn.

Don't look down, don't look down, don't look down . . .

As it turned out, scaling a castle wall was every bit as treacherous as she'd imagined it would be. She'd barely made it a quarter of the way down before her hands froze, and then her feet kept slipping. At one point she was hanging from her hands, her feet scrambling for purchase, and to add insult to injury one of her shoes slipped off her foot and landed with a muted thud in the snow far below her.

She cursed herself for a reckless fool a dozen times over as inch by inch, hand by hand and one foot after the other she made her way down until somehow, damp, shivering and with her heart threatening to beat out of her chest, her feet touched the ground.

She'd done it! Somehow, one small step at a time, she'd gained her freedom, and goodness, how glorious it was!

There was only one problem.

She had no friends, no money, an insufficient cloak, a lost shoe, and no place to go.

Very well, then. She had a multitude of problems.

What was she going to do now?

CHAPTER 8

There was something magical about snow at Christmastime.

Gabriel stood in front of the stained-glass doors in the conservatory, gazing out at the formal gardens covered in a downy blanket of new snow. The worst of the storm had passed, and the flakes drifted from the midnight sky like white rose petals floating on a summer breeze.

It was quiet in the conservatory this evening, the trickle of the fountain splashing gently into the pond the only sound that disturbed the silence. Behind him a dozen lamps glowed in the dim light, their golden halos hazy in the reflection in the glass.

It was perfect, but for one thing. Stella was missing.

He hadn't been concerned by her tardiness at first. She'd been delayed by Lady Featherstone's whims before, but she'd never been as late as this, and he'd seen Lady Featherstone and her daughters enter the ballroom earlier.

Stella was no longer attending them. What, then, could have become of her?

He abandoned his post in front of the doors and paced restlessly from the pond to the citrus trees and back to the pond again, his pocket watch clutched in his hand.

It was ten o'clock. The ball had started nearly an hour ago.

He'd waited long enough. Something was wrong.

He hurried toward the conservatory door. He'd check her bedchamber first, and if she wasn't there, he'd see if any of the servants had seen—

"Good evening, sir! Why, what extraordinary luck that we happened to find you here!"

God above, what the devil were they doing here?

Not a dozen steps away was Lady Featherstone, standing between him and the conservatory door, her elder daughter by her side.

What was the chit's name? Caroline, perhaps, or Cressida.

Of all the people he might have encountered at this moment, Lady Featherstone was the very last one he wished to see.

"This is a lovely conservatory!" Lady Featherstone edged closer, blocking his way out. "My dear Cornelia is excessively fond of plants. She's made a thorough study of them, and insisted we come see your . . . er, that is, the Duke of Hawthorne's lovely . . . tulips."

"Tulips." For a young lady who'd made a thorough study of plants, Cornelia's expression was remarkably vacant. The girl looked as if she didn't know the difference between a tulip and a violet.

"Oh, yes! Cornelia is excessively fond of tulips. Aren't you, Cornelia?"

"Yes, Mamma."

For God's sake, what was the woman on about? "I beg your pardon, madam, but this isn't a convenient time. I have an urgent matter to attend to."

"I'm sure you can spare a few moments for such a lovely plant enthusiast!" Lady Featherstone nudged the girl forward. "Go on, Cornelia, dear."

Lovely plant enthusiast? That was doing it a bit brown. What in the world were the two of them doing here? Why weren't they at the ball like the rest of his guests?

Unless . . . of course!

Somehow, Lady Featherstone had discovered he was the Duke of Hawthorne, and now she was trying to thrust her daughter upon him.

And at the same time, Stella had gone mysteriously missing.

It couldn't be a coincidence.

He took a step toward Lady Featherstone, his hands clenched into fists. "What have you done with Stella, Lady Featherstone?"

"Stella?" Her eyes widened innocently. "I assure you, sir, I haven't the vaguest notion what you're talking about."

"*Stella*, Lady Featherstone. Your lady's maid. Where is she?"

"I don't see what difference it makes." Lady Featherstone raised her chin. "Estella is of no consequence."

"She is of great consequence to me, madam."

Lady Featherstone drew herself up with a huff. "Very well, if you must know, I've locked her in her bedchamber! The girl is a liar and a thief, and I won't have her—"

"The key." He held out his hand. "Give it to me, or I'll see you and your daughter escorted from my castle at once."

Lady Featherstone's mouth dropped open. "There's no need to be—"

"The key to the attic chamber, Lady Featherstone. I won't ask you again."

Lady Featherstone's face twisted with anger, but he was the duke, and this was his castle. There was little she could do but hand over the key.

"Very well. Since you insist upon it, Your Grace." She reached into her reticule, snatched up the key and dropped it into his palm. "You'll soon find out your mistake. There's nothing special about Estella. She's as common as—"

"You promised me, Mamma," Cornelia interrupted. Her lip was trembling, and her cheeks had turned a rather startling shade of red.

Lady Featherstone rounded on her daughter. "Promised you what, you silly girl?"

"That I would become a duchess! You said if we came to Scotland, I would become the Duchess of Hawthorne!"

"For pity's sake, will you hush, Cornelia? Wait, Your Grace!"

But Gabriel had had enough of Lady Featherstone's games, and he didn't wait. He brushed past them without a second glance. He had to get to Stella at once.

Behind him, Cornelia let out a deafening wail, but he didn't stop. The girl was always wailing about something.

"I insist you stop at once, Your Grace!" Lady Featherstone's voice had risen to a hysterical pitch, and she chased after him, dragging Cornelia with her. "My child has been stung by a bee!"

Gabriel turned back to them with a sigh. "Cease that infernal screeching, Miss Cornelia. Loud noises disturb the bees."

"It's too late for that!" Phillippa snapped. "Why, just look at her!"

Cornelia had been stung near her right eye. Her eyelid had turned bright red, and the side of her face was beginning to swell.

As far as Miss Cornelia Featherstone was concerned, the Christmas ball was over, along with any chance she may have had to marry a duke.

Perhaps the chit had finally learned her lesson. "Take Miss Cornelia to her bedchamber. On your way, ask one of the housemaids to bring a cloth and a basin of cold water to your rooms. The compress will bring the swelling down."

"That's it? That's all you have to say?" Lady Featherstone stamped her foot. "What sort of gentleman keeps bees in his conservatory? I demand to know what you intend to do about this!"

God above, had there ever been a more troublesome personage than Lady Featherstone? "Do? Not a blessed thing. The damage has been done."

Lady Featherstone sucked in a deep breath, but before she could launch into a harangue he turned and left her and her sniveling daughter to do as they pleased.

All he could think about was Stella. It had been hours since he'd last seen her. Had she been locked up in her attic prison that entire time?

He took the stairs two at a time, the thud of his footsteps drowned out by the ragged sound of his breath rushing through his head.

Up, up, up he went, flying past the second-floor landing to the back staircase that led to the servants' quarters. It was deserted up here, with the castle's servants scurrying about downstairs for the Christmas Eve ball.

The corridor was silent, not a sound coming from Stella's bedchamber. If she'd been pounding on the door and calling for her freedom, she'd since given up.

It wasn't a good sign.

He didn't pause, nor did he knock. He fitted the key in the door and turned the knob with a wrench. It flew open with a protesting squeal, and he rushed inside. "Stella?"

The word emerged from his lips in a puff of frosty air.

God above, why was it so cold in here? "Stella? Are you here?"

It was a foolish question. The bedchamber was the size of a pocket handkerchief, the only furnishings an iron bed with a miserably thin mattress, and a battered washing stand with a chipped basin on top of it.

Dear God, what a miserable room.

There was no place to hide. If she were here, he'd have seen her at once.

He stood in the middle of the bedchamber, his heart pounding. This didn't make any sense. Where was she? She couldn't have gone out the door. It had been locked from the outside when he got here, and there wasn't any other way out of the bedchamber, so how . . .

The window. It was wide open, the tattered drapes billowing in the wind.

No, it was impossible. Hawthorne Castle was forty feet high!

But what other explanation was there? His heart rushed into his throat as he strode to the window, visions of her crumpled body far below flashing in his mind.

God, he couldn't look, but he couldn't *not* look, either.

There was no moonlight tonight, but the lanterns in the entryway had been lit for the ball attendees, and the dim glow illuminated the shower of snowflakes swirling in the wind.

He squeezed his eyes closed, braced his hands on the sill and leaned over the edge.

He opened his eyes, his breath leaving his aching lungs in a rush.

There were no twisted bodies lying in the snow below, but there *was* something there. He couldn't see it properly from here, but it looked like . . .

Fresh footprints in the snow.

He turned and flew out the door, into the corridor and back down the stairs, the heels of his evening pumps thundering against the floorboards.

A small throng of servants were scurrying about in the main hallway, but he squeezed past them without a word and flew out the front door into the dark night, droplets of freezing water prickling the back of his neck as he raced around to the western side of the castle.

Good Lord, but it was dark out here. It took him longer than it should have before he was directly underneath her window and up to his ankles in snow, squinting into the darkness far above him.

There was only one way she could have made it from her bedchamber to the ground without breaking her neck.

She'd climbed down the Glastonbury thorn. It was the only explanation.

The branches were more than thick enough to hold such a petite lady, but it must have taken her ages to make her way to the ground from such a distance.

The strength it must have taken, the determination . . .

If he hadn't already been madly in love with her, he would be, now. But this wasn't the moment to indulge in romantic musings.

She couldn't have gotten far in this snow.

He turned, but just as he was about to rush back to the castle he spotted something dark half-buried underneath a shrub.

It looked like . . . a shoe?

He rummaged in the shrubbery and pulled out a worn black half-boot, half covered in snow. It was hers. He recognized the broken silver buckle. It must have slipped from her foot as she was climbing, and then when she reached the bottom she couldn't find it.

Stella had certainly gone out the window, then. Here was the proof of it, right in his hand. God, how desperate she must have been, how frightened!

He searched the ground, and after a bit more flailing and fumbling in the dark, at last he found a shallow set of footprints rapidly filling with falling snow.

They were pointed east, toward the front drive.

He snatched up the shoe and raced back to the castle and through the first door he came to, which happened to be the kitchens.

A dozen heads turned in his direction and a dozen mouths fell open at the sight of their wild-eyed master standing before them, covered with snow and waving a shoe about.

"Your Grace?" His cook, Mrs. Hazelton, hurried toward him, her eyes wide. "Is something amiss?"

"Yes, Mrs. Hazelton, there is. Please have Brooks ready the sleigh as quickly as the thing can be managed. I'll need hot bricks as well, and plenty of blankets."

Mrs. Hazelton, bless her, didn't ask a single question, but leapt into action at once. "Yes, Your Grace, right away! Quickly, George! Find Mr. Brooks and tell him the duke needs the sleigh!"

George dashed off, leaving Gabriel pacing between the staircase and the front door in an agony of impatience until at last—at last—he heard the tinkle of bells echoing in the night air.

He threw open the front door. The sleigh was in the drive. Brooks leaped out and handed the reins to Gabriel. "Ready to go, Your Grace!"

"Good man, Brooks." Gabriel hurried through the door and leaped into the sleigh, Mrs. Hazelton chasing after him with an armful of blankets, and calling over her shoulder to the two footmen behind her to make haste with the hot bricks.

Within moments they were tearing down the drive, snowflakes swirling around them and Gabriel's heart beating in time with the jingling bells.

He'd find her. He wouldn't stop until he did.

This had been a mistake.

Stella hadn't even reached the end of the drive before she was forced to admit the humiliating truth—one small lady in a threadbare cloak with only a single shoe was no match for a Scottish snowstorm.

She'd have to go back. It was either that or freeze to death. Her hands were numb, and her left foot was . . . well, perhaps it would be best not to dwell on the state of her left foot. It wouldn't do to lose her courage now, when she still had to find the strength to trudge back up the drive.

It was an extraordinarily long drive, too, because of course the Duke of Hawthorne must have the longest drive in all of Scotland.

But there was nothing to be done. She'd simply have to take it one step at a time.

Three steps later she paused again, her ears pricking. Were those sleigh bells? Or had she become delirious with cold?

No, those were certainly sleigh bells. They were coming from the direction of the castle, and . . . were they growing louder? She peered into the darkness, but the snow swirled around her, and it was impossible to see a thing.

"Stella!" A deep voice broke the silence. "Stella, wait!"

A sleigh was barreling down the drive, Gabriel at the reins.

He'd come after her.

She forgot her frozen fingers, her numb toes and wet cloak and the melted snow dripping down her neck, because her heart . . . oh, her heart had always known what it wanted, even before her mind had.

He'd lied to her, yes, but there was no naysaying her heart. As soon as his voice reached her through the darkness, the irrepressible organ swelled with joy and love.

"Stella, thank God!" Gabriel tossed the reins aside and leapt from the sleigh.

Oh, dear. Now she'd have to explain that she'd climbed out her window and shimmied down his prized Glastonbury thorn! He would think she was mad. "Gabriel, I—"

"Shhh. Not now, love. We need to get you warm." Without another word he gathered her into his arms as if she were no heavier than a snowflake and carried her back to the sleigh.

"Here we go." He sat her down in the seat and with a tender affection that made her heart swell, he wrapped his greatcoat around her. "There are hot bricks by your feet, and plenty of blankets."

"Gabriel, wait. I must ask you something." She caught his hand. "You're not the Duke of Hawthorne's gardener, are you?"

He'd been busily tucking blankets around her, but his hands went still, his gaze meeting hers. "No. I'm Gabriel Ambrose Christopher Scott, the Sixth Duke of Hawthorne."

"The Sixth Duke of Hawthorne." Phillippa had been telling the truth, then.

"I should never have lied to you, Stella. It was wrong of me, and I sincerely beg your pardon. Do you think you can ever forgive me?"

"I already have. But why did you lie? Why not tell the truth from the start?"

"It was foolish of me, and I've made a mess of it, but I had to be certain . . ." He looked down, avoiding her gaze. "I want a lady who would love me for myself, rather than one who simply wants to be a duchess."

"I see." She laid her hand against his cheek and turned his face back to hers. "And did you find such a lady?"

"I did." He turned his head and pressed a kiss to her palm. "I found the lady I've been dreaming of my whole life. I'm in love with you, Stella, and I never wish to be apart from you again. Will you be my duchess, and make me the happiest of men?"

There were a dozen reasons why she should refuse him, a dozen reasons why it could never work. They'd only just met, and he couldn't make a servant his duchess—

But she wasn't a servant. She was Lady Estella, the daughter of Lord Featherstone, who'd been an honorable gentleman, and an earl.

She wouldn't explain it to him now. Not when he was gazing at her with so much love shining in his beautiful green eyes.

There would be time for that later. A lifetime.

"I love you too, Gabriel. I never wish to be parted from you, either." Her hand found his, and the cold receded as his fingers curled around hers.

"Then I have nothing more to wish for."

He leaned closer, and everything faded to a soft blur around them as his lips met hers in a soft, slow, devastating kiss.

When he released her again, they were both panting.

"Let's get you back to the castle and get you warm." He pressed a final quick kiss to her lips, then took up the reins, the bells ringing in the cold night air as he took them back up the drive.

"You never did get your dance this evening." He jumped out of the sleigh, then took her hand and led her into the castle. "It's not too late. Shall we go into the ballroom, announce our betrothal, and claim our celebratory dance?"

It *was* tempting, but Stella shook her head. She didn't need the congratulations of people she hardly knew. All she needed was him. "I heard that Hawthorne Castle does the best figgy pudding in Dumfriesshire. I believe I was promised a slice of it."

"Wonderful idea. Figgy pudding it is." He took her arm and led her down to the kitchens.

"It smells heavenly in here," Stella murmured, inhaling the scent of nutmeg and warm brandy.

It smelled like Christmas. Not Christmas as it had been these past two years, but Christmas as it used to be before her father died, like the Christmases she recalled from her childhood, Christmases filled with laughter and warmth and joy.

"Mrs. Hazelton's famous figgy pudding awaits your judgment, Miss Harley." Gabriel strode to the long wooden table in the center of the kitchen and pulled out a chair for her. "She bakes a dozen puddings for the church raffle every year. Last year Lady Ellenton and Mrs. Harnish nearly came to blows over the last remaining pudding."

"Ladies coming to blows, at Christmastime?" She sank into the chair with a grateful sigh. "Surely not."

Gabriel's eyes were twinkling. "Annan may appear to be a quiet, sleepy village, but it's a teeming miasma of scandal and intrigue underneath that serene surface."

"My goodness, how shocking." A laugh slipped from Stella's lips, and she paused, surprised by the sound.

Her stepmother had locked her in an attic prison this evening. She'd come close to tumbling from the uppermost window of a duke's massive castle and lost one of the only pair of shoes she owned. Her right foot was wet and her left foot numb and her hems were soaked, yet despite all this, another laugh followed the first, a burst of giddy joy.

Gabriel had been rummaging about at the sideboard, but he turned to her, his lips curved in a soft smile. "You have a lovely laugh, Stella. I look forward to hearing it more often."

Stella pressed her hands to her burning cheeks, her heart leaping at the softness in his eyes and her head swimming with the scent of currants and spices.

"And an even lovelier blush." Gabriel joined her at the table, setting a plate with a thick slice of Christmas pudding beside a small pitcher of clotted cream. He handed her one of the two forks balanced on the edge of the plate. "Here you are."

The fork slid easily through the dense cake, revealing a wealth of currants and almonds, just the way she liked it best. A proper Christmas pudding must have lots of goodies hidden inside. Christmas was no time to skimp.

She scooped the generous bite onto her fork, closing her eyes with a groan as the rich flavors melted on her tongue. "My goodness, this is lovely! I've never tasted a nicer Christmas pudding."

"There's one other thing." He rested his fork on the edge of the plate, reached into the pocket of his greatcoat and plucked something out. "I believe this is yours?"

"My shoe! I never thought I'd see it again. Wherever did you find it?"

"Buried under a bit of shrubbery." He dropped to one knee. "May I?"

"Yes, please." Tears rushed to Stella's eyes as he slid her poor, battered shoe onto her foot.

One floor above them, the grandfather clock chimed the midnight hour.

"Look at that." His gaze met hers, his green eyes shining with love. "It's a perfect fit."

Epilogue

Hawthorne Castle
One year later

"It's nearly three o'clock, Gabriel! What could be keeping them?" Stella braced her hands on the windowsill and peered down into the empty drive below. "It will be dark soon. Do you think the weather has delayed them? There was snow in Dumfries last night. What if they—"

"Patience, my love." A pair of warm, solid arms wrapped around her waist. "I think," Gabriel murmured against her ear, "that you should cease fretting. Beatrice wrote that they likely wouldn't arrive until dusk, didn't she?"

"She did." She melted against him, a shiver of pleasure skipping down her spine at the brush of his lips over her ear and the fresh scent of cedar that enveloped him. Had there ever been a gentleman who smelled as divine as her husband? "I can't wait another moment to see her! It's only been six months since their wedding, but it feels as if an age has passed since we saw them last."

What an eventful year it had been!

If anyone had told her she would become a duchess this year, she would have thought them mad. After two long years at Phillippa's mercy she'd nearly given up on ever knowing happiness again, but now here she was, the Duchess of Hawthorne, wed to the kindest and most handsome duke in all of Scotland, and every day was more delightful than the one before it.

Goodness, life was a funny thing, was it not? It was filled with twists and turns, disappointments and triumphs, and—when one was tremendously lucky—a love that illuminated every corner of one's heart.

"I'm anxious to see Rowan, myself. Did you notice Lady Bruce frowning at my cravat at church yesterday?" Gabriel chuckled, the deep rumble in his chest vibrating against her back. "Gordon does his best, but he doesn't have Rowan's sartorial flair, I'm afraid."

"Oh, bother Lady Bruce! You're the handsomest gentleman in all of Dumfriesshire, and that remains true whether or not your Gordian knot is perfectly tied."

He chuckled again, his arms tightening around her. "Thank you, Your Grace, but methinks you're too partial to be trusted."

"Nonsense. I'm as judicious as any lady who's madly in love with her husband."

"So you are." He dropped a kiss on the top of her head. "It's strange how much can change in so short a time, isn't it? I stood at this same window at this time just last year, watching in horror as the guests arrived for my Christmas house party."

"Horror? Didn't you want to have a Christmas party?"

"God, no. Rowan talked me into it. He was worried I would end up a lonely old recluse rambling about inside this enormous castle, so he set out to find me a duchess, and I must say he did an outstanding job of it."

"And he found himself his own wife in the process. How wonderfully clever of him."

"Yes, well, Rowan's always been terribly efficient."

"He certainly made quick work of courting Beatrice. I confess I would never have predicted a match between them, but now they're wed, I can't imagine how I didn't realize at once that they're perfect together."

But then love was a funny thing, too. Goodness knew she hadn't wanted to come to Hawthorne Castle last year. She'd left Chester with a heavy heart. Who could have guessed a gentleman as lovely as Gabriel was hiding in a castle in the wilds of Scotland? Not her, but love had found her when she least expected it, and in the last place she ever would have thought to look for it, and it had turned everything topsy-turvy in the best possible way.

Just like a fairy tale.

To think, only a year ago she'd thought fairy tales didn't exist! But if there was another, less fanciful explanation for an orphaned servant-turned-duchess becoming the proprietress of the prettiest castle in southwest Scotland, not to mention mistress of a thriving colony of honeybees, she had yet to hear it.

As for Rowan and Beatrice, they'd married just six months ago, much to Phillippa's fury. Why, the woman had nearly had an apoplexy at the thought of one of her daughters marrying a lowly valet, but Beatrice was too wise and too much in love to pay the least attention to her mother's harangues.

Neither Phillippa nor Cornelia had attended Beatrice's wedding, and good riddance to them. It had been a lovely, intimate ceremony, and better for their absence.

Stella certainly hadn't missed them. Not then, and not now.

The last she'd heard, Cornelia's much-anticipated London season had ended without a single offer. She and Phillippa had returned to Chester in a cloud of fury and bitter disappointment, and there they remained, wallowing in their discontent.

She hadn't taken any satisfaction in Cornelia's failure, but it had occurred to her more than once that in the end, one tended to reap what one had sown.

In the end, after years of existing only in Cornelia's shadow, Beatrice was the one who'd triumphed. Soon after they'd wed, Rowan had made up his mind to take orders, and with a bit of help from Gabriel, he'd been offered a lucrative living at St. Michael's church in Dumfries, which was only fifteen miles from Annan.

They were on their way to Hawthorne Castle now and would spend all of Christmas here before Rowan took possession of the living at the end of January. It was to be a lovely, cozy holiday with good company, much cheer and, of course, Mrs. Hazelton's incomparable figgy pudding.

After all, it wouldn't be Christmas without figgy pudding.

Figgy pudding, and family, that is. She'd always longed for a sister, and though it had taken years, she'd found one in Beatrice. Oh, they'd been compatriots of sorts for many years now, but in the way of two prisoners under the thumb of a particularly brutal jailor.

But now . . . well, it was different now. She and Beatrice had struck up a lively correspondence after Beatrice's marriage to Rowan, and Stella had found a kindred soul in her stepsister.

"Look, my love." Gabriel nodded at the window. "It's snowing."

"So it is." Delicate white flakes as light as feathers were drifting from the sky, the fluffy flakes gilding the drive below in a carpet of silvery white. "How pretty!"

"Mmm." Warm lips pressed to the sensitive skin at the back of her neck. "Quite the prettiest thing I've ever seen."

She closed her eyes, her breath catching at the maddening drift of his lips over her eager flesh. She turned in his arms, sinking her hands into the soft hair at the back of his neck. "I can think of one way to pass the time while we wait for—"

She was interrupted by the cheerful jingle of bells and the clop of horses' hooves, and she opened her eyes to find a carriage making its way up the drive. "Oh, dear. What dreadful timing!"

"Later, my love." He tweaked one of her curls, his green eyes shining with love as he gazed down at her. "We have all the time in the world."